D1132707

JUN 9 2008

SURVIVORS

SURVIVORS
THE

A NOVEL

GREGG LUKE

Covenant Communications, Inc.

Cover Photograph by Sexto Sol © Getty Images, GettyImages.com

Cover design copyrighted 2007 by Covenant Communications, Inc.

Published by Covenant Communications, Inc.
American Fork, Utah

Copyright © 2006 by Gregg R. Luke
All rights reserved. No part of this book may be reproduced in any format or in any medium without the
written permission of the publisher, Covenant Communications, Inc., P.O. Box 416, American Fork, UT
84003. The views expressed within this work are the sole responsibility of the author and do not neces-
sarily reflect the position of Covenant Communications, Inc., or any other entity.

This is a work of fiction. The characters, names, incidents, places, and dialogue are products of the
author's imagination, and are not to be construed as real.

Printed in United States of America
First Printing: May 2007
13 12 11 10 09 08 07   10 9 8 7 6 5 4 3 2 1

ISBN 978-1-59811-160-6

To my father,
Clinton Lemar Luke (1925–90),
who taught me that the more you know,
the more you know you don't know.

ACKNOWLEDGEMENTS

First, I would like to thank my Heavenly Father for my innumerable blessings, and His son, Jesus Christ, for the gifts of the Resurrection and Atonement. Second, I would like to express my gratitude to all my friends who helped me on this project, including Julie Luke, David Dickson, Kirk Luke, Ryan Goodrich, Gary and Leann Durfey, and the wonderful, patient staff at Covenant Communications. I also wish to express my gratitude to the McMaster family and the Randall family for allowing the use of their lyrics in this work.

ONE

It was my own stupid fault, although I refused to accept the blame. My head spun with too many conflicts vying for immediate resolution. Embittered and confused, I had engrossed myself in a Tom Clancy novel in an attempt to distract my thoughts from the disturbing note the hotel concierge had given me. It was an ultimatum from my wife.

With note in hand, I had immediately called home. When no one answered, I left a short, urgent message on the machine asking her not to make any rash decisions before we had a chance to talk. Then, because my thoughts continually vacillated between the novel, corporate mandates, and the note, I lost track of time. Before I knew it, I found I only had fifteen minutes to get to an airport thirty minutes away.

I crammed everything into my carry-on and fled the hotel room, cursing my careless time management along the way.

A woman in her midtwenties drove the taxi I hailed. Probably a college student working evenings to pay for her premed courses, she sported a professional look atypical for a taxi driver: a short, contemporary hairdo; no-nonsense eyeglasses; starched blouse. A tattered copy of *Gray's Anatomy* lay on the passenger seat next to her.

I yanked opened the door, tossed in my carry-on, and dove into the backseat.

"Step on it. I need to get—" I stopped midsentence, wondering if my words were reaching anyone's ears but my own. A thick Plexiglas divider separated the cabby-would-be-physician from her passengers—a safety device mandated by the cab company, no doubt. An intercom on the panel in front of me crackled and hissed as we left the hotel roundabout and melded into the traffic of Phoenix's nightlife.

"Nice bit of rain we're having, isn't it?" a monotone yet polite voice asked.

I had little patience for pleasantries. "Whatever. Just get me to the airport quickly," I said, wondering if I had to push a button to communicate with her.

"Which one? Scottsdale? Falcon Field?"

"Phoenix Sky Harbor, and hustle it some. I'm terribly late," I snapped, sounding rather terse, but not caring.

I caught the driver's slow, weary blink in the rearview mirror. Her shoulders lifted and slumped in an obvious sigh from having to put up with another perpetually rude passenger. I was about to apologize but decided the effort would be wasted. She'd already made up her mind about me, and I really didn't care what her conclusions were.

"Right," was her blunt reply; however, our speed did not increase one fraction as we cruised steadily along the rain-slick interstate.

I quickly retrieved my Palm Titanium planner and connected it to my cell phone to access the airport registry via the Internet. Despite a quick, desperate plea to a God I didn't really believe in, my flight to São Paulo, Brazil, was right on time. I cursed inwardly. A delay might have allowed me to catch the flight. My company had insisted I be there within twenty-four hours. I had learned about this mandate only a few hours earlier.

My career with BioCraft Pharmaceuticals was a love-hate relationship. I loved what I did, but hated the numerous, sporadic, spur-of-the-moment meetings I had to personally conduct. I was a senior field analyst, which sounded impressive, but which really meant I had garnered a little prestige and a lot of sky miles. I earned my B.S. in anthropology at the University of California, Santa Barbara. From there I attended UCLA where I obtained a double Ph.D. in ethnobotany and pharmacognosy.

BioCraft's mission was to assay new chemicals from field studies for the ever-growing biopharmaceutical industry. My expertise in rare plants was supposed to place me in a highly specialized, highly compensated employment echelon. However, instead of landing me in a plush, multimillion-dollar laboratory, BioCraft had flagged me as the gofer that ran between the States and anywhere else on the planet that boasted the discovery of a new, potentially revolutionary, miracle drug.

This was one of those times. It didn't matter to my superiors that it was the day before Thanksgiving. BioCraft insisted that I immediately leave the conference I was attending in Phoenix and head to São Paulo. Supposedly, a small research lab had discovered an unusual chemical, which they claimed improved the symptoms of—and might even cure—Alzheimer's disease. And if BioCraft didn't get there first to personally seal a contract, someone from Pfizer or Merck certainly would. To say that my numerous departures and conspicuous absences were eating away at my marriage was an understatement. But first-come, first-served was the credo BioCraft lived by, and if I failed to land a contract on the drug of the century, it wouldn't matter how many years I had faithfully served the company or how many contracts I had secured in the past. Nor would the current state of my marriage come into play. I was almost certain my position as senior field analyst would be up for grabs.

To the corporate board of directors, neither the ultradetailed storyline and scientific rhetoric of Tom Clancy, nor the pleadings of a husband trying to save a shaky marriage, would excuse the loss of a multimillion-dollar—make that multi*billion*-dollar—opportunity. The only explanation BioCraft would accept was if I called in dead, and the Policy and Standards Committee would exhaustively review even that request. That's how unforgiving my employer was.

"You gonna miss a flight, mister . . . ?" the cabby asked.

I looked up and scowled. "Kirkham. David Kirkham. And if you don't drive any faster, I'll miss more than just a flight."

She slowly shook her head. "Well . . . traffic's light. Won't be much longer."

"Seconds count here, babe," I groused. I silently chided myself for being so terse. It really wasn't her fault I was late, but I had no other avenue in which to vent my frustrations. "Look, it would mean the world to me if you could put the pedal down a bit," I added, trying to sound more engaging but coming across more abrasive.

"Yeah, the world waits for no man," the young woman said, almost to herself.

I clapped my cellular shut and turned off my Palm.

"Nice night for a drive though," the cabby continued, as if light chitchat would ease my tension. "I love these fall thunderstorms."

"Look, miss, I've got a hundred-dollar bill with your name on it if you can get me to Sky Harbor in ten minutes," I nearly shouted.

She scratched her chin reflectively. "Let's see . . . a speeding ticket would cost about 150 dollars, plus there's the extra gas from pushing it. Reckless driving could be another 300 dollars, plus a bail bond if we're taken in. Death, on the other hand, should we get in an accident, would be free, except to the insurance company . . . "

I slumped back hard. "Great. I get an economics major for a driver."

"Premed," she corrected.

I knew it. I didn't vocalize. "Listen, I'm in a crisis situation here!"

"Somebody gonna die?" she asked, only half interested.

"Yeah, me."

"You sick?"

"No, there's just a very important business meeting I can't be late for."

She shook her head again. "Look, buddy, I'm sorry about your problems. But a lack of preparation on your part does not constitute an emergency on mine."

Great. A premed philosopher. I bit my lip and said no more. She was right, though I refused to admit it.

* * *

Choked with the usual melee of Thanksgiving passengers, Phoenix Sky Harbor bristled with anxiety and foul tempers. Adding mine to the fray, I fought my way to the check-in and threw my ticket on the counter. The attendant patiently reviewed my ticket and apologetically handed it back to me.

"I'm sorry, Mr. Kirkham, you have already missed boarding that flight," she said from behind horn-rimmed glasses. She looked more like an English teacher from the fifties than an airline hostess.

"Is there another flight to São Paulo?" I asked in a placating tone.

She checked her computer screen and randomly tapped a few keys. "I am sorry, sir. All major airlines are booked up. It *is* Thanksgiving, after all."

I was about to tell her just how aware I was of the holiday at hand, but held my tongue. I had missed the last two Thanksgivings with my wife and daughter, and had promised on my own grave I would be home for this one. The mandate from BioCraft came so quickly I hadn't even had time to make a proper apology to my wife about missing the holiday—again. *If I could just get to São Paulo by morning and secure the contract tomorrow, I might at least make it back in time for leftover turkey and all the trimmings.* Of course, even if I did, I wasn't sure my family would be there when I returned.

I stared at the airline hostess in mute silence for a time, not knowing what to do. The finality of her words left little room for negotiation. After meeting my sorrowfully empty gaze a minute or two, she adjusted her glasses and rechecked her monitor.

"There *is* a smaller plane, an economy shuttle service heading to Corpus Christi, Texas. From there you might get a flight to São Paulo, or perhaps to Miami, then down to Brazil. Not many people go across the border for Thanksgiving. I don't believe it's celebrated in South America."

"Fine," I said, taking the ticket and heading toward the appropriate gate.

The shuttle service was Southern Skies Ltd.; the *limited* perfectly described the small aircraft I boarded on the wet tarmac. Hunkering under a storm-tormented umbrella, I didn't catch the manufacturer of the plane, but once inside, I concluded the designer was a skinny man with shortened legs and a penchant for torturing claustrophobic travelers. Actually, the plane was very clean and orderly, but as I was used to first-class accommodations on nothing smaller than a Boeing 747 or a DC-10, this aircraft seemed distressingly small.

Undoubtedly, this matchbox of a plane was another of fate's punishments for my tardiness.

The commuter plane seated about thirty people, with only a flimsy, accordion-like partition separating the cockpit from the cabin. Luckily, I was one of the first passengers to board and promptly ensconced myself in a seat midway down the fuselage. The lone flight attendant sat directly behind the partition, chatting with the pilot as the passengers helped themselves to the available seats. Buried beneath a pile of charts, the copilot spent his time in animated conversation—over a headset—about the weather. I chanced a look out the window at the swollen rain clouds that continued to moisten the ground. The gloom outside matched my feelings within.

"Excuse me, sir, but could I sit here?" a young voice asked.

A little girl, probably ten or eleven years old, was looking at me with raised eyebrows and a hopeful smile on her face. She wore a silly denim hat with a yellow sunflower on the front and a matching denim jacket. I looked at the seat and realized my carry-on was filling the spot. I wasn't much in the mood for a companion on the three-hour flight, but being so late in the evening, I figured the little girl would probably fall asleep anyway. I nodded and stuffed my carry-on under my seat as the girl buckled herself in snugly.

"Thank you very much," she said with another winning smile. She then busied herself with a small backpack she carried. At least she was polite.

A disturbing shudder ran through the fuselage as the plane's engines roared to life. I looked out the window again and saw—*propellers?* The aircraft was a turboprop! I didn't think they even made commuter planes with propellers anymore. The noise was almost deafening. The whole aircraft vibrated as if in an epileptic fit, and I found my stomach churning with nervous apprehension. I've never been afraid of flying, but then I've always traveled in aircraft much larger than this. This one resembled little more than the leftover tube from an empty roll of toilet paper. If my spent nerves had heretofore needed soothing, now it was medically necessary.

I hailed the flight attendant, who was helping an older couple with a blanket. *Didn't this thing even have a heater?*

"Yes, sir?" the thirtyish woman said.

"Can I get a drink?" I asked, trying to smile pleasantly.

"You bet. As soon as we are in the air I can get you a Coke or a Sprite, or some orange juice if you'd like."

"I'd like a Sprite, please," the little girl next to me said.

"How about a scotch?" I asked.

The flight attendant smiled congenially. "Yes, sir, I'll get you a mini-bottle as soon as we get airborne."

Another delay. That's just great! Apparently, my luck was not going to get any better in the immediate future. "Fine," I answered through clenched teeth.

The flight attendant nodded and continued down the aisle to help seat the remaining passengers. From the corner of my eye, I noticed the little girl looking at me with an expression of genuine surprise painting her face. I tried to ignore her, but she continued to stare at me as if I had a glob of that evening's cheeseburger stuck on my chin. Finally, she put words to her expression. "You drink alcohol?"

At that moment, a loud clap of thunder boomed across the lowering sky, as if the heavens acknowledged the magnitude of her question.

I forced a smile to lighten the implied gravity of her query. "Just when I'm nervous, kid. Why, don't your parents drink?"

"No, sir, they don't. We're members of The Church of Jesus Christ of Latter-day Saints."

"The who?"

"Most people know us as Mormons. But our prophet has asked that we not use that title anymore because we belong to Christ's Church, not Mormon's."

For an instant I felt defensive, bracing myself for the lambasting I was about to receive from an adolescent teetotaler. But the young girl simply smiled her perfect little smile, with eyes twinkling up at me, and then returned to the paperback she had retrieved from her backpack—a book from the *Little House on the Prairie* series.

My heart softened. There was something downright disarming in her smile, and her innocent demeanor told me I was not under any condemnation, that in spite of her earlier astonishment, she accepted me for who I was (at least as far as she knew me). At least the little girl was not going to preach to me about her religion.

I had never been much of a religious man. I knew my fair share of Mormons, but never thought much about looking into their beliefs. One of my best friends in high school, in fact, was a Mormon. I remembered Matthew Christiansen as a cool guy, well liked by his peers and respected by his teachers. And he was good. I mean, almost *too* good. The guy never drank or smoked or, as far I knew, fooled around with girls. How he could thrive as a teenaged straight arrow in Southern California had always mystified me. I usually found it easier to meld with the in-crowd rather than stand out in it. Matt, on the other hand, had never seemed bothered by it; rather, he seemed to grow more self-assured, more confident because of it.

The young girl sitting beside me had the same self-confidence. She radiated a maturity I found intriguing, especially in one so young. Still, I was not in the mood for any conversation at that moment, particularly one on religion. My worries lay elsewhere: my job with BioCraft, my family, and my sanity onboard this tin-can airline.

I exhaled a labored, woe-is-me kind of sigh and laid my head against the curve of the cabin wall. I closed my eyes and tried to relax and remain optimistic about my miserably uncontrollable future. A quip I once thought humorous came to mind: "If it weren't for bad luck, I'd have no luck at all." Presently, that saying rang too true to be funny.

TWO

"My name is Melodee, spelled with two *e*'s instead of an *ie* or a *y*," the young girl said.

I opened my eyes and turned to face her. Her raised eyebrows and impish grin highlighted clear blue eyes that sparkled. Despite my current ugly state of mind, I found it impossible not to return the smile.

"Hi," was my inane reply.

We taxied to the end of the runway and awaited permission to take off. I had already consigned myself to three hours of misery, but my temporary companion seemed bent on making it otherwise.

"My parents named me that because they said when I was born I was singing instead of crying. But they wanted to spell my name differently, so they did the *ee* thing instead of the regular spelling. I still love to sing. Do you?"

I chortled and shook my head. "No, Melodee-with-two-*e*'s. I can't carry a tune in a bucket. But I envy those who can."

She smirked and tilted her head slightly. "Anyone can sing," she stated matter-of-factly. "In *The Music Man*, Professor Harold Hill—his real name was Greg—said that singing is just sustained talking. And I know you can talk, so you can sing, too."

How could I argue with that logic? "Okay," I conceded, "but my sustained talking would make a catfight sound like an operatic duet."

I heard the pilot "roger" something in his headset. He nodded to the copilot, who turned to the passengers, fifteen of us in all, not including the flight attendant. "We're going to take off now. Be sure you're buckled in tight. I'm afraid this storm is going to make things a little bumpy at first."

He addressed us as if we were a bunch of kids piled in a minivan. Perhaps he was simply trying to add a personal touch to their "limited" service. Well, at least the guy wore a uniform.

"I hope you're not too scared, mister," Melodee said to me. "You look pretty nervous right now. If you like, we can talk about something else. Sometimes it helps to talk about other things—you know, to get your mind off of flying."

I couldn't decide whether this little girl was mocking me or simply being overly friendly. Still, her offer touched me. I wondered if my little Paige, only five years old, would grow up to be like Melodee.

"That's very kind of you, kid," I said. "Maybe later."

The airplane lurched forward as the pilot released the brakes and the turboprops accelerated to a speed where they wailed like banshees. A machine-gun-like pelting of heavy rain rose to a cacophonous din as the small plane sped down the tarmac. I cast a glance out the window and saw flames belching from the rear of the turboprops. *Was that normal?* The sight significantly enlarged the knot in my stomach, and I vowed never again to fly in anything that did not have jet engines.

The plane shook violently as our speed increased, and I began to wonder if we would successfully break the grasp of earth's gravity before vibrating apart. A plastic shade that covered the window clattered against its frame as the noise of our takeoff rose to a level so deafening I could scarcely hear my own thoughts.

I glanced at Melodee to see if she seemed as nervous as I was. The little girl had her head bowed and her hands folded in her lap, as if in prayer. *Not a bad idea*, I thought, but couldn't bring myself to do the same. The pretense would feel too hypocritical.

As I watched Melodee pray, I noticed something odd. Having removed her hat, she revealed a hairstyle that did not at all fit her persona. Cropped in an uneven, blotchy cut, her golden blond locks stood out in random disarray. It looked like a punk-rocker hairstyle from the eighties, without the Mohawk or fluorescent coloring. The harsh style struck a stark contrast to her innocent countenance. It made me wonder how my little girl would style her hair in a few years.

A terrifying jolt in the plane's momentum caused me to notice something else peculiar. Little Melodee did not seem to be praying out of nervousness or fear; she smiled as though she was actually communicating with someone and enjoying the conversation. She did not appear to be pleading with God to save her young life; rather, she looked as if what she were saying had nothing to do with the strength and aerodynamics of the Southern Skies Ltd. aircraft or the intensity of the thunderstorm.

As the plane finally broke contact with the runway, the slow, weightless sensation of leaving terra firma pulled at my body. It was not a comforting feeling, and, to add insult to injury, the buffeting and lashing of the storm seemed to intensify as we clawed our way into the thick, black sky. Lightning flashed all around us as if our presence were offensive to the clotting storm clouds. We were trespassing in their domain, an unwelcome intruder, and the cumulous creatures were determined to make our stay unforgettably miserable. We seemed to gain little altitude as the plane sporadically plunged several feet then jerked back up in whiplash-causing leaps and bounds. The vagaries of wind and air pressure created solid thermals from which our little plane would ricochet from one side to the other. I heard strained gasps and muffled cries from the passengers around me, and drew comfort from the fact that I wasn't the only one fearing for my life.

I tried to concentrate on something else, anything to get my mind off flying through these tornado-spawning clouds. Another flash of lightning drew my attention to the window, but I refused to look out for fear of seeing a small house flying alongside us, and a black-clad spinster riding a bicycle in midair, screeching venom-laced oaths about getting the pretty girl and her little dog, Toto, too.

A tremendous clap of thunder rocked the plane so violently that my head smashed against the cabin interior. I believed that if I touched the moist spot above my right eyebrow my fingers would come back red with blood. I gingerly daubed my forehead anyway while stealing a glance out the window. At first, I thought there was someone outside staring back at me, but it was only the reflection of my own bloodless face and fright-filled eyes, and I sternly chided myself for being such a wimp.

The spot on my forehead was indeed tender, but there was no blood present, only a generous profusion of cold sweat. A few women in the plane were softly crying now, and a feeling of dread filled the narrow tube in which we were strapped. I was certain that at any moment Melodee would grab my arm, desperately seeking comfort.

Another burst of lightning caused the plane's interior lights to flicker off. An unrestrained scream came from someone in the back as our fears uniformly reached their zenith in the sudden darkness. Clicking on a flashlight, the flight attendant rose from her seat and began a mantra of comforting statements and assurances while she struggled to maintain her balance in the narrow aisle. I doubted anyone truly believed her warbling, not-so-sure-herself comments. I know I didn't. The copilot then rose and braced himself next to the flight attendant.

"Okay, everybody," he began. "I'm not going to try and fool you into a false sense of security. We are in the middle of a severe electrical storm, and that last lightning burst shorted out some of our systems. But I can also tell you that we are in no immediate danger. This is a well-designed airplane, and even if all our electrical systems crashed . . . *oops*, excuse me, bad choice of words." When no one chuckled at his ill-conceived humor, he continued, "Even if all our electrical systems went out, we could still fly the plane with manual controls."

An audible sigh went through the small cabin, although I wondered how many of us felt reassured. He smiled briefly and patted the stewardess on the shoulder.

"In the meantime," he continued, "I suggest you all stay buckled in and try to stay calm. It's going to remain bumpy for the rest of the flight, and the worst may be yet to come. If you need blankets or pillows just ask Jenny here, and she'll assist you as best she can."

I was the first to raise my hand. When Stewardess Jenny stumbled over to me, I requested anything that contained alcohol. She obliged. Melodee had long since finished her prayer and had donned her hat. She no longer wanted a Sprite and instead scrounged for something in her backpack.

It was some time before the pitch and roll, rise and fall of the commuter plane seemed commonplace enough that I could cease worrying about imminent death. And although the flight was now slightly less traumatic, my mini-bottle of smooth Tennessee scotch did little to help smooth out *anything*, least of all my harried nerves.

All this time Melodee did not utter a sound. She tried valiantly to read from her book using a small penlight she had scrounged from her backpack, and seemed content that we were still aloft and in one piece. She appeared comfortable in her solitude, which, at her young age, baffled me.

Solitude. It occurred to me that she had never mentioned anything about where her parents were, or any other traveling partner, nor had she spoken to anyone else while boarding the airplane.

"Are you traveling with someone on this plane?" I asked over the roar of the turboprops and the howling of the storm.

She placed a marker in her book and closed it. "No," she replied while looking up.

"You mean your parents let you fly by yourself?" I asked, impressed with her independence.

"Yeah. So?"

"Well . . . aren't they afraid of something happening to you?"

"It's not like I'm the one flying the plane," she retorted with a sarcastically playful tone.

"True, but . . . well, how old are you?" I could think of nothing else with which to argue.

"I'm twelve and a half." She then smirked. "I've done this before, you know."

I did not respond, just gawked.

"So . . . how old are you?" she asked with conversational innocence.

Just then, the commuter plane seemed to fall straight down at least twenty feet. With my stomach in my throat, I fought to keep a scream in check. I was certain my face had blanched an even lighter shade of white than it already was. I took another quick pull from my mini-bottle. As I felt the plane begin a gradual climb, I flippantly said, "That was fun."

When Melodee did not respond, I answered her question. "I'm thirty-nine and a half. And I've done this before too."

She gave me a half smile and an incredulous look. "Are you sure? You seem awfully tense so far, just because of a little turbulence."

A little? As if by command, the airplane lurched upward, causing my stomach to leave my throat and slam into my guts. My knuckles turned white as my hands gripped the armrests with viselike force. Melodee's arched eyebrow inched a fraction higher.

I nodded. "Believe it or not, I have more frequent-flyer miles than Amelia Earhart and Neil Armstrong put together. It's just that I usually fly in much larger planes. I'm not used to airborne sardine cans like this one."

Apparently satisfied with my answer, she said, "I can't afford to fly in a big plane, so I'm used to these bumpy rides."

"And just how often do you fly?"

"About once every year or two. I've been staying with my grandpa in Phoenix for a few days. Kind of a last-minute vacation of sorts. I might not ever see him again."

"An illness?" I guessed.

"Yeah. Now I'm heading back home to Corpus Christi for Thanksgiving. I saved up and paid for my ticket to Phoenix, but Grandpa helped pay for the trip back. Luckily, the flight between Arizona and Texas is not that expensive. My parents rarely come because they're too busy, and Grandpa can't spend Thanksgiving with us this year because he's going to Uncle Scott's—he's their weird son."

"Every family has at least one."

"Yeah, I guess. I think he's kinda funny. It was actually my younger brother's turn to visit Grandpa this year, but he let me go instead because it might be the last chance I get to see him. My older brother can't go 'cause he's on a mission. My older sister went last year, and my younger sister is still a baby."

A mission? "What do you mean, 'a mission'?"

As soon as I asked the question, I remembered the tradition of nineteen-year-old Mormon boys going on voluntary, two-year proselytizing missions for their church. I recalled Matt talking about preparing for such service, and I reflected on my original curiosity as to why he would spend his money on that instead of a new car or college tuition. The whole mission experience was something I had never really understood.

"Is that where they go off into some jungle to convert the natives?" I asked with only a minimal touch of sarcasm in my tone.

She laughed a delightful, mirth-laden laugh. The sound was like an alien presence in the cabin full of fear and anxiety.

"I guess some do," she confessed, "but most go to normal cities and towns. My brother is in the Osaka Japan Mission. He loves it there because he sticks out so much."

"Why, because he's an American?"

"Partly that, but mostly because he's got blond hair and blue eyes and is six feet six inches tall."

I had been to Japan three times for BioCraft and could see her point. The Japanese people, while big of heart and humble dignity, were not very large physically. The average man stood about five feet four inches. A blond *gaijin* over a foot taller than the norm would indeed make a lasting impression.

"Oh, I see."

The conversation lulled at that point, and Melodee returned to her book. Another violent shudder shook the plane as we bobbed mercilessly on the unseen riptides of wind and rain. And although my conversation with the brave young girl next to me distracted my mind somewhat, it did little to ease the anxiety and queasiness that our flight through this aerial maelstrom caused in me. The cabin lights remained out as we catapulted over thermals and plunged into pockets. Lightning flared all around us, and I wondered why we didn't simply fly above the storm. Probably because the plane was too small to gain the necessary altitude, I guessed.

Just then, a horrific electrical *pop* blasted next to the plane, and we lurched painfully in the opposite direction. Again my head whacked against the cabin wall, and a new dull pain throbbed within my skull.

I decided the only way to survive this tortuous flight with any sanity was through chemical intervention. Since this shuttle service only offered low-proof beverages as refreshment, I rummaged through my carry-on for the sleeping pills I knew were there.

Halcion was a drug I didn't like to use often, but after many trips across uncounted time zones, my biological clock was beyond the point of recalibrating itself naturally, and a little help from Upjohn's pharmacopoeia never hurt anyone. I swallowed the tablet with the remainder of my scotch. I knew that this class of drug shouldn't be combined with alcohol because of extreme synergistic effects. But the angst and short-circuited sparks coursing through my nervous system would undoubtedly negate one pill alone, and I felt total oblivion was the only way to get through this flight. My neurons were so spent I didn't even taste it. The chemical brew worked fast. The last thing I remembered was the sight of Melodee reading from her book, a slight smile playing on her face as if she were reading under a shade tree on a soft, summer day.

The next images I saw were straight out of a nightmare.

THREE

Smoke.

Screaming.

Falling.

I remembered reading that Halcion could cause some wild dreams, especially when mixed with alcohol, but this was so . . . *real*. My dream was what many God-fearing souls deemed their worst nightmare: one of plummeting down an eternal chasm, ever accelerating, surrounded by fire and smoke and endless torments.

Someone was shaking my arm. Small hands. A young voice—one filled with dread. The smoke was not thick enough to impair breathing, but it tainted the air with an acrid, rubbery stench. The heavy, noxious odor partially blended with the cerebral fog in my head. The drug-induced stupor that benzodiazepines were famous for was working its magic on my intracranial neurons, eliciting a blissful, distant, antithetic ambience to the hysteria surrounding me.

More screaming.

Crying now, too. People in abject horror awaiting an imminent doom. Innocent souls prematurely condemned well before their allotted time on Earth was fulfilled, as if standing before a blood-thirsty tribunal like the Spanish Inquisition of the thirteenth century, knowing of their innocence while pleading guilty. Guilty by assumption. Guilty by happenstance. Guilty because they chose a small, economy commuter flight instead of a high-priced airline. Maybe. Some, like me, were guilty simply because the Thanksgiving holiday had created a lack of any other option.

"Mister!" A small voice pierced my cranial haze. Pleading. Urgent.

I tried to open my eyes against the powerful medication but couldn't. I thought that perhaps I should try something vocal.

"Yesth?" I heard myself slur from about five miles away.

"Mister, bend forward and hold this pillow over your head," the young voice commanded.

Why is she yelling? Why is everyone on the plane yelling?

A loud *whumph* sounded from the turboprop on the opposite side of the airplane. The whole fuselage lurched to one side, but to me it felt more languid than it probably was in reality. At that moment, I wasn't sure *what* reality was. The sensation of falling grew more real as I felt the ambient pressure in my ears increase at a rate that didn't allow for comfortable decompression. I wished I had a couple cups of coffee or a six-pack of Diet Vanilla Coke. I couldn't have been out for more than an hour as we flew over the plains of Arizona and Texas, but who knew? My nerves, having been frayed and shredded by a devastating note from my wife, a slow cabby, and a white-knuckled plane ride, were prime targets for the sedating—and hallucinogenic—effects of the pill I took.

"Mister, please," the small voice called again.

I knew it was Melodee, but she sounded almost like my daughter, Paige. Quite a bit older—but still quite young. Innocent.

"I don't want to die!" a woman screamed from the back of the plane.

That was my feeling too, except that in my present condition it didn't seem to matter anymore. I was happy simply floating in my seat, held in place only by the nylon belt fastened tightly across my lap, which provided a constrictive, somewhat unpleasant sensation. Normally I am a control freak, having to be in command of everything around me. But being bound to a seat that was tilting forward at an alarming angle, with several people around me crying their spoiled eyes out, was definitely something beyond my control.

No, that isn't quite right either. It's funny how the mind works when under chemical influences. This crying was different. It wasn't a spoiled cry, but a panicked, end-of-the-world, we're-all-gonna-die kind of cry.

"Please, mister, you've got to lean forward!" the small voice called again, choking on the last words as the smell of smoke grew thicker around us.

Concentrate, I told myself. *What was she asking? To lean forward? But . . . why?*

"Hurry. Lean forward and put this pillow over your head."

"Is sthomething wrong?" I heard myself slur from some uncharted quadrant.

"We're going to crash!"

"Crash?" I asked, removing the pillow from my head but still unable to get my eyes to open.

"Yes!" the anguished young voice answered.

Just then, I sensed the plane struggling to level out. A metallic retching moaned through the cabin like the remorseful groaning of a thousand forgotten souls. I felt the plane list to one side and crab through the air at an impossible angle. Then came a shuddering of such magnitude that I thought I was in an earthquake.

Somehow, I managed to pry one eye open and saw nothing but darkness all around me. From the window came a yellow-orange flickering from some unchecked fire outside. In the pulsating light, I saw the young girl next to me leaning forward, pressing a pillow over the back of her head. I also noticed that she had donned her backpack.

Another shudder and more metallic groaning followed. The airplane plummeted as if the wings had suddenly vanished, yet the fuselage remained fairly horizontal. A shrill whine cried from the turboprop on my side, followed by an ear-shattering explosion.

An autonomic force within me took over with presence of mind enough to follow the little girl's example. Then the plane hit something. Slammed into it, really. I felt a bone-crushing jolt and a sudden draft of fresh air. We began turning, cart-wheeling, totally out of control. The motion was slowed by the drugs in my system, but I knew exactly what was happening.

I was aware of a violent, whistling gale coming through the place where tempered glass had filled the window casing moments before. I heard myself tell the girl to hold on—as if she weren't doing so already.

Then a high-pitched, nauseating rending screeched behind us and grew until it was directly over our heads—then suddenly ceased, as if secreted away by some powerful force to an unknown destination.

Then a new noise began, but it was different somehow. Not so much a tearing sound, it was more like scratching, like someone dragging a fork across a tin plate. I felt the hairs on my arms stand up and a shiver course down my spine as if that same someone were simultaneously raking their fingernails across a grade-school blackboard. The only other sound was the harsh keening of a fierce wind that seemed to come from all directions at once.

Suddenly the scratching turned into a splintering sound, like the snapping of tree limbs, and my ears began to ring with unrestrained tinnitus. I then felt a new sensation—moisture, probably rain, thickening the air and pelting my body with fat, heavy drops.

Then, quite suddenly, we came to an abrupt, vicious stop.

The loud, abrasive noises subsided into hushed, nocturnal sounds. I no longer heard human voices, crying or otherwise.

I sensed my arm was no longer around the little girl, but could feel nothing more.

With the absence of stimuli, my mind and body eased into a chemical slumber devoid of dreams or random thoughts.

FOUR

The first thing I sensed was moisture on my face—a soft, misty, dewlike wetness that had no origin or direction of flow. It was not rain, but it condensed on my skin in a manner best described as precipitation. And it was warm, not at all like the chilly rain I knew back home.

Thousand Oaks, California, was hundreds of miles away and was probably drenched in a winter storm about now. It always rained on or around Thanksgiving, and when the rains came in from over the chilled Pacific, as they always did, they brought with them a refreshing humidity laced with a faint saline quality.

The moisture presently daubing my face, however, was not the chilled precipitation of a southern California winter, nor was it the subtropical rain one felt in Corpus Christi, Texas. Instead, this was a warm, sticky wetness that clung to my skin like maple syrup.

Then there was the pain: dull, throbbing, and resistant to any stoic grin-and-bear-it tactics my mind attempted. I tried to move my left hand to wipe the water from my face but found it would not cooperate with my brain. Instead, the harder I tried, the more intense the pain became. My right hand felt functional, but it seemed to be pinned underneath something, and I could not budge it. I opened my eyes but could see nothing more than a soft, orange-yellow glow flickering behind a mass of dense vegetation.

I found myself still buckled into the Southern Skies Ltd. seat, but the rest of the plane seemed to be missing. My seat was still mounted to a piece of deck, as was the seat in front of me. Lying on my side with my feet tucked under me, I sensed that my head rested in the cavity of the window, which had lost its glass sometime earlier. Immediately, I recognized the smell of bunch grass, ferns, and rotting vegetation, and perhaps the hints of something burning and a petroleum distillate of some kind. No light from the evening stars or ambient moon glow penetrated the heavy clouds that seemed only a few feet from the ground on which I lay. Yet the oppressive blackness that crowded around me made it clear it was night.

I closed my eyes against the pain in my skull and tried to concentrate. How did I get here, and exactly where was *here?* It occurred to me that I might still be experiencing the effects of my alcohol-Halcion stress mix, but I doubted it would cause the pain that slowly intensified throughout my entire body with each passing second.

I shivered uncontrollably in the unusually warm, moisture-shrouded night, a sign that I was sick or injured somehow. Attempting to raise my head to look around caused a painful shock to shoot down my spine, followed by incapacitating spasms of vision-blurring agony in my left arm.

I laid my head back down on the soggy earth in the window frame and squinted against the misery pulsing through me. It was all I could do to keep from crying out. However, because of the unusually thick feeling of my tongue and the coppery taste of blood in my mouth, I knew any sound I produced would be more animal-like than human, more like a hapless creature caught in the steel maw of a poacher's trap than a human crying out for the help of another.

I swallowed hard against the bitterness in my mouth and tried to slow my hyperactive breathing. I forced my eyes open and struggled to orient myself so I could determine my current whereabouts and condition. If I concentrated hard enough, I believed forthright scientific deduction would reward me with the answers.

Logic was something I prided myself as having in ample amounts. The ability to see things for what they were and then do something about it to gain advantage was a skill I had possessed since middle school. I had headed many a debate team that never lost a contest thanks to my ability to view any argument clearly, objectively, and with intimidating confidence. But hard as I tried, I could not even begin to organize the conundrum of disjointed clues that presently surrounded me. I did remember the shattering of glass and the sensation of falling into a black abyss. And the panicked sound of a little girl's terrified voice.

I shivered again and concentrated on clearing my mind and relaxing. I thought of calm, tranquil beaches, of tropical breezes and the creamy taste of piña coladas coating my mouth. I willed my muscles to loosen and let my mind drift to pleasant scenes made up from personal memories mixed with pictures from magazines and vignettes from favorite movies and books. It was a technique I had learned while in college to enable me to fall asleep almost instantly—a power nap some called it—to catch up on sleep I had denied myself while cramming for an exam or finishing a paper due the next morning.

And it was working. The pain pulsing through me seemed to take second place to the imagery displayed in my mind. I knew the pain was still there, but it did not deter the pattern of events I had trained my subconscious to conjure up. Often, my wife was with me on the beach. A vision of loveliness herself, Dyana always looked a perpetual twenty-nine years old, in the peak of physical condition, with her hair and makeup done to perfection—even though we were on a desert island thousands of miles away from any amenity like running hot water or room service. My daughter was usually with us in these dreams. Always cheerful, never bratty or sick, Paige would run along the beach collecting shells and oddities, laughing and squealing in delight with each new discovery she made.

She's coming toward me now, my little Paige, with her sandalwood hair and chestnut eyes. She seems to be searching, but she doesn't look happy. As she gets closer, I can see something is wrong. Her shoulders are not bobbing with laughter, but with sobs of anguish. I turn to Dyana—but she is no longer there. I try to reach out to Paige to comfort her, but my arms refuse to move. Then she looks toward me, as if I had suddenly appeared out of nowhere, and a fleeting glimmer of hope fills her eyes. She approaches me slowly, cautiously, as if she were coming up on a new discovery that could be either a wondrous delight or a heartbreaking disappointment.

"Mister, are you alive?" she asks me shakily.

What a silly question. Of course I am. I'm right here in front of you, aren't I?

"Mister?" she asks again. "Please tell me you're alive."

My heart burns with a sudden pang of sorrow. How could she be asking such a saddening question? Again, I try to reach out to her, but I cannot. I see tears running down her cheeks, tracing rivulets of salty moisture that crease her soot-covered face. My own eyes burn with emotion as I long desperately to let my little girl know I'm still here for her, that I would do anything to take away her pain and make her happy again.

"Mister, please," she sobs uncontrollably. "Don't leave me all alone."

Oh, Paige, I would never do that, I ache to say.

As she drops to her knees and buries her face in her hands, her shoulders tremble with the convulsions of pure sorrow.

I cannot bear to watch. I close my eyes but continue to see her. I try to listen to the rolling surf and the gentle scraping of palm fronds against each other, but I only hear her gasps and sobs.

I open my eyes again and force myself to speak.

"Don't cry, honey," I hear a hoarse voice croak—a voice that sounds remotely like my own.

She looks up in surprise and disbelief. I try to smile, try to show her some inkling of happiness, but I'm not sure if the muscles in my face respond the way I want. Without warning she wraps her arms around my neck and shoulders and continues to sob, but no longer in sorrow.

Her touch shocks me with a jolt so intense it's as if all my sensory receptors have fired simultaneously. Hot, searing sparks ricochet from my skull to my toes, triggering staccato bursts of unbelievable pain. I groan loudly, suddenly gasping for breath. The little girl crouches back on her heels while an embarrassed, shy smile breaks through her sooty face.

"Sorry, mister."

I try to smile back. "It's okay, Paige."

A labored laugh forces its way through her sobs of grief. She pouts playfully. "My name's not Paige," she says. "Don't you remember? It's Melodee."

FIVE

The cool dampness of morning penetrated my clothing and gave me a chill that made my body crave movement. I opened my eyes and found I was reclining in an airline seat, propped against a banyan tree. At first, I thought I was still dreaming. But the myriad of sounds permeating the heavy mist around me and the chilled dew moistening my pants and shirt told me this was no dream. Besides, if this was just my imagination, it was more akin to a nightmare than a dream.

My left arm was in a splint and sling; my right arm was burnt and sore. My head pounded like drums beating in perfect cadence between my temples and around the base of my skull. I knuckled the sleep from my swollen eyes and squinted. As my environment came into complete focus, my breath instantly caught in my chest.

All around me was thick primordial jungle, a tropical rain forest enshrouded in a perpetually shifting mist, like some forgotten other-world where dinosaurs roamed freely and human clothing was limited to mastodon kilts and reptilian sarongs. Animal voices murmured in a chaotic clamor, a primeval symphony that was at once disjointed and harmonious. Before me were random bits and pieces of debris, the scattered remains of a doomed commuter flight—a scrap of metal here, a bit of cloth there, but nothing that resembled a once-intact airplane. It was as if the jungle had engulfed the turboprop aircraft in a single gulp, leaving only a hint of its former existence.

A disturbing emptiness engulfed me as I suddenly realized I might be alone. The rumpled blanket, black and singed at the edges, covering my lap, and my splinted arm were the only solid evidences of anything connected with human intervention. Remaining in my seat, I looked around for evidence that someone else had survived, but I saw no one, living or otherwise, who could claim to be a former Southern Skies Ltd. passenger. A partially bent seat leaned to one side directly in front of me. In its pouch was a plastic-coated card describing recommended procedures to follow in the event of a plane crash. I scoffed and swore. That the plane had crashed was obvious; how I had survived the crash was still a mystery. I couldn't remember anything about the accident itself and only snippets of sounds and impressions leading up to it. I recalled taking a heavy-duty pill . . . I had a few chemically induced dreams . . . and now I was here, reasonably intact, sitting in an airline seat as if I were awaiting the flight attendant's beverage cart and small bag of pretzels. I couldn't recall putting my arm—obviously broken—in a splint and sling, or how I even got in—or if I had ever left—the airline seat. Yet here I was with a blanket over my lap, as if Mom had come and tucked me in before saying good night.

Then I heard a light groan, like someone stretching after a fitful night's slumber. Slowly, a young, dirty face appeared above the listing seat in front of me. It was my former seat-companion, Melodee. And she was smiling.

"Good morning," the young girl mumbled. Her face was blackened on one side by smoke and dirt, and her once-shiny blond hair looked more like the unkempt beginnings of dreadlocks.

"How did we get here?" was my inane first question.

She gave me a *duh, are you stoned?* kind of look, then answered simply, "We crashed."

"You think?" I shot back in a perturbed tone while forcefully rubbing my eyes. I don't know why her blatant honesty annoyed me so much, but the last thing I needed was prepubescent sarcasm. "I guess what I meant was: *Why* did we crash?"

"I don't know," she answered, not appearing bothered by my harsh tone. "I think we were hit by lightning or something. All I know is there was a lot of flashing and noise, and then one of the engines blew up and we crashed. Are you feeling okay?"

"I feel like crap," I said, grimacing against the pain in my head. "Is there anyone else around?"

Melodee looked away, focusing on nothing as her eyes misted up. "I don't think so. Most everybody I've found is . . . gone."

"Gone? You mean they're all dead?" I asked, not wanting to believe her.

She nodded quickly, causing a tear to trace down one cheek. The magnitude of her revelation struck me with such force that it emptied my lungs of breath. How and why did all of the passengers die except us? The odds of such a survival rate would make a Las Vegas bookie salivate with anticipation—or cringe, depending on which side of the bet he backed. It was more than amazing, more than incalculable. It was a miracle.

"Surely someone else survived."

Melodee remained silent.

"Who put my arm in this splint?" I persisted.

Without returning my gaze, she answered softly, "I did."

"And you're sure no one else is alive?" I gasped, vainly trying to rationalize the irrational information surrounding our near-death experience.

The young girl choked on a sob. "I tried to help them—but I—couldn't—do—it."

"Shh, hey, it's okay, Melodee," I said, realizing the young girl was in no condition to be grilled with painfully blunt questions. But my curiosity was overpowering, and my need to catalogue everything in a precise sequence of events was tantamount to maintaining my sanity. I could feel my temper rising with each sob on which the young girl choked. It was aggravating. The crash had happened. Nothing could be done to reverse that fact. Why couldn't she be more mature about this situation? What we needed now was cool heads and sharp wits, not sniveling, flighty emotions.

"I'm sure you did all you could," I said with minimal sincerity. "You're a very brave little girl."

She looked at me with moist, weary eyes. Then she came quickly from around the seat and wrapped her arms around my neck. My head throbbed from the added pressure and my broken arm exploded with pain, but I didn't ask her to stop. I warmed to her embrace and patted her back, trying to console her. After a moment, she released me and sat on the ground next to my seat. She wiped her face, smearing spent tears over her soiled cheeks, and tried to smile.

"What do we do now?" she asked with an expectation in her voice I knew I couldn't satisfy.

I scratched my head. How could I answer honestly without sounding like all was lost? I had absolutely no clue what to do now, but her childlike trust of an older person—an adult probably about the same age as her father—buoyed me with a resolution to protect her and make everything right. I didn't begrudge the responsibility, but I had no idea how to fulfill it. Normally I would lay out all the options in front of me, no matter how depressing they might be, and examine each one with sensible logic and scholarly aplomb. At that moment, however, such a meticulous, systematic approach seemed banal instead of academic. I had to figure out how to help both of us survive in the middle of a jungle and eventually find a way home. Yet I didn't want to come right out and say that our chances were next to impossible. Even though the variables were astronomical, our resources limited, and my own abilities handicapped, I took some courage from Melodee's trust in me.

"I guess we should first figure out where we are," I said with mock bravado. I wanted to sound sure of myself, confident, but in reality, I had no idea where to start. The only solid facts were that the two of us were in less-than-perfect health in some time-forsaken jungle in the middle of who-knows-where with little more than the clothes on our backs.

"I think we're in Mexico, or somewhere in Central America," Melodee offered.

That made sense. Of course it did. We were flying in a plane that had a limited range—1800 miles at best. We were heading southeast toward a city that was only a hundred and twenty miles north of the Mexican border. And a few hundred miles to the south of that border, at the extreme edge of the commuter plane's range, were the tropical rain forests of deep Mexico. If we had crashed anywhere near the border, we would be in more of a desert environment. This was anything but that.

"I think you're right," I concurred. "We might even be somewhere in the Yucatán Peninsula."

Melodee smirked. "Thanks for agreeing."

I flinched. *Was that a slam?* No. She was too innocent for her remarks to be sarcastic. Impressed with her deductions, I said, "You're pretty smart for a . . . how old are you again?"

"Twelve and a half."

Her smirk spread into a warm smile, full of pride. The smile was in direct contrast to the oppressive situation in which we found ourselves. I decided to encourage the first emotion.

"How'd you get to be so smart for a twelve-and-a-half-year-old?"

She shrugged her shoulders. "I read a lot. That's how I spend my free time. My mom says I should try other things besides reading, but she lets me do it anyway. My dad says you can never learn too much. He says the more you know, the more you know you don't know."

"That's pretty profound," I chuckled. "I think I agree with your dad."

I leaned forward, preparing to stand, when an unexpected wave of nausea surged up my throat. I suppressed it with some deep breathing and leaned back in the seat. The thought crossed my mind that I might have internal injuries as well as a broken arm, perhaps even a serious head injury. If that were the case then things would soon turn from bad to worse.

"You should probably take it easy for a while," Melodee said with doctorlike authority. She reached around her seat and hefted her backpack onto her lap. "You hit your head pretty hard when we crashed. You might even have brain damage."

"My wife accuses me of that all the time," I scoffed lightly.

She smiled politely. "You should drink some water, and I'll get you something to eat if you'd like."

"Some water would be nice, but I don't like the idea of you wandering off and getting lost."

She gave me a sassy look as if to say, *Who found whom out here?* I quickly added, "I'm really not very hungry right now anyway."

"It's okay. I know right where to go," she said as she retrieved a small squeeze bottle from a pouch on the side of her backpack and handed it to me. "I won't get lost."

"You mean you already know your way around here?"

"Of course. We've been here for two days, you know."

"Wh—at?" I croaked, gagging on the swig I'd just taken.

"This is our third day here," she stated. "We crashed night before last."

I was speechless. Sensing my confusion, Melodee explained, "We crashed Wednesday night. If you look at the day on your watch you'll see it's now Friday."

I did. She was right.

She continued, "At first I thought I was the only one who survived. The plane pretty much blew apart when we hit. Our section must have broken off from the rest of the plane. When we stopped, my seat was stuck in a bunch of gooey moss or something, over there by the stream." She pointed as she talked. "You really smacked your head hard, and at first I thought you were dead. I found you on your side right here." She nodded at a divot of gouged grass and soil. "There was a man and a lady beyond those trees over there . . . but they died." She paused a moment, then continued in a much quieter voice. "I found a couple of others a lot farther away, but it was too late to help them. I don't know where everyone else ended up."

"But we were sitting right next to each other. Why did . . . how?" I found it impossible to form a complete question. Finally, I asked, "How did we end up so far apart?"

She shrugged. "I don't know. Your seat and this one," she patted the tilting chair in front of me, "broke off with the wing when we hit. I think mine split off from yours just before we stopped rolling. It's a good thing you had a pillow over your head, or your skull would have cracked clean open when it broke the window."

I gingerly touched the large lump on my head. "I vaguely remember you putting the pillow there for me."

She ducked her head slightly. "Well, you were pretty sleepy. I thought you looked kinda drunk. Maybe it was that little pill you took, or the alcohol. That's why our religion teaches us not to drink, you know. You're never in complete control when you drink, my dad always says."

"Your dad may be right." An illuminating realization swiftly filled my mind as I took another pull from her water bottle, a realization I was loath to admit, but did so anyway. "You may have saved my life, young lady."

She blushed warmly through the soot on her face. "I doubt that. I bet that pill made you so relaxed that you just flopped around when the plane broke apart."

"Yeah. The alcohol may have had a little to do with it, too." I furrowed my brow in mock resolution and stated, "I may just give up drinking because of you."

I wasn't serious, of course, but the way her face radiated with pride at my false declaration made my conscience wither in shame. If this little Mormon girl thought she was close to converting a lost soul like mine, she was grossly mistaken. I was pretty well entrenched in my beliefs about life on Earth, and religion had very little to do with my philosophies and conclusions. Still, considering our current situation and the fact that Melodee quite possibly *did* save my life, I thought it best to play along and not dampen her ardor.

"That would be great," she beamed, "but you really don't owe me anything."

"I think I do, and I want to honestly offer you my thanks."

"Well, you're welcome."

There was an awkward pause as we stared at our feet, wondering what to do next.

"So, what happened after the wing came off?" I asked.

"I don't know exactly. Like I said, there was some fire and stuff, and we flipped over a bunch of times, and when we finally stopped, there wasn't much of the plane left anywhere."

"How far does the crash spread out?"

"Pretty far. All over, in fact, but most of it is on the other side of those trees," she pointed. "That's where the other bodies are," she added softly.

"How many have you found?" I asked just as softly.

"Just six—some old people and the stewardess. I don't know where the others are. I think they weren't wearing their seat belts or something, and got thrown out when the plane ripped open."

"And you're sure they're all dead?" I asked, still not believing we were the sole survivors.

She nodded as tears again welled in her tired eyes.

"It's okay, Melodee. No need to dwell on bad things we can't change. But let me ask one more question. If you and I are the only ones around, who put my arm in this splint?"

She gave me another "Duh!" look and said, "I already told you: I did."

She was right; she had said that before. Only it hadn't sunk into my addled brain. This little wisp of a girl had somehow righted my seat and put my broken arm in a splint and sling. "Where did you learn first aid?" I asked, admiring the crude but effective triage.

"At girl's camp. I know CPR, too."

"Wow. You *are* pretty smart."

"No, I'm not. I just like to read and learn."

I smiled and shook my head, wondering if my daughter would grow up to be as incredible as this young girl was. Then my thoughts drifted to another question. "If we crashed Wednesday night, what have you been doing for two days?"

"Cleaning things up, mostly. You've been unconscious most of the time."

"Apparently."

My thoughts raced to organize all the pertinent information affecting our current situation. The contract I was sent to negotiate for BioCraft was probably lost, or maybe just delayed because of the storm—if the storm had reached that far south. Hopefully, the people expecting me in São Paulo had reported my absence, and anyone checking the flight records would see I had missed the scheduled Delta flight. A name search might show I had booked a last-minute seat on Southern Skies Ltd. Or perhaps the airline hostess/English teacher look-alike might remember suggesting the shuttle flight. I shook my head. In the confusion of countless holiday travelers, she'd probably forgotten my name the minute I left her sight. Why I hadn't called in to report my missed flight, I didn't know. My mind was elsewhere at the time, I guessed. But even the crash of a small commuter service would have to be reported, and a search would undoubtedly be initiated. They should already be looking for us, especially since a couple of days had lapsed since the crash.

Melodee reached into a pocket and pulled out a small bag of pretzels. "Here, happy late Thanksgiving."

I stared at the small bag that contained a dozen pretzels at best—and my heart sank. The fact that my company would be furious at my failure to make São Paulo by Thanksgiving was nothing compared to the anger my wife would feel at my inability to make yet another promised holiday appearance. Especially this one.

Thanksgiving was Dyana's favorite holiday. She loved what it represented: family. She had always cherished Thanksgiving because it bespoke all the things the pilgrims had left the religious oppression of England for, including the right to raise their children by whatever religious credos they deemed best. To my wife, Thanksgiving was a time to be thankful, not so much for the bounties we had garnered or for the easy life we enjoyed, but for the very country in which we lived. To her, the holiday represented the courage of a few brave families who had risked everything for future generations. It had as much patriotic substance as the Fourth of July. Thanksgiving was in celebration of our country's first patriots, the pilgrims. It was in honor of them. And I had failed to honor my family by not being home for yet another Thanksgiving—three times in a row. Three strikes and you're out. I began to wonder if my family would even notice my absence, they were so accustomed to it. And even though this time it was not my fault—mostly—I still could not think of an appropriate way to sufficiently justify missing my wife's favorite time of year.

I thought of Melodee's family, too. They would be devastated not knowing where their daughter was or even if she were still alive. What would they be thankful for? Nothing. My family was used to my absence . . . but hers? I choked on the emotions that stirred inside me as I saw in my mind an empty plate at a holiday-festooned table, and somber, tear-stained faces trying to be stoic in spite of the horrible news from Southern Skies Ltd. and the FAA.

I thanked Melodee for the pretzels. "Are you sure you don't want them?" I asked.

"No, I've had plenty. There were bags all over the place. It seems right when I get hungry, another bag shows up."

"And this is all you've eaten for two days," I stated.

"No, I had a sandwich in my backpack, and there's a banana tree right behind you, but they're kinda green."

"What a lousy Thanksgiving," I snarled with double meaning, angry at life while trying to be sympathetic toward her unstated melancholy. "I'm sorry there's not much to be thankful for."

But she didn't seem remorseful at all.

"Yes, there is," she corrected rather sternly. "We have a very obvious reason to be thankful."

"Oh?" I scoffed, thinking only of our present miserable state.

"Hello! Isn't it obvious?"

Missing my family's favorite holiday—*again*. Dreading the verbal (and perhaps monetary) reprimand I'd get from BioCraft. Lost in a rain forest with a broken arm and a possible head injury. *Yeah, those are the kind of things for which I'm always grateful.*

"Tell me, what the—" I choked on the harsh expletive I was about to use, and instead asked, "Exactly what I should be thankful for? There's no turkey, no stuffing, no pumpkin pie and whipped cream."

"No, but those things can always be had later. We're fortunate that way. No one else on the plane will ever have them again. We should be thankful because we're alive."

It hit me like a full-on punch in the stomach. So what if we had missed one holiday—albeit an important one—with our families? Who cared if we did not have the goodies with which to stuff ourselves like pigs being fattened for slaughter? We had so much more to be thankful for than anyone else on the Southern Skies Ltd. flight to Corpus Christi.

We were alive!

SIX

The day warmed significantly as it wore on. I napped often and tried my best to stretch my cramped muscles, but was only able to stand up for brief periods. Nausea and vertigo limited my mobility, and I found the best way to deal with the pain was to sleep through it.

One could hardly construe the wreckage in our immediate area as a major crash site. Even the most highly trained FAA forensics expert would meet his match trying to identify the various bits and pieces of debris scattered around us, let alone determine what fragments came from which part of the airplane. A scrap of metal here, a bit of cloth there, sundry wires, and shards of plastic littered the forest floor, resembling a scaled-down version of a New York City ticker-tape parade. There were also fragments in the trees above us, scattered randomly throughout the canopy like the metallic nests of countless robotic birds. Luckily, the only remnants we didn't encounter were the corpses—whole or otherwise—of those who didn't survive the crash, except the few Melodee had found.

The young girl had covered the bodies, or what remained of them, with tattered and singed blankets she'd found. Having landed fairly close together, the bodies lay in unnatural positions, and I figured the kid simply didn't want to touch them. I couldn't blame her. I hadn't seen the makeshift funeral proceedings, but I guessed it was a fairly gruesome undertaking. Undoubtedly, she had offered a prayer over the deceased. If that gave her some comfort, fine. As for praying over dead tissue, I simply didn't put much credence in wishing for things you couldn't change. Asking a God she had no proof of to watch over the departed souls of our flight was like praying that a certain lottery ticket was the ten-million-dollar winner. The lottery of life had already determined their winnings. I'd say they lost.

The following day we tried to dig graves for the deceased, but with my recent injuries and Melodee's limited strength, the best we could accomplish was a few shallow depressions in which we laid the bodies. My little companion prattled on incessantly about her family and her schoolwork as we performed the grisly task. I figured it was her way of keeping her mind from the horrible nature of such an odious chore. Several clues in her ramblings led me to believe she had a photographic memory—or something very close to it. She denied the claim, but I perceived it was due to embarrassment rather than an error of fact.

Melodee had done a good job of gathering every item she could find, useful or not. She had even discovered an unopened mini-bottle of vodka, which she gave to me without comment. Remembering how she felt about alcoholic beverages, I decided not to drink it in front of her. As an afterthought, I deemed it prudent to save the alcohol until it was medically necessary. I handed the small bottle back to her and asked that she keep it safely in her backpack.

What I had hoped to find was a first-aid kit. I needed some pain medication for my head and arm. Both were disrupting my concentration with disorienting waves of pain and random surges of dizziness and nausea. I could do little to quell the symptoms. Mostly I tried to just grimace and bear it. As far as nursing my broken bones, Melodee had already done all that could be done.

I examined the crude splint and sling again. She had braced my arm between two stout sticks and wrapped the assemblage with strips of cloth she'd found. From the look of the gingham pattern, the fabric had probably come from a woman's blouse. The sling was a portion of pillowcase that wrapped around my neck and cradled my arm. I could not discern how badly my arm had been broken, although I remembered earlier seeing it bent where no joint naturally occurred. Had Melodee set it correctly? I really didn't want to remove the splint to find out. I figured the best way to keep my pain at a minimum was to simply not mess with it. A doctor could sort it out later, with me blissfully under the wondrous effects of general anesthesia and a morphine drip.

With the speed of a lethargic snail, I made my way to a fallen tree trunk blanketed with thick, spongy moss, took a seat, and looked around. Ordinarily I would have thought this environment a captivatingly beautiful place. Abundant shades of green created a kaleidoscope of patterns, punctuated by occasional bursts of brilliantly colored tropical flowers. Considering our current circumstances, however, I could not keep my eyes, my mind, or my heart focused on the pleasant scene. There were simply too many negatives. And the intense isolation and forced captivity of the crash site elicited a decidedly unwelcome feeling.

Melodee had just finished combing over a small clearing and was coming toward me. She had a slight limp and was sweating profusely, more so than would be expected even in this humid environment. Other than that, she seemed fine. The fact that she came out of the crash without a scratch seemed beyond the most creative imagination. I had already asked question after question about how she walked away from the tragedy unscathed, but she said it all happened so fast that she remembered very little of it. At first, I found her stoicism frustrating, as if she were trying to show off how well she had fared compared to my pitiful state. Then I remembered reading about the ability of young children to block severe traumatic events from their memories so they would not have to relive the angst and fear that accompanied such episodes. I was certain Melodee had done just that. Her light frame and weight also gave her advantage over the older passengers by allowing her body to bend and twist in ways that would cause severe damage to persons much older than her. I reflected again on the fortuitousness of being chemically inebriated at the time. Like numerous car crashes where the undeserving drunk who caused the accident ends up being the sole survivor, my sedative-alcohol mix had literally kept me from a blanket shroud and a shallow grave. It was also pure luck that I wasn't irreparably crippled, consigned to relive the terrifying experience every day for the rest of my life. A broken arm was a very acceptable price to bear considering the alternatives.

"Are you sure you're not hurt?" I asked Melodee for the umpteenth time, still inwardly perturbed at her ability to shrug off this disaster.

"Yep, I'm fine."

"Well, you look pretty worn out to me. Pretty tired, too."

"Yeah, I get that way sometimes, but it usually passes."

I kicked at a rock by my foot. "If you say so. Still, I'm glad neither of us was seriously hurt in the crash."

Her eyes narrowed, as if she sensed an emptiness in my words. "Really? You seem more upset than glad," she stated with razor-sharp honesty.

"Trust me, I'm plenty glad. It just baffles me that we're the only two who survived. There had to have been about fifteen people on that plane, including the pilots."

"I think Heavenly Father was watching over us," she said with such nonchalant confidence she could have been answering the question, "What is one plus one?" She wasn't preaching or trying to show off her unshakable faith; she was simply stating a fact. The unbeliever in me wondered why God hadn't "watched over" the others too, but I didn't voice my pessimism.

Instead, I shook my head and said, "He may have been watching out for you, but I doubt He even knows my name."

She snickered. "You're funny. Of course He knows your name. Heavenly Father knows everyone, although He might not be as pleased with some as He is with others," she added without accusation.

I shrugged. "Perhaps."

Actually, I had serious reservations about her forthright state-ment, yet I doubted she would understand. Having never been a religious man, I only *sort of* believed in a higher power—some governing influence that organized the universe in which we lived. I was a man of science. I knew the ins and outs of many biological, geological, and even medical processes. I could work chemical equa-tions in my head as if merely an afterthought. I could regurgitate the taxonomy of thousands of flora and fauna without pause. I accepted things that made sense: the tangible, the verifiable, things proven by fact and scientific experimentation. But I simply could not accept the existence of an all-loving, all-knowing "father" in heaven.

I wasn't an atheist per se. I could acknowledge the concept of a godlike entity; I just couldn't understand Him. If He had infinite love for all His children, why did so many terrible things go on in the world? Our plane crash was a perfect example. It didn't make sense. Accepting that disaster—and our mysterious survival—as part of God's plan required a kind of blind faith I couldn't condone. The kind of myopic obedience mandated by most world religions—to accept things because "that's the way God wants them"—bordered on ignorance and skirted close to idiocy. I was certain Melodee's understanding of such things came straight from the Bible or some Sunday School teacher's pious interpretation. That was fine for her.

Not me.

My wife, Dyana, a college graduate with an accounting background, had a religious conviction of sorts. Often, she would attend various services on Sunday, but she never joined a specific denomination. She never felt completely satisfied with any one doctrine or philosophy. Paige accompanied her and seemed to enjoy the association with parishioners her age, but I wondered how much she truly got out of it. Occasionally, Dyana even dragged me across a church's threshold—for a Christmas service, a wedding, or the christening of a friend's baby. Yet I never felt comfortable in such places.

In my youth, Matt Christiansen had asked a number of times if I'd like to go to a Mormon worship service with him. I finally gave in once—and thought it was the weirdest meeting I'd ever attended. Nestled tightly in hard-backed pews, the noisy children of several large families spent their time coloring pictures and fighting over Cheerios rather than listening to the sermon. Adjacent to them, teenagers filled the air with excited whispers and incessant, nonreligious chatter. To add further distraction, the occasional odor of an over-ripe diaper wafted past my nostrils, averting my attention from the proffered message. And their minister—I think Matt called him a 'bishop'— didn't even do the preaching! Instead, a member of the congregation gave an insufferably long speech about food storage—not God or Jesus. Matt later explained that the Church was interested in *all* aspects of our lives, and that food storage was mostly about obedience, not simply being prepared for emergencies. Still, I found it very strange.

I had always believed church meetings should be solemn and reverent, where a preacher pontificated on some timeless lesson from the scriptures: faith and brotherly love, hellfire, brimstone, forgiveness, damnation, or a do-unto-others kind of sermon. Matt said they got that stuff too, all the time in fact, just not on that particular Sunday. If you had the same lesson repeatedly crammed down your throat (my words, not his) meeting after meeting, things would get real boring real fast. I had to agree.

As I watched Melodee rummage through her backpack, I wondered if she attended similar meetings back home. I could understand why God would want to spare her life. She had a purity about her that bespoke a faith in the Almighty and a love of her fellow man. But why me? Why did I survive too? I was much too bitter and egocentric for that kind of heavenly gratuity—if such a thing existed.

"Do you think it's possible to figure out exactly where we are right now?" she asked, snapping me from my wandering thoughts.

"I'm not sure. We know we were heading south because we're in this rain forest, which we both assume is in Central America."

"Makes sense to me."

"What I really want to know is how we got this far off course."

Melodee put a finger to her temple in rapt concentration. "Well . . . remember when the lights went off after we got hit by lightning?" she stated. "The copilot said something about the electric systems going down. Maybe that broke the direction finders and we drifted off course."

So the lightning shorted out the VORTAC compass and GPS navigational equipment. Which means we have no way of finding out where we are . . . "A smaller plane like ours probably didn't have a redundant system or any kind of backup, and with the storm being so bad, there were no visual landmarks to go by," I continued to reason, this time aloud.

"Yep. I bet that's how we got here," she said as if she were simply choosing which pair of shoes to wear that day.

"I agree," I said, trying to mimic her happy-go-lucky attitude.

Considering our bleak circumstances, I would have thought a girl her age would be trembling with fright, but Melodee seemed so at ease with the situation that I felt foolish worrying about anything at all. Still, my analytical nature told me we had little chance of survival without proper equipment or supplies. Yet I didn't want to frighten the little girl by voicing the obvious. I thought it best to try to instill some confidence in her—actually, more for me than for her—by listing the things we knew for certain.

"Let's make a plan, shall we?" I suggested.

"Okay."

"First off, we have a good guess where we are, and we have a valid assumption on how we got here."

"Yep," she said, returning to her backpack.

"I guess the next thing is to determine which direction to go to get out of here." Tilting my head to one side, I watched her pilfer through her backpack, mildly annoyed that she was ignoring my dissertation. "Are you paying attention?"

"Of course."

I frowned. "What exactly are you looking for?"

"A way to get out of here."

Perhaps she wasn't ignoring me after all. "From inside your backpack?"

"You said we need to find which direction to go, right?" She looked up as she continued to search the depths of her backpack by touch alone.

I nodded. "Yeah. You have something in there that will help us do that?"

"Yep," she answered as her eyes lit up with the elation of success. Withdrawing her hand from the pack, she said, "Here it is."

In her small hand was a black-rimmed, solidly built compass. It was the kind many Boy Scouts carried when venturing into the woods for an outing of camping skills, merit badges, and ghost stories. I couldn't have thought of a better item to have at that moment, except for maybe some Lortab or Tylenol III, or a Double Whopper with cheese and a chocolate milkshake. But a compass in the backpack of an adolescent girl baffled me. I would have thought her possessions would be comprised of a pink diary with a white unicorn airbrushed on the cover, a Pez dispenser (empty), a matching comb and brush, some preteen makeup, and a pocket CD player loaded with Brittany Spears' latest platinum-selling bubble-gum music. A compass, and a good one by the look of it, was by no small means a miracle possession.

"This will help guide us on our journey home. It will be our Liahona."

"Our what?"

She stood and played at finding true north while turning slowly in a circle. "Our Liahona. In the Book of Mormon, the Lord commanded a man named Lehi to take his family out of Jerusalem to a promised land that was to be their new home. And Lehi was guided by a compass called the Liahona. But it only worked when his family was obeying the commandments."

The words she spoke had a familiar ring to them, maybe relating to something Matt had told me long ago, but the obvious importance they played in Melodee's life had absolutely no bearing in mine.

"Lehi?"

"Yeah, the prophet Lehi. From Jerusalem," she said pointedly, as if repeating the names would bring to remembrance something I had learned as a youth.

"Oh, *that* Lehi," I said, trying to sound encouraging, but not grasping an iota of what she was talking about.

"Yep."

I smiled cheerfully. I did not want to belittle the valor this brave girl was showing or frighten her with a stiff dose of reality. The compass—or whatever she wanted to call it—would help us find direction in this labyrinth of dense jungle. It was a massive stroke of good luck which offset the equally massive bad luck that had landed us here. And I was very glad she had it.

The next big question was, would her compass help us get out of the rain forest before we died from physical exhaustion, starvation, or worse?

SEVEN

One minute it was day, the next, night. Since we were at the base of countless tall trees, which formed a dense, multilayered canopy, the rising and setting of the sun was merely acknowledged instead of witnessed. The only way to view the sky was to find a small clearing and look straight up. This I did and saw an ominous portent.

Dark clouds swelled with torrential foreboding and promised a miserable night if we didn't find shelter soon. The stifling humidity saturated our clothes and soaked us to the bone. Despite the imminent storm, night sounds erupted as if on cue the moment the sun disappeared. Frogs of various timbre, crickets, cicadas, and countless unidentified insects filled the air with sounds so numerous it made one dizzy trying to pinpoint any particular species.

There were other sounds, too. Dangerous sounds. Ululations I wished I couldn't hear, yet which found their way through the din of lovesick bugs and amphibians like a horrific nightmare makes its way through the cloak of blissful slumber. The deep, throaty sounds of large predators caused a mental sign to flash: *Warning. No Loitering.* Why I had treated it with minimal consideration before infuriated me, but the scent of blood from the former living, breathing members of our doomed flight was sure to attract scavengers that would not care if their meal was long dead or still kicking. Night was a time of feasting for most of the jungle's carnivores. Our recent tragedy provided new fare to their menu, and I had little desire to be the *especial du jour* that evening.

After she produced the compass, Melodee and I policed the area in search of any last item that might prove useful. I found a ballpoint pen and a disposable butane lighter. At first, we had considered staying with the wreckage in hopes that a search plane might spot us. However, knowing that we had crashed in a particularly dense section of rain forest, we acknowledged the futility of such a hope.

With our policing complete, we took a moment to organize a plan. Despite the threat of storm and predator, we were both cool-headed enough not to go running pell-mell into the forest with unchecked hysteria. But in being carelessly placid, we had lost track of time—our most precious asset. Now, shadowed by the last light of dusk ebbing into blackness, we forfeited all hope of making our way more than a few feet without falling off a cliff or bumping into a voraciously hungry creature long on teeth and short on patience.

On top of that, my broken arm was clouding my thoughts with throbs of pain so intense I often had to hold perfectly still and take several deep breaths to keep from passing out. We found no coveted first-aid kit or other items that might help with my injuries. My carry-on, which had a plethora of medicaments within its depths, had disappeared. How my seat remained intact, yet my carry-on stowed under it had not, was a mystery worthy of Sherlock Holmes himself. Nevertheless, I was not one to dwell on things I could not change, and instead began looking for certain plants that would help my pitiful state.

Earlier that day, I had found a native willow which has certain salicylates in its bark—medicine that would help with both pain and inflammation. But getting the drug from the bark would require a distillery of sorts. Instead, I scraped a bit of fiber from the inner cambium layer and washed it in a clear stream, then chewed it briefly. I rinsed my mouth immediately afterwards to reduce the chance of ulceration from the caustic substance. Fortunately, it did help—a little—and I suffered no ill aftereffects. Of course, it may also have been a simple placebo effect, but at that point, I didn't care.

Several times, I considered drinking the mini-bottle of vodka, but I didn't feel that total oblivion—as tempting as that sounded—was wise. Our precarious situation in the deep, dark middle of nowhere warranted a sharp mind and sharper reflexes. I needed my wits about me, and a stiff shot of alcohol was one sure way to lose them.

As the night pressed harder on the clouds overhead, the first few fat drops of rain beat a *rat-a-tat-tat* on the leaves around us.

"We'd better find some shelter quickly," I said to Melodee.

"Okay."

A small river to the east had several large mangrove-like trees on its banks. The roots of these trees began some three to five feet above the ground, some higher, which arched away from the main trunk enough to create a small hollow. We found a suitable tree whose roots extended into the river on one side and over a good portion of dry ground on the other. We gathered some large taro leaves and, laying them on top of the arching roots, created an instant shelter. I placed more elephant's ear leaves on top of these and used some small stones to anchor everything in place. Melodee did her best to sweep out the interior and make it as pleasant as possible.

Just as we settled in, the rain came in earnest, a thundering torrent that seemed more like a waterfall than drops of precipitation. My thoughts turned to the river a few feet away. If the storm did not rescind its Noah-like deluge, the river would undoubtedly overflow its banks and wash us away like so much driftwood. I decided not to share this insight with Melodee, figuring she would be more concerned about my safety than her own. She impressed me as that kind of girl. It was an equally annoying and admirable trait.

What we both needed was to clear our minds of any immediate concerns, have a nourishing meal, and get a good night's rest. But as the rain continued, the thoughts of scavenging for food were quelled. Moreover, the potential for predatory animals gravitating toward the crash site kept my eyes glued to the entrance of our little grotto. It was all too apparent we would not get a refreshing rest that evening.

I sighed heavily and peered out at the pulsating clouds, backlit by occasional bursts of sheet lightning. *Great.* All we needed to make this night totally unbearable was lightning and thunder the likes of which got us here in the first place. "That'd be just my luck," I grumbled under my breath.

As if in response, the bloated clouds belched out a long, tremulous, bass reverberation so spectacular it would have made the timpani section of the Philadelphia Philharmonic green with envy.

"Cool," was Melodee's awe-filled response.

"Yeah," was my unenthusiastic concurrence.

We sat for a time watching the celestial light-and-sound show. I don't know if it was the odd shadows cast by the lightning, but Melodee had a haunted look about her, a sickliness around her eyes and a gauntness hollowing her cheeks that I hadn't noticed before.

"You okay?" I asked.

"Fine," she replied without emphasis.

As I attempted to settle into a more comfortable position, Melodee suddenly wrapped her arms across her stomach and winced. She rocked tenderly back and forth and breathed slowly yet forcefully through clenched teeth.

"Are you sure you're not hurt?" I asked again with a heartfelt sincerity that surprised even me.

She rocked a bit more before gathering enough breath to answer. "I'm okay. I'm just hungry, that's all." It wasn't a complaint, just a statement of fact.

I'd thought a lot about food. I knew that in times of severe stress the human body can compensate for normal daily needs by deadening its sensitivity. But as soon as Melodee made her declaration, I could no longer ignore the vast emptiness inside my stomach. I realized we had gone four days without a real meal. The fact that Melodee had not complained about living on pretzels and a few green bananas was a wonder to me. From the look on her face, she was suffering more than she had let on.

"I'm hungry too," I said. "But then, I could stand to lose a few pounds." I patted a succinct drumroll on my belly, trying to lighten the mood.

She smiled but didn't laugh. Instead, she began rummaging wearily through her backpack, again searching more by feel than by sight. Within a minute, she pulled out a gorgeous, large Red Delicious apple. "Here," she said, placing the fruit in my hand.

"Where'd this come from?" I asked, gawking at the fruit.

"My backpack, silly."

"No, I mean . . . why didn't you eat it earlier? You must be starving by now."

"I've been saving it for later," she replied. "Besides, I don't have that big of an appetite."

Emotionally overwhelmed, I tried to refuse the apple. "No, Melodee, I can't take—"

"It's okay," she interrupted. "Apples aren't fattening."

I wanted to laugh and cry at the same time. "No, it's not that. You need this a lot more than I do. You eat it."

"I'll be fine until morning," she said with a wan smile. "I just want to get some sleep now."

"But you're hungrier than I am," I protested. I had to admit that part of me wouldn't allow a little girl to one-up me. But I also took comfort in the feeling that I truly did not want her to suffer from hunger on top of everything else she'd gone through. Maybe it was my parental instincts taking charge. Maybe it was just stubborn pride. Whichever the master, I was willing to be the humble servant and let this brave girl have what could very well be our only decent food for a very long time.

She gave me the look a weary parent flashes an exasperating child. Then she reached into her backpack again and pulled out a red Swiss Army knife, one of the big ones that had everything you could ever want on it and a few things you had no clue what to do with.

"How'd you get that past airport security?"

"I don't know," she said with unquestionable innocence.

"Didn't they x-ray your backpack?"

"Of course."

I waited for an explanation. None came. "Was the knife in it at the time?"

"Yeah. I keep it in my pencil tin."

That would explain it, I reasoned. The metal container would hide a pocketknife. I marveled at the irony of the situation. If Melodee had been caught with the knife, she would have been detained, and undoubtedly would have missed the doomed flight. She would be home now, safe, healthy, and happy. I decided not to share this insight with the little girl. She might just conclude her luck was as bad as mine.

Melodee opened the largest blade and took the apple from my hand. "We'll share," she pronounced as she sliced the apple cleanly in two.

I took the proffered half, but could not take my eyes from the young girl sitting next to me. What wouldn't I give to have had her maturity at that age? As a youngster, I had been a roustabout, a would-be naturalist and explorer, an adventurer who had little interest in being good and setting proper examples. I remembered being more a source of embarrassment and consternation to my parents than an emblem of pride. I began to wonder what kind of environment Melodee came from. What were her parents like, and what had they done to raise such a remarkable girl?

"Would you consider this our supper?" Melodee asked with a serious expression sharpening her face.

I looked at my luminescent wristwatch. It was nearly twelve a.m. "It's more like a midnight snack, I'm afraid."

She shrugged. "Either way, perhaps we should say a blessing on it, like it was our supper."

Her suggestion struck me as a rather childish thing to do. What good would a prayer on a halved apple do for us? It's not as if it replaced our Thanksgiving dinner. If blessing our food was that important, why were we forced to miss a semi-religious meal with our families in the first place?

As if Melodee could read my thoughts, a forlorn, weary pout reached her eyes. "I take it you don't you pray over your meals."

I lowered my eyes. "I guess I never thought it was that important."

A deep, angry rumble rippled through the storm above us, adding to the chastisement of my unbelief. Melodee was undaunted. "Well, I'm going to bless mine. You can bow your head if you want."

She closed her eyes and held the half apple in her hands as if she was cradling a delicate heirloom. In the darkness, I saw her lips move in silent prayer as she thanked her god for the meager meal before her.

She soon lifted her head, said, "Amen," and then took a big bite from the fruit.

I echoed a shy, "Amen," and followed her example. The tangy sweetness of the apple exploded in my mouth as if I had never tasted one ever before. What an incredible sensation! It was the best-tasting apple I could remember eating. Ever. I patiently tried to savor the fruit, but instead I greedily finished my half in three bites, core and all.

"Thank you, Melodee," I said, licking my fingers where a trace of juice had trickled. "That was a wonderful supper."

She smiled as she snuggled into a fetal position. "You're welcome," she said through a stifled yawn.

It was some time before the rain lightened. I drew a concealed sigh of relief, deciding that my earlier fears of a rising river were moot. As the endless night wore on without incident, I felt that we were temporarily secure in our little homemade shelter. Nonetheless, deep inside I knew we were far from being truly safe.

EIGHT

I watched Melodee's form in the darkness and thought again about her family back home. I wondered if they were grieving the certain death of their beautiful little daughter. My emotions twitched as I wondered if my family was grieving as much as hers was. I'm sure Dyana and Paige went on with Thanksgiving dinner as they had in years past, knowing I was somewhere completing a business deal that had a significance they couldn't understand but believed was important because I said so. Well, maybe not believed, but accepted. The more I dwelt on the thought, the more I wondered how I had remained married all these years.

My wife had done an amazing job keeping up with Paige's rearing and development. It seemed like each time I'd come home after a brief trip, my little girl would have aged not days but months, years. One day she was in a crib, sucking on a pacifier and reaching for the tropical fish mobile that hovered over her crib just beyond her reach. Then the next day I'd come home to see a ruffle-festooned infant crawling on all fours, wide-eyed and giggling at every little thing. I would lift her into my arms and kiss her neck. She would accept the kiss and then squirm from my embrace to be off in another direction, exploring the house and babbling excitedly, as if each corner she rounded revealed new territory. My wife, who never aged, would beam with a warm, radiant glow when I took time to play with Paige. She relished those moments, as did I. But it was inevitable that as soon as that precious time began, the phone would ring and BioCraft would have some critical need for my expertise. Then I'd hang up the phone, and my daughter would be walking. The lapse of time between those events was a blur of redundant memory, scintillated with brief vignettes of happiness at the dinner table and occasional birthday parties, and muddied with recollections of the same old excuses and droll rationalizations for my absence.

What grade was Paige in now? How many preschool activities had she attended with her mother but not her father? What finger-painting masterpieces taped to the fridge had I overlooked while getting a snack? What pride-filled accomplishments had she tried to share with me only to be waved off because I was too busy, or never shown me because I wasn't there?

My mind flashed to a sampling of Paige's artwork my wife had thrown in my face, not caring what shame and embarrassment it caused me. Dyana stormed out of the room before I had a chance to examine the crayon drawing. Had she stayed, she would have witnessed my breath catch deep in my chest and tears brim in my eyes. It was a drawing of a Christmas tree with ornaments and tinsel galore. Next to the tree were images of Paige and Dyana opening numerous gifts, with huge smiles filling their faces. Daddy was nowhere in the picture. My daughter had drawn the scene from her memory. *Fatherless* was the only kind of Christmas she knew. The insight was devastating.

My heart sank whenever I thought of that drawing, and each time I vowed to do better, to spend more time with Dyana and Paige, and less time trying to impress the upper echelon of BioCraft. However, I could not recall actually attempting the change, of honestly turning the tide of my career-dominated life and taking time for those who were dependent on me for financial support. *After all, if it weren't for my efforts, they wouldn't have a roof over their heads or food on the table,* I argued. That's what fathers were for, wasn't it? If I didn't successfully battle the dragons of the monetary world—Mortgage, Insurance, and Debt—then my wife would have to join the Career-Mom Society, and our daughter would be relinquished to the care of rented parents and television companionship.

Neither of us wanted that, so I worked hard. Extra hard. And because of that, I felt being blamed for a faltering family wasn't completely fair. Dyana wanted the big house in the upscale neighborhood as much as I did. She preferred owning a Lincoln Navigator to driving a Nissan sedan. Additionally, she wanted recognition for more than a clean house, a beautiful daughter, and a mildly profitable home-based business. I knew she hated riding my coattails, of being known as "David's wife" instead of Dyana Kirkham, successful number cruncher for some megacorporation in Thousand Oaks. She wasn't a hardcore career woman per se. She liked mixing two lifestyles: being a stay-at-home mom with Paige while keeping books for a couple of local dentists. But she also wanted me back at six o'clock every evening, with weekends off, and home for every holiday that graced the calendar. She expected life to be like a Norman Rockwell painting. I told her Pablo Picasso better represented reality. You simply can't have the "good life" on a more-or-less single income without making other cuts. Unfortunately, my family was often what lay on the chopping block.

Remembering Dyana's note, I pulled the slip of paper from my pocket. The light in the crude shelter was not conducive to reading, but it didn't have to be. The hotel concierge's block letters were easy enough to make out.

THIS IS THE LAST STRAW. NO MORE EXCUSES. IT'S OVER.

Melodee stirred and moaned quietly in her sleep. I could not tell if the moan was from pain or weariness. I wished there was more I could do for her. I knew her parents were making every effort to find out what had happened to their daughter's flight, and most certainly, offering prayers in her behalf. My family was asleep after spending the holiday weekend doing who-knows-what and snacking on Thanksgiving leftovers. Paige might accept the fact that Daddy was not home, but Dyana was silently cursing my name. *Way to go, David. Another family holiday down the drain.* If word had not reached them about the plane crash, they would naturally assume Dad was in Brazil, whooping it up at the company's expense, celebrating another financial victory for the omnipotent BioCraft Pharmaceutical Corporation.

But they'd be wrong. I had never enjoyed the time away from my wife and daughter. Yet each time I tried to explain this, the words sounded like insincere excuses. Whenever I attempted to validate my convictions, it seemed the phone would ring again, and my words would once again be invalidated. I had let my career take precedence in my life and had done nothing to change it. My family didn't miss me the way Melodee's missed her. And the fault *was* all mine.

I looked at Melodee and my eyes began to burn. A tear trickled down my cheek. I wiped it away and stared at the salty droplet on my finger. I was amazed to know I could still cry. It hadn't happened in so long. But it felt good. It was an awakening of sorts, an epiphany. And I swore that I, David Kirkham, would from hereafter be a better father and husband . . . *if* we got out of this jungle alive.

NINE

Putt-putt-putt-putt . . .

I awoke to whispers . . . and something else, a mechanical sound of some sort. The whispers came from Melodee. The other sound I couldn't figure out. And then it was gone.

Melodee was on her knees just outside our makeshift hut. She was praying again. I watched her for a moment, hearing nothing more than a subtle breathiness. All else seemed quiet in the early morning hour, as if the jungle were respectfully acknowledging the solemnity of her communication with her Maker. Out of respect for Melodee's beliefs, I waited until she was finished before I stirred. She still looked gaunt and weak, but I assumed that would change once we found some decent food.

The day promised to be a glorious one. The patches of sky we could see through the canopy were a brilliant robin-egg blue. Not a cloud in sight. The sun was just beginning its inexorable trek across the sky, and the warmth of its presence radiated throughout the jungle. Weaving tendrils of steam rose from the rain-soaked forest floor, mimicking the roots which hung from the branches of the banyan trees.

The sodden air was thick and claustrophobic. I inwardly moaned as I thought of how the rising sun, while filling us with warmth and hope, would also cause the jungle humidity to rise to such an insufferable level that it would quickly drain us of all remaining energy. Heat *and* humidity can do that to a body more rapidly than heat alone. And we had precious little energy to draw on. The day was indeed going to get worse before it got better.

Yet more unsettling than the weather was the sound I had just heard. The saturated atmosphere did little to muffle the natural noises of the waking jungle. But mixed with the myriad of bird, monkey, and insect calls was something unnatural, something alien to these primeval surroundings—a metallic timbre not created by indigenous animal life.

"Amen." Having finished her prayer, Melodee raised her head.

I cleared my throat politely. "Morning."

"Good morning, mister," she said cheerfully. "Did you sleep well?"

I couldn't remember falling asleep, but it was obvious I had. "I guess so," I answered with a yawn. My body ached from head to toe.

"Me too."

I crawled out of our shelter and stretched as much as my sling would allow. My broken arm throbbed again with renewed vengeance, but it was within the threshold of tolerability. I wondered: if I were home at that moment, would I bear the pain with as much stoicism? Or would I revert to being the typical male who became a simpering boob whenever he was sick or hurt? I shook my head. *No. Of course I wouldn't.*

Putt-putt-putt . . .

There was that sound again. I cocked my head, trying to concentrate on what it might be. The sound was so faint it was almost imperceptible, but I knew it didn't belong in the rain forest. It was a repetitive mechanical sound of some kind. I waited a moment, but the sound vanished as quickly as it had come.

"I'm really getting hungry," Melodee said, staring at me with more wistfulness in her eyes than I recalled seeing before. It was the closest to a complaint she had ever come.

"Me too, kid," I said, looking around for any possibility of nourishment. "Perhaps if we followed this river some we'd—"

Putt-putt-putt-putt . . .

My words caught in my throat as I heard the sound again. *Ah-ha!* I instantly recognized the noise as the distinct sputter of a two-stroke engine. Its spits and coughs echoed along the smooth surface of the river, originating from somewhere upstream. I smiled at Melodee as I made my way to a clearing a few yards up the riverbank. I could not see much of anything up the river, but I was certain the sound was getting closer. Perhaps we would not have to spend much time in this miserable jungle after all. This turn of fate seemed too good to be true.

The engine noise filtered in and out as the boat rounded corners and motored between steep embankments, and its steady *putt-putt-putt* grew louder each time we heard it. Normally a grating, distasteful din, at that moment it was the most beautiful music I had ever heard.

We gathered our few belongings and waited by the clearing at the water's edge. If the boatmen—whoever they were—could get us to civilization, I could phone BioCraft and have us out of Central America in a matter of hours.

The idea of telephoning my company was obviously one of the first things that crossed my mind after the crash. However, in searching my pockets and the crash site, I realized my cell phone had vanished along with my carry-on. Finding it would have proven to be the kind of luck I was not accustomed to anyway. My cell phone, my Palm, my Internet service, and my personal pager were all things that kept my life moving faster than time could account for. It was simply the way things were. I gained some comfort, however, knowing I was not alone in this regard. Current societal norms fairly mandated the use of these high-tech gadgets, and anyone who did not have a minimum of four telephone numbers and email addresses was considered Neanderthal, or at least mid-Victorian and way behind the times. Yet, while the modern world had many things that claimed to simplify our lives, it seemed that society had grown too dependent on those conveniences, so much so that their unexpected withdrawal often caused our personal worlds to grind to a halt.

Putt-putt-putt-putt . . .

It didn't matter much now. Help was on the way. Perhaps our four days in the jungle would end up being nothing more than an anecdotal conversation piece at dinner parties, which was okay by me. Still, it would have been exciting and somewhat vindicating to have made a call to Dyana from the crash site to explain my absence at Thanksgiving dinner.

I patted my empty pockets again for the thousandth time and cursed my misfortune. It would still be some time before I could tell my wife what had happened. If I could get just one break—any minor, little break—I would be content, I vowed, and would never complain again.

Melodee brought me back to reality when she took my hand and squeezed it firmly. "They're almost here," she said excitedly.

I felt a perceptible increase in Melodee's grip as she spoke again. This time her voice had a nervous edge to it. "What if they're head-hunters or cannibals?"

I chuckled lightly, then drew a short breath. The thought was at first humorous, but carried with it a profound dose of reality. I didn't think there were any such people in this part of the world, but who was to say the boat owners were not militant rebels with a loathing for anything American? Or closer to Melodee's concern, a boatload of loincloth-clad natives who had an innate mistrust of anyone not affiliated with their tribe—especially two white-skinned strangers? The jungles of Colombia and Brazil had many remote peoples of that kind, not unlike the Yanomamo Indians of Venezuela who call themselves "the fierce people" because of their craving for constant warfare. But here in Central Mexico? No.

"I don't think we have to worry about being eaten by anybody," I said lightly, "even if it does turn out to be a boatload of natives." I swallowed hard and forced a smile.

Putt-putt-putt-putt . . .

The boat was definitely coming toward us, but it was hard to tell when it would arrive. Whoever was operating this craft was taking his time. The sound grew steadily stronger but by small, almost imperceptible decibels. A worrisome apprehension churned in my stomach as we listened to the engine's rattle. Something inside me warned of danger, an instinctive foreboding I could not explain. I tried to reason it away, thinking it was simply not knowing what lay ahead, mixed with the unsettling events of the past few days. Yet it was something more than that. A dark something.

"What's the first thing you're going to do when you get home?" Melodee asked, breaking me from my premonitions.

I smiled. This time it was not forced. "I'm going to hug my wife and daughter and tell them I love them."

She nodded in affirmation. "I'm going to hug my parents, too, and my brothers and sisters, and then ask to get a huge pizza with everything on it, and eat it all by myself."

The thought of biting into a slice of gooey pizza with all its cholesterol-laden constituents, accompanied by a large helping of greasy garlic bread and gallons of draft beer, sounded great right then. But food was only one of the things that had been inundating my thoughts.

Throughout the past couple of days, having Melodee as my only link to humanity, I was acutely aware of how uniquely she behaved. She was not the typically spoiled, egocentric preteen who wanted everything and gave nothing in return. This young girl had a maturity beyond her years—beyond the years of many of my associates. It was more than the resounding confidence of faith in a religion such as Mormonism or the uncanny ability to memorize reams of information. I sensed it was something very personal, something I had no business knowing about. Still, I felt I had to know.

I looked down at Melodee and smiled. "The second thing I'm going to do is thank your mom and dad for raising such a remarkable young lady."

Melodee ducked her head, but I could see that her smile ran from one ear to the other. "You don't have to do that," she said softly, still smiling.

"Oh, I think I do. In fact—"

Putt-putt-putt . . .

I looked up and saw the bow of the boat edge into view. Expecting a rush of excitement, I was instead horrified at the first glimpse of our salvation.

It's amazing how fast the brain can process information, draw conclusions, and incite reflexive action—faster than many super-computers can calculate simple equations. In an instant, a whirl of facts registered in my mind, and a red flag of danger blazed across the back of my eyes.

Still holding Melodee's hand, I yanked her forcefully into the covering of some dense ferns. She opened her mouth to question my actions, but I covered it quickly with my good hand. I then placed my finger to my lips in a motion to be quiet.

We both had to be as silent as a grave, or we'd end up in one.

Putt-putt-putt . . .

The boat motored into the wide arc of the river where we could see it more clearly. But that meant the occupants of the boat might be able to see us, too. If our luck held out, that wouldn't happen.

"Why did—"

I placed my finger on Melodee's lips and silenced her for a moment longer.

There were three men in the boat, a wide, minimum-draft flatboat designed for moving cargo through shallow waters. Each man looked to be of South American nationality. They were surly-looking characters with faces that radiated a foul disposition and a seething hatred of everything about their lives. At the rear of the boat, one man operated the long-handled throttle that regulated the outboard engine's speed. The other two men sat in the bow, looking forward. Both held shotguns at the ready. The cargo in the center of the boat was loosely covered with a camouflaged tarpaulin, but enough of the product extended beyond the covering that I recognized it immediately.

Erythroxylum coca, the coca shrub used to illegally manufacture cocaine.

"What's wrong?" Melodee whispered anxiously.

"Those men are drug runners," I whispered back.

She frowned at me, and then turned her attention to the boat creeping past us. "How can you tell that?"

"They have a boatload of coca leaves. Probably taking it to a hideout where they will make it into cocaine."

She frowned more deeply at my words, not as if she recognized the imminent danger we were in, but more as if I had just revealed that a neighbor down the street regularly took the Lord's name in vain. She was not afraid, but rather, displeased.

"Do you understand what I'm saying?" I whispered urgently, wanting her to comprehend the magnitude of our precarious situation.

She nodded. "Yeah. Those are bad men."

Her gross understatement actually hit the proverbial nail on the head. They were bad men—men who would not think twice about killing a couple of innocent American plane-crash survivors and dropping their bodies in the river. Men who actually killed thousands of Americans by selling a highly addictive substance to kids as young as Melodee for a profit, not caring what permanent damage it did to their brain cells, nerve tissues, immune systems, cardiac muscles, optical fibers, and sinus tissues, not to mention their personal and social lives and self-esteem. All those men cared about was money. And they would kill us to protect that money as easily as they would swat a mosquito on their arm. That they would eventually kill countless people with their illicit product probably never crossed their minds.

Knowing that my blue shirt and white pillowcase sling did not blend well with the surrounding plant life, I tried to crouch a bit lower. It was unfortunate irony that the foliage density in this rain forest was probably some of the thickest in the world, yet the hiding place I had chosen seemed pitifully sparse. Our best defense was to remain quiet and perfectly still, so as not to attract any attention.

As the boat steadily moved away from us, its noisy two-stroke motor continued to corrupt the pristine, tranquil jungle. The man closest to the riverbank was eyeing the mud along the shore. Had we left any footprints? My line of sight did not allow me to see the embankment, and I could only hope that fate would lean in our favor on this one. But it didn't.

The nearest gun-toter mumbled something to his partner in the bow. That man then turned to say something to the man at the tiller. As he was speaking, he casually looked in our direction.

Our eyes locked. I tried to turn mine away but knew it was too late. A trancelike bond formed instantly between his eyes and mine, like a person who comes upon a severe traffic accident with crumpled bodies involved—they want to keep moving and not dwell on the gruesome scene, but they cannot peel their gaze from the tragedy. I wished I could avert my stare to break the eye lock with his, but my strength of will could not overpower the force that bonded our eyes to each other's.

The gunman's eyes grew steely, as if in rapt concentration, then widened in sudden recognition. How he could have pinpointed my stare in the midst of the ferns I couldn't fathom. My eyes were in deep shadow, and thick vegetation obscured most of my face and body from sight. Nevertheless, he saw my eyes and apparently recognized them for what they were: human.

In a flash, the man swung his shotgun toward me. "¡Párate!" he yelled.

I rolled back, dragging Melodee with me just as a violent, concussion-rending blast erupted from his shotgun with enough volume to make my ears ring. Hundreds of pellets shredded the foliage around us. An instant plume of leaf shards filled the air like a blizzard of green snowflakes. Melodee let out a chirplike scream as she had not seen the blast coming. It sickened my stomach to think she may have been hit, but now was not the time for even a cursory examination.

"Run!" I cried in a subdued shout, not wanting to confirm to the gunman that he had seen what he thought he saw.

There was more shouting as the boat's two-stroke motor shut off.

"Vi a alguien," the man yelled in Spanish. "¡Allí!"

He had seen us! Melodee and I were on our feet, running into the jungle, following whatever trail we could find. We tried to remain as silent as possible while distancing ourselves from the drug runners.

It's nearly impossible to run along a narrow, convoluted, vine-choked jungle trail with the tiniest element of grace. It's even more difficult when holding an adolescent's hand. Yet I had no other choice. I couldn't very well leave Melodee behind and, to be honest, I wasn't sure she wouldn't outdistance me anyway. My faltering gait, brought about by my slinged arm, regularly caused me to smash into encroaching shrubs, vines, and branches. We needed stealth as much as speed, neither of which was in great supply.

After a few yards, it was painfully clear we had to change tactics. I suggested to Melodee that, instead of my holding her hand, she follow close behind me as I blazed the trail, but even that did not diminish the level of noise we made crashing through the underbrush. As I concentrated on distancing ourselves from the drug runners, I found focusing on that—and sheer panic-born fear—masked the pain in my arm remarkably well.

We eventually fell into a cadence that allowed us to move through the dense forest with minimal noise. Melodee followed close behind as I shadowed faint paths and hints of animal trails. We seemed to be going in no particular direction, a tactic that concerned me. If a straight line is the shortest distance between two points, then I wanted the line between the drug runners and us to be as long and un-straight as possible. I told Melodee I wanted to forge ahead. She nodded in affirmation. My intent was to guide us to safety, but I didn't know where to find it.

Initially, I thought of making a wide circle toward the crash site. It was the only destination I knew. It seemed logical at first, but as my racing mind fought to bring a semblance of order to my jumbled emotions, it occurred to me that leading the drug men to the crash site would solidify the fact that foreigners were in the area. It would further incite their cartel to do whatever was necessary to keep their operation a secret. Therefore, I veered toward the river again, and ran straight ahead—or attempted to do so. The trouble was, the closer we got to the river, the thicker the vegetation became.

We did our best to remain silent, but with little success. What may have been only the muted snapping of twigs or the mashing of dried leaves sounded to me like a stampede of rogue elephants running through an aluminum pot factory. Yet, because of the density of plant life and the scantiness of the trail, the only way to quiet our progress would be to crawl at a sloth's pace, which would not serve our purposes in the least. Our only hope was that the men would lose our trail in the primeval undergrowth of the rain forest floor.

At last we reached the river. I wondered if this was the same river we had camped next to, but it didn't matter. One branch would lead into the other, and I felt our best chance of getting out was to follow any quickly flowing tributary to the main waterway, and then follow that to the sea. We paused to catch our breath and listen for sounds indicating our pursuer's location.

"How—do you know—they are—following us?" Melodee asked between gasps of breath.

"I don't. But—I don't want to take—any chances either."

"I know they are—bad men, but—are you sure they—they couldn't help us get out—of this jungle?"

I dropped to one knee and took both her small hands in mine. "Melodee, listen, those men are not interested in helping anyone but themselves." I paused to steady my breathing, then said, "We represent a threat to everything they have, and they would not hesitate to do anything necessary to keep their drug-running operation a secret. That's why they shot at us without asking questions."

She frowned a bit and said, "You mean even if they knew who we were, they'd kill us anyway?"

I nodded. "It wouldn't surprise me if they've killed others before."

She pondered the significance of my words, tilting her head to one side. "But they don't even know us," she said, mostly to herself.

"I know."

"So, why would we be a threat to them?"

"Because we're Americans. Foreigners like us are generally not welcome here."

"Why?"

I sighed, not in weariness from her barrage of questions, but at my inability to answer them sufficiently. "I don't really know. I just know they would."

She was silent for a moment, staring off into the jungle at nothing in particular before she asked, "How do they know we're Americans?"

The same question had been running through my mind ever since the gunman pulled the trigger. Did they know? It was obvious my eye contact with the gunman had betrayed our presence, but unless he had seen our clothes or the color of our hair and skin, he would not know if we were American, Mexican, or a local denizen from some indigenous Indian tribe.

"You've got a good point there, kiddo. But it wouldn't be smart to simply wait and find out. I think we're safer if we stay out of sight."

She nodded in agreement.

I looked up and down the embankments of the river. It was characteristic of many of the waterways in the rain forest: a slow-moving, semiwide confluence that meandered for miles through the vegetation with little, if any, whitewater. In fact, the landscape we'd seen thus far was a consistent miasma of dense tropical forest with little in the way of mountains, valleys, or even rolling hills—at least that we could see. What we needed was to get a visual bearing on the topography around us. I looked at the enormous trees overhead. Climbing one would certainly give us a better perspective on the terrain. I touched my slinged arm and shook my head. The next best thing was to find a rise of some kind, a knoll or other elevated jut of earth that would allow a better view.

The width of the river permitted a bit of clearing that brought into view a densely overgrown yet prominent escarpment to the north. A few jagged portions of volcanic stone jutted through the vegetation, suggesting the possibility of mountains nearby.

"Look, there's a trail over there," Melodee said, bringing me from my wandering thoughts.

Sure enough, while I was concentrating on seeing things beyond my view, I had overlooked a well-worn, clearly modern trail on the far side of the river. Where it led was anybody's guess, but it was definitely more than an animal trail or a footpath reserved for natives. To get to it would require some effort, especially with an arm in a sling. But it was heading in the same direction as the escarpment, so it seemed a logical choice.

At that moment, I heard the crunching of foliage a short distance behind us. Apparently the drug men were still on our trail, and they were getting closer. An echolike word or two filtered toward us, as did the sounds of crushing leaves and snapping twigs, but the verbiage was nothing I understood. Even if I did hear their conversation clearly, my Spanish was rudimentary at best, and I doubted I would be able to translate the meaning. Getting the gist of their tone, on the other hand, was easily done, and I understood only too well that they were not pleased with this detour in their schedule.

"Do you think you can swim?" Melodee asked.

The river was about twenty-five yards across but ran slow and smooth, indicating a deep bottom. I was confident I could swim it, even with one arm immobilized.

"Sure. Piece of cake—" My head jerked around as the dull crack of a wet branch snapped not fifty feet behind us.

"Perdí sus huellas," a husky voice called out. "Pero pienso que pasaron por aquí."

Melodee's eyes widened with fear, as I'm sure mine did too—not at what they were saying, because I didn't understand much of it, but at the nearness of their voices.

"Let's go," I whispered.

We entered the water with cautious steps. The bottom was soft and muddy, but we did not sink beyond the ability to pull our feet free from the brown-black muck. The water was tepid but refreshing. I looked back and saw clouds of silt billowing from the riverbed where we had stepped. With the slow progress of the water, the plumes of mud and silt would be a dead giveaway as to which direction we went.

"Lift your feet and swim," I said, pushing forward and floating away from the embankment.

I struggled to gain forward movement at first, and then succeeded by doing a sidestroke with one arm. It wasn't a fast stroke, yet it wasn't long before we were halfway across. I let Melodee swim ahead a little as I glanced back. There was no one at the water's edge. Yet.

If our luck could hold out just a bit longer . . .

"Hey, mister," Melodee whispered between ragged breaths. "Do you think—there are piranhas—in this river?"

That was one thought that had *not* crossed my scientifically astute brain but should have. A school of piranhas, vicious little disc-shaped fish with razor-sharp teeth and voracious appetites, could tear apart a good-sized animal in a couple of minutes. These waters were their ideal habitat, and I should have considered that before venturing into their domain like a sheep going to slaughter. And there were many other animals which posed a potential threat. Anacondas, huge snakes that could grow to fifty feet in length, could squeeze the life out of a man my size and swallow a girl like Melodee whole. Hungry crocodiles, sporting ghostlike stealth and hundreds of bacteria-coated teeth, could strike without warning. Electric eels, poisonous snakes of several species, leeches, disease-carrying microbes, and others all considered these waterways home. And we not only were trespassing, but we afforded fresh meat in the process.

I smiled halfheartedly. "No, I don't think so," I lied. "Just keep swimming as fast as you can."

"Okay."

Even though the river flowed smoothly with little current to alter our course, we found ourselves approaching a tangle of roots and vines instead of the sandy beach on the other side. I suggested we head into them and then pull ourselves to the clearing. Just as we ducked into the shadows of the roots, the sound of clear, distinct voices slid across the water's surface.

"Can you see them?" a man asked in Spanish.

"No. But they had to come this way."

They'd spoken slowly enough that this time I more or less understood what they'd said. I peered out from the tangle and saw two men with shotguns scanning the river. They looked angry and tense, and were clearly bent on finding us.

I eased back into the shadows, not wanting to repeat the eye-contact incident that got us into this situation. I motioned for Melodee to keep silent. We watched the two men move up and down the opposite embankment as far as the vegetation would allow, their eyes constantly sweeping the surface of the water. They looked directly toward us a couple of times but did not see us.

After a time, the two men seemed to relax, and they talked quietly with each other. They looked across the river one last time before returning up the jungle trail.

Melodee and I waited a few more minutes in breathless anticipation. After what seemed like hours, we heard the boat's two-stroke engine cough and sputter to life and slowly fade into the jungle.

Upon leaving the river, I noticed Melodee was still carrying her backpack. How she had managed to transport it across the river baffled me.

"It's watertight Gore-Tex," she explained. "When I zip it up it acts like a float."

I rubbed the back of my neck. "Wow, you're more prepared than an Eagle Scout," I chuckled.

"Thanks," was her short reply.

Overall, we came through our ordeal unscathed. The only animal we had encountered was a leech that had stuck itself to my calf, but I easily pried off the bloodsucker with Melodee's Swiss Army knife.

No longer feeling the need to run for our lives but still very much on edge, we headed down the trail at a much slower pace. I wondered if the drug men would send back a search party. It didn't matter. By that time, I anticipated being as far away from the crash site as possible.

TEN

With compass in hand, Melodee led the way as we followed the canopied trail through the jungle. Neither of us spoke much. I felt confident that the drug men were no longer chasing us, but I knew we were far from safe. Melodee watched the orange-colored arrow of her Liahona, as she called it, occasionally looking up at the sky and the path before us. What she was thinking I couldn't tell, but it seemed obvious she was concerned about our direction of travel.

Finally, she asked, "Mister, are you sure we should be going this way?"

I shrugged. "No, but it's opposite from the direction the drug men were heading, so it seems like a good idea, don't you think?"

"But if they came *from* this direction, wouldn't you think that somewhere up ahead was where they got the cocaine plants?"

Her pattern of logic made sense. "It's possible. But they were following the river, and they might have started up a different branch."

She frowned. "So how do you know there won't be more of them where we're headed? They could've grown the plants anywhere, I mean."

"Yeah, so?"

"So we're in danger pretty much wherever we go, right?"

Her questions had merit, I thought to myself. When we had crashed, I was at first concerned with getting out healthy. With the new threat of drug runners, I was now concerned about staying alive.

"We'll be all right as long as we can stay out of sight," I said, as much to comfort myself as to comfort her.

Suddenly Melodee stopped and turned to face me with a frown. "Hey. How did you know what was in that boat, mister?"

I had to chuckle at her unvoiced accusation. "I guess you wouldn't know what I do for a living, would you?"

"How could I?" she said, not changing the intimidating quality of her scowl. "I don't even know your name."

I flinched. She was right.

All the times she'd called me mister, I thought she was trying to be polite—that it was simply out of respect. In part, I'm sure it was. But only then did I realize I had never introduced myself to her. In all her politeness toward me, I had neglected to reciprocate.

I extended my right hand. "My name is David Kirkham. Pleased to meet you."

She took my hand and gave it a surprisingly firm shake. "I'm Melodee Braithwaite. Likewise, I'm sure. But you still haven't told me how you knew what cocaine plants look like."

I chuckled again. "I'm a botanist. I study plants. My company makes drugs—useful, legal drugs—from plants and the chemicals they produce."

She continued to scrutinize me as if I were a wolf in sheep's clothing. After all, exactly what does a botanist look like anyway?

"A botanist, huh?" she said coolly. "Okay, which plants contain licorice flavoring?"

"What?"

"If you know plants, then you'll know which kind licorice flavor comes from."

I chuckled awkwardly. She didn't. Apparently, I was on trial.

I cleared my throat. "Two plants are typically used, though there are several that have licorice scents and other characteristics. The licorice plant itself, genus *Glycyrrhiza,* has flavorful roots, and anise, or *Pimpinella*—from the parsley family, believe it or not—has licorice-flavored seeds and leaves."

There was an uncomfortable pause as she digested my answer. I laughed to myself at how nervously I awaited her response.

"Okay. That sounds right," she said.

"Swell," I said. "Now I get to ask how *you* would know I was right. Unless you're an avid cook or a candy maker or something."

"As a matter of fact, I make very good homemade candy, but never mind that. What plant do they make chocolate from?"

I couldn't believe I was having to prove my innocence to a twelve-year-old child, but at the same time, I enjoyed the challenge. I was certain her parents had lectured her on the evils of recreational drug use. She may have learned about drugs already, through a science class or a middle school D.A.R.E. program. It was probable some dealer may already have offered her some illicit substance, though I doubted she would have accepted any. After all, she was a Mormon.

From the little I knew about Mormon culture, illegal drugs were not something often found around good Mormon families—*often* being the operative word. Although high moral standards were passed down from generation to generation in many religions, including Mormonism, youth will be youth, and I knew that many unfortunate families had gone through the misery of having their children fall prey to the offerings of street dealers.

"Chocolate comes from the chocolate tree," I said. "In the *Sterculiaceae* family."

"Wrong!" she snapped.

I blinked in confusion. "You think?" I said, scratching my head. "I could have sworn the family was *Sterculiaceae.*"

"Chocolate doesn't grow on a tree," she argued. "It comes from a bean, the cocoa bean."

"Well, yes, that's right, but where does the cocoa bean come from?"

She didn't answer, but continued to glare at me with accusatory eyes.

"The cocoa bean comes from big, reddish seed pods that grow on a tree. It's called *Theobroma cocoa* in Latin. A long time ago, the Aztecs showed Cortez how to make a drink from it, and he took it to the Old World where it became known as the 'drink of aristocracy.'"

She softened somewhat as if embarrassed by the harshness of her tone, but still stayed on the defensive. "Nice history lesson, Mr. Kirkham, but everyone knows the story of Hernando Cortez and the Aztecs. How does that prove you're a botanist or chemist or whatever?"

"Ask me something else," I said, enjoying the sharpness of this young girl's mind.

"Okay. Does chocolate have caffeine in it?"

"What? Why's that important?"

"Just curious. A lot of my friends say it's loaded with caffeine."

"Well it's not; not literally, anyway. Chocolate contains a chemical called theobromine which is structurally related to caffeine in that they are both methylxanthenes and therefore have similar effects of stimulation and euphoria."

She stared at me for some time before speaking. "I'm not sure what you just said, but I think it was good news."

"How's that?"

"Well . . . if I'm not supposed to eat or drink anything with caffeine in it, I can still have chocolate, can't I?"

"Sure," I said, somewhat confused by her question.

"So why do some people say hot chocolate has as much caffeine in it as coffee?"

"I don't know. Perhaps because most tests that determine the caffeine content of a product only test for xanthenes in general and not for which specific xanthene it contains. You actually have to assay the xanthenes—that means break them down to their individual chemical structures—to find out if it's caffeine, theobromine, or theophylline. All three are chemically pretty much alike."

"So chocolate is okay then?"

I was still confused at her concern over the caffeine content of chocolate, but I answered her question without asking why. "Sure. Chocolate's perfectly safe."

My answer had a magical effect on her demeanor, and she instantly returned to being the precocious, inquisitive young girl I first met on the plane.

"Good. That's something I've always wanted an expert's opinion on. Thank you, Mr. Kirkham."

I scowled playfully at her. "Truth be known, it's actually *Doctor* Kirkham. But I'd prefer it if you called me David, okay? We're not in school now."

"You're a teacher, too?"

"No, no. I'm much too dry and boring for that. I'm a scientist— a botanist. I couldn't teach fish how to swim."

She giggled. "Well, you taught me something about chocolate I didn't know before. That makes you a teacher."

"Okay," I said, not wanting to diminish her infectious enthusiasm.

She continued to beam at me with weary but sparkling eyes. Then her gaze locked on an imaginary point by her feet as her mind focused in rapt concentration. "Now I've got to teach you something so we can be even," she stated, mostly to herself.

I snorted softly. "Now, what could *you* possibly teach me?"

Her eyebrows knitted together as she considered my question. Then she smiled and her eyes radiated with pure happiness. In fact, the sickly pallor of her skin seemed to vanish as her entire being exuded a perceptible joy and warmth.

She dropped to one knee and rummaged through her backpack, then pulled out a scuffed, somewhat worn book.

I smiled and tilted my head for a better look. The book was approximately five by seven inches, with a black cover and embossed with gold lettering—in both large and small print. The large letters spelled out *The Book of Mormon.*

"I can teach you the truth," Melodee stated. Then, holding up the book, she asked, "Have you ever read this?"

I chortled, "No."

She handed me the book upside down. I turned it over to read the small print. *Another Testament of Jesus Christ.*

I don't know why, but a strange mix of emotions ran through me as I looked from the book's cover to Melodee's anxious eyes. I felt defensive . . . and curious. Annoyed . . . and pleased. Leery . . . and inquisitive. That Melodee felt she could teach me what she considered to be the truth somehow touched me and irked me simultaneously. I could never see myself becoming brainwashed by the preaching of any specific religion, including Mormonism. Science was my religion, and a darned good one for me. I was comfortable in my intelligence, happy in my knowledge of things. The fact that this young girl considered a religious book to contain the truth—assuming the finality of her tone meant it contained the *full* truth—was to me a sign of a simple, innocent, yet unenlightened mind. Not to say she was stupid or "thick," as my grandmother used to say, but that she had none of the training to organize, analyze, deduce, and conclude when presented with a collection of facts.

A religious book containing the truth? Well, perhaps it had some good suggestions about how to live with one's fellow beings and such, but that would be the end of it. Personally, I had little use for such books.

I smiled and handed the book back to Melodee. "Thanks, but no. I have a pretty good grasp on things as they are."

Melodee was uncertain about my refusal. "You mean you *have* already read it," she stated more than asked.

"No, no. Look, I don't want to offend you, kiddo, but I have no interest in religious works."

"But, how do you know what it says if you haven't read it?"

"Well . . . the cover says The Book of Mormon, right?"

"So?"

"So this is a copy of your Bible, isn't it?"

"No."

I paused and waited for a more elaborate explanation, but she offered none. The book was clearly the same type that my friend Matt had carried with him throughout high school. He had offered it to me a time or two, and I had graciously declined it then, too. I never felt I had time for *Thou Shalt This*, and *Thou Shalt Not That*. When it came to new information, I consulted a textbook. As far as uplifting reading, I felt I could get more out of a Michael Crichton, Robin Cook, or Tom Clancy techno-thriller than a Mormon Bible. Melodee, as if reading my thoughts, grew more crestfallen by the second.

"Listen, I don't mean to be rude, kid, but I honestly have no interest in your book."

"But . . . you're a scientist, right? You spend your life searching for sources of truth, right?"

I shrugged. "Well, yes, but—"

"Then you could consider this another source of the truth." She held a finger up to accentuate her next statement. "If you prejudge something before studying it fully, then you're not much of a scientist."

And with that, she shoved the book back into my hand, hiked her backpack onto her shoulder, and headed off up the trail.

I blinked hard.

"Remember, you can't judge a book by its cover," she called over her shoulder.

I blinked again.

ELEVEN

The afternoon temperature rose quickly, as did the accompanying humidity. Our steps were labored and our breathing raspy. We did not encounter any more drug runners, and we talked very little with each other—not from lack of conversational material, but from sheer fatigue. As evening approached, the painful gnawing in my stomach surpassed the dull throb in my arm. Even Melodee had slowed considerably, and frequently stumbled over roots and stones on the trail. We were both terribly hungry and thirsty and near complete exhaustion.

There is a misconception perpetuated by Hollywood movies and romance novels that belies the hostile environment tropical jungles present; that is, that in these lush and aesthetically beautiful settings one can find a plethora of edible plants and fruits and abundant clear streams from which to drink. In reality, although there are a number of edible plants and roots, there are precious few at which you'd look twice. Moreover, although water is plentiful, the various streams and ponds one encounters are usually so choked with algae, silt, and detritus that they are rarely potable. Fortunately, fresh drinking water could be obtained during a rainfall by using large plant leaves to channel the water into your mouth.

But too much moisture causes other problems. Because of the constant presence of high humidity and tropical showers, we soon found that keeping dry was an insurmountable task. Our feet began to itch and stink, and our clothing chaffed against our skin. Additionally, in the thick, insufferable heat, the thought of adding more layers of clothing to protect us from incessant precipitation was the furthest thing from our minds. No wonder many natives throughout these jungles wore little more than loincloths.

Adequate nourishment was my biggest concern. I tried to mentally calculate the number of calories we were burning with each mile we trudged through the rain forest, and knew that we simply would not make it more than a few days without a good source of beneficial food. I was able to knock down some papaya with a long stick. They were a bit green but wonderfully refreshing. I also found a few wild onions along the way. But that was the extent of our sustenance. After only four days, my pants hung loosely around my waist, necessitating taking up a notch on my belt. I smiled as I made the adjustment. Dyana was always after me about getting more exercise and losing a little weight. I wasn't clinically obese, but I wasn't happy about the thirty-pound spare tire I carried above my beltline either. I just never seemed to find the time to exercise. And with my frequent trips to companies that prided themselves on lavishly spoiling their clients (or me spoiling them to get a contract) with sumptuous luncheons and dinner parties, my college physique was regrettably a thing of the past.

An angry rumbling pealed from dark clouds that had collected overhead without warning. As if in reply, my stomach growled back in a challenge of one-upmanship. It looked like it was going to rain. Again. Rain rarely starts slowly in these forests. One or two drops are all the warning you get before a deluge of precipitation obscures everything from view. When the first drop hit my face, I immediately began looking for shelter. Melodee was ahead of me doing the same. She caught on quickly to the rhythms of the jungle, which didn't surprise me.

"Over here," she said, pointing up a steep embankment.

Melodee had found a deep, stony overhang masked with a veil of morning glory vines. We entered and found it surprisingly clutter free. Melodee doffed her backpack and began to stretch her sore muscles, leaning forward and touching her toes, then pulling her feet behind her one at a time and touching them to her rump.

"I haven't been able to do that in years," I chuckled.

"It's important to keep healthy and limber," she replied.

"Yes, it is," I agreed, looking out through the curtain of vines at the water cascading over the rock ledge. "I'm glad you saw this place. This storm is a whopper. We would have drowned out there."

"Probably," she said while stretching her arms and lower back.

"You got any other surprises in there?" I asked, indicating her backpack, not really expecting a positive answer.

"Just some stuff I take on trips."

"Anything edible?"

She sighed and shook her head. "Not unless you consider pills food."

"Pills? Like Tylenol or something?" I asked, wondering why she hadn't offered me any.

"No, just some stuff I take."

"A prescription med?"

She nodded, but didn't say any more. I didn't see the point in pursuing a topic she obviously considered boring or too personal.

My stomach rumbled again. As if responding, Melodee's also gurgled loudly. Then a contorting knot brought a flash of pain across her face. Just watching made me wince. I asked Melodee if I could do anything for her. She shook her head.

I knew what she really needed was rest and wholesome nourishment. The hollowness encircling her eyes told me she was near starvation. My concern for her had already grown very deep—considering what we had gone through and what she had done for me. Now, with her health diminishing exponentially, I felt an urgency to get her to civilization as quickly as possible.

Luckily, her mind was still sharp and her attitude indefatigable. But a dullness now paled her skin and glazed her eyes. She was hungry and thirsty to the point of physical pain.

I took my arm from the sling and worked it carefully to test its condition. The pain was definite but not unbearable. The dull throb reminded me I'd had a serious injury, but my body was doing what it could to heal itself.

During our frantic escape from the drug runners, Melodee had lost her plastic water bottle. It probably floated away when we forded the river. I reached for a large pathos leaf and fashioned it into a cup. Then I held it out in the rain, quickly filling it with wonderfully clear, clean rainwater. I offered it to Melodee, who took it without comment and drank deeply. My worry grew even more. Normally, her manners ran close to being obsequious. The fact that she took the proffered drink and downed it without a "thank you" was a poignant sign she was weakening. I filled the leaf-cup again and handed it to her a second time. She placed a pill on her tongue and drank again, then smiled at me as best she could.

"Your turn next," she said weakly.

I drank several "cups" of water and felt much better. The amount of hydration one loses when sweating from sunup to sundown is mind-boggling. It constantly amazed me how dehydration hospitalized so many people, especially in climates where water abounds. When massive amounts of moisture are lost through perspiration and coarse breathing, a simple drink of water can be lifesaving.

I watched the rain for a while before stating, "I think our first concern should be finding some decent food in the morning. What do you think, kiddo?"

Melodee's head lay drooped on her chest. She was fast asleep. I gently pulled her down and let her head rest on my lap. She curled into a fetal position and sighed deeply. I watched the rain, listening to it pound the earth like a perpetual drum roll.

My mind wandered as I sat in our little hollow. Dull, opaque light transfused through the thick clouds and jungle canopy, giving the place an oppressive, lackluster feeling. In a hypnotic trance, I stared without acknowledging the blurry scene through the curtain of water obscuring our hideout. Moisture mixed with briny sweat beaded on my face and stung my eyes and cracked lips. As I picked up my sling to wipe my face, the book Melodee had given me fell out. I had forgotten it was in there.

The Book of Mormon. Clearly a religious text, undoubtedly filled with prophetic warnings and omens which dictated a nearly monklike, exclusionist lifestyle for faithful Mormons to follow—or so I thought. I turned the book over a few times before opening it. I listlessly began reading the title page. I wasn't honestly interested in the tome. I simply figured I didn't have anything else to occupy my time at the present.

The title page stated that the book was handwritten on some kind of plates by a guy named Mormon and that it was translated by Joseph Smith Jr. *That's interesting.* I had always assumed that Smith had written the thing himself. The word *translated* gave it an entirely new appeal. The rest of the page stated the text was a history, or rather, a compilation of histories about certain groups of people descended from families originating in the Old World, near ancient Israel and Babylon. Perhaps this wasn't simply a top-ten list of Mormon dos and don'ts after all.

Admittedly, I consider myself a history buff, mainly because so much history revolves around scientific discovery. If this book were a historical document, it might prove entertaining reading. On the other hand, if it were a compilation of quotes from overzealous prophets and preachers, I knew I'd tire of it quickly. Yet the title page, written in verbiage similar to that of the Bible, said that this was an abridgment of *records* kept by various peoples from the Old World. Therefore, it had to be a history.

Melodee stirred and moaned softly. The little girl was suffering but she would not admit it. She had a stoic maturity that reminded me of orphans who were forced to grow up too quickly, skipping the joys of adolescence and teenage years to become responsible, self-sustaining adults in child-sized bodies. Yet Melodee had parents and a solid, functional family, so her deeply rooted self-confidence had to come from somewhere else.

My thoughts then returned to the book in my hands. Like the deluge that inundated the landscape outside our grotto, the words Melodee threw at me earlier that day flooded my mind. *If you prejudge something before studying it fully, then you're not much of a scientist.*

As painful and humbling as it was, I had to admit she was right.

On the following page of the Book of Mormon, an introduction further dissected the work. I read on, trying not to become interested but finding myself intrigued by the words. The next thing that caught my eye was a declaration that the last remaining group of people in the book—Lamanites, it called them—were the principal

ancestors of the American Indians. I concluded that that was
possible. Most historians theorized that Native Americans came
from across the Bering Strait by way of Alaska and that they were
descendants of the denizens of Siberia and present-day Russia, or
perhaps even wanderers from China or Mongolia. But the inconsistencies in physical traits and social customs never substantiated that
theory. The characteristics and habits of ancient North and South
American cultures often mimicked many of those found in the Old
World, so it made sense that they were descendants of ancient Israel.
I could accept things that made sense.

The rest of the introduction talked about how the present-day
Book of Mormon came to be. It got a little too churchy for me, but
did bring out two intriguing points. The first was that Joseph Smith
translated the ancient record from plates of gold. I tried to recall
everything Matt had told me about their church's founder, young
Mr. Smith. I remembered he was a farm boy back East somewhere.
He had a vision from God and formed a church . . .

I rubbed my eyes. For the life of me, I could not remember Matt
saying anything about Smith's knowledge of Semitic languages, or
any higher education or advanced linguistic training. How then had
he translated a record such as this? Reading on, the introduction
said it was simply "by the gift and power of God." I scoffed
inwardly. Once again, religionists fall back on their timeworn
"power of God" explanation of things. To my way of reasoning, even
God would use materials found in the universe and known laws of
physics to do His wonders. I made a mental note to ask Melodee
how Joseph Smith went about translating these ancient writings.

The second thing that piqued my curiosity had a similar theme
but a different timbre to it. Toward the bottom of the page, the
introduction stated: "We invite all men everywhere to read the Book
of Mormon, to ponder in their hearts the message it contains, and
then to ask God, the Eternal Father, in the name of Christ if the
book is true."

Then it added this promise: "Those who pursue this course and
ask in faith will gain a testimony of its truth and divinity by the
power of the Holy Ghost."

That was a pretty bold statement. It was a promise, a guarantee of sorts, that anyone who read the book and asked (in prayer, I assumed) about its validity would be told of its truth. It didn't qualify only those who were exceptionally faithful or pious, or those who were churchgoers to begin with—it said *anyone*. Even my employer could not make a promise that solid about any of its pharmaceutical products—that it would always work for everyone with the same efficacy and outcome. This promissory line in the introduction was succinct and blunt. No holds barred, no punches pulled. Anyone who read it and asked would be told whether it was true or not.

I smirked. This was my out-clause, my vindication, my escape route. If I read it and asked but didn't get an answer, then I could honestly say I was still a scientist and had used my analytical training to determine the accuracy and validity of the book. I could tell Melodee that I gave it my best scientific effort and came up inconclusive.

On the other hand, if I read it and got an honest-to-goodness answer that it *was* true . . . then what would I do?

TWELVE

I can't remember if I was dreaming of smoke before I sensed it was real or if I simply eased from subconsciousness when its acrid fumes assaulted my sinuses. Either way, I knew I smelled a fire without needing to open my eyes to confirm it. It wasn't an unpleasant odor; rather, it carried with it a musty tang, a bitter sharpness, and . . . something else, something that added a palpable, aromatic flavor to its fragrance. Then the fire's voice, the characteristically cheerful hiss, pop, and crackle, permeated the fog in my head.

I opened my eyes and found I was alone. I was lying on my side against the moss-covered wall of the hollow with my hands folded gently under my head. Melodee was not in the grotto. Just inside, a tiny campfire spat noisily as it tried to burn through wood too moist to be good fuel. A thick, bluish-white smoke arose from the flames, further testifying that the wood was anything but dry. Beyond the fire, the sun showed painfully bright. Not a direct glare from unchecked solar rays, but an omnipresent illumination, as though light came from everywhere at once, transmuted through a fine mist that diffused details with an edge-softening shroud, giving them the ambience of a Thomas Kinkade painting.

When I tried to move from my resting place I found my body rebelling at the very thought. I ached from head to toe, especially my feet, as if I had had the misguided enthusiasm to run a twenty-six-mile marathon in patent-leather Italian dress shoes. A sarcastic snort escaped my nostrils. The distance my little companion and I had hiked yesterday was probably not much shorter. Or so it felt.

"Good morning," Melodee said as she entered the grotto to stir the fire with a stick.

With my eyes squinted against the harshness of the outside light, I could only see the silhouette of her small frame, but I knew by the sing-song tone of her voice that she was feeling much better. I wished I could say the same. I sat up, stretched painfully, and moaned, "I'd say that statement is the most-often-used oxymoron in the world."

"Oxy-mormon?"

"Oxy*moron*. When two contradictory words or ideas join to make a single phrase. You said, 'Good morning.' It's morning all right. It's the *good* part I'm questioning."

She giggled the mirth-filled laugh I enjoyed but hadn't heard in a while. I immediately wondered what had brought on this miraculous change. Surely, it wasn't just a peaceful night's slumber. I recalled her being so weak last evening that she seemed on the verge of collapse. Still, I wasn't about to diminish her spurt of good health with probing questions that would dampen her spirits.

I squinted in pain as I slowly tried to touch my toes. They seemed so far away. "Where have you been?" I groaned.

"I found some breakfast."

It was then that I identified the unique smell from the smoky campfire. My eyes blinked open and focused on the glowing coals and dancing flames. Melodee was holding a stick over the fire, turning it slowly. On the end of the stick was a saucer-sized fish. I didn't recognize the type of fish, and right then I didn't care. The scent of the coal-brazed fish knotted my stomach, reminding me that it had been empty for some time. There were also a few berries on a large, flat pathos leaf next to the fire.

"Do you like fish?" Melodee asked.

I rubbed my eyes and forcefully shook my head, as if trying to clear a surreal dream that was currently overpowering my consciousness. I found it impossible to believe. I shook my head again, and deeply inhaled the delicious smell.

"No?" she continued. "Too bad. They're really kinda good."

"No, no," I said, holding my palms up as if signaling a truce. "Fish is great. I love it. I'm just trying to determine if I'm still dreaming or not."

"You're not," she said with unmeasured frankness.

"Good. So, where did you . . . ?"

"I think Heavenly Father is still watching out for us."

When I responded with a soft snort and a wry smile, she continued. "When I went out this morning, I found a couple of puddles by a stream, and there were fish in them. They're tiny but they still taste pretty good."

Her story seemed truly miraculous, but I knew it was merely coincidence. I figured the stream must have risen above the bank during the rainstorm, then gone back down again as it ran off, leaving the fish trapped in the puddles.

The fish on her skewer resembled a perch. She had cleaned it and removed the head and tail using her Swiss Army knife, and was doing an excellent job of searing it evenly over the fire. "You want one?"

"Absolutely," I said.

"Okay."

I watched silently as Melodee cooked the fish. My mind tried to distill the scene in front of me and put some sense to it all. Too many inconsistencies presented a scenario too fantastic to accept as simply the beginning of a new day.

"How did you make the fire?" I asked, massaging my sore arm. "Rubbing two sticks together?"

"Nope. I tried that once at girl's camp, but nothing happened. It's nearly impossible."

"Then how . . . ?"

"I got some matches from the 7-Eleven around the corner. Duh. I used the lighter you found at the crash site."

Smart-aleck brat. She must *be feeling better.* "And the dry wood?"

"There's a pile of big old rotten logs just outside. The ones near the bottom weren't too soggy, and they fell apart really easy. The inside stuff was dry enough to burn, but it could be better. It's like everything in this jungle is wet all the time. I had to use a couple of pages from my book to get the fire started."

I glanced at the fire and only then noticed some singed and blackened leaves of paper. My heart beat a painful staccato as I thought of Melodee burning her Book of Mormon. I was truly shocked. And disappointed. I had emotionally built myself up—got myself honestly excited in fact—to read the book, as if embarking on a new scientific quest that would reveal a mysterious truth or dispel a widely accepted myth. And I was the lone scientist who could perform the experiment. I wasn't excited to read the book for the sake of gaining greater knowledge, and I certainly wasn't delving into it from a religious viewpoint. But the fact that my mind had been set and my emotions so geared up for the venture, the thought of the book being immolated filled me with angst and remorse.

"You burned your book?" I asked in an arid, breathless voice.

"Just part of it," she explained. "I had to. Nothing else was dry enough to catch fire."

"But it means so much to you."

She cocked her head to one side and frowned with a *what are you talking about?* expression distorting her face. "I can always get another one," she said flatly.

That might be true, but it did not alter the fact that it was a book of *scripture* to her—a holy text whose sanctity supposedly equaled that of the Bible. That she could put a flame to it without a second thought astounded me, and for some reason, made me slightly angry, not only because it robbed me of my planned dissection of its contents, but also because I had come to expect better-than-adult behavior from this little girl. To have her display such childlike disrespect galled me.

"But . . . don't you consider it sacred?"

Her frown deepened as she scoffed, "No. I mean I really like it, the whole series in fact, but it's not *sacred.*"

"The whole series? You mean there's a Book of Mormon II and III and so on?"

Her eyes danced with pent amusement before she lost control and rolled back laughing, nearly dropping the skewered fish into the small fire. Her laughter elicited a coughing fit, which proved she wasn't one hundred percent well; however, that did not seem to dampen her infectious humor. I couldn't help but smile until she regained control enough to speak again.

Melodee wiped her eyes. "I didn't burn my Book of Mormon, you silly goose." Pointing into the flames with the sizzling fish she said, "That's one of my *Little House on the Prairie* books, *The Long Winter.* I would never burn my Book of Mormon."

The relief that washed over me surprised me. I can't explain why, but knowing her copy of the Book of Mormon was safe and unharmed warmed me inside in much the same way that one warms to a fond reminiscence or a child's embrace. My scientific side chided the rest of me for taking pleasure in those feelings, yet somehow I knew I shouldn't deny them. I let loose an unconvincing *I knew it all the time* chuckle.

"Uncle David, you get funnier every day."

Melodee had taken to calling me "Uncle" because she didn't feel right using my given name alone, conversing with an adult on such a personal level. I said it was okay because otherwise she would have continued to call me Mr. Kirkham, which would make me feel older than I wanted to admit I was. And every time I heard, *"Uncle David,"* I liked it even more.

"Most people find me more boring than funny." I reached out and plucked a crisply browned page from the coals. "Were you able to finish the book before burning it?"

"Oh, I've read them all before. Three times in fact."

"Really? Do you have the whole *Little House* series with you in your backpack?"

"No. There's not that much room. *The Long Winter* was the only one I had with me—besides my Book of Mormon, that is."

"Oh." I looked around. "Then . . . where is it?"

"What?"

"Your Book of Mormon."

"In my backpack. I thought you were done with it, so I put it there for safekeeping. Here, your fish is done."

The perch was wonderful, as were the few berries Melodee had found. I asked her if she knew what kind of berries they were. She didn't—she only knew that they looked good. Of course, I chastised her for carelessly eating something about which she had no knowledge. I knew that there were hundreds of toxic species in these rain forests, and to randomly sample any portion of the abundant plant life was asking for a violently cramped stomach, incapacitating diarrhea, respiratory depression, and even death. Luckily, the berries she had gathered were a species of currant, and although somewhat bitter, were perfectly safe to eat.

"I saw a bunch of monkeys eating them, so I figured they were safe," she said.

Pretty smart, I thought. "Well, that's usually okay, but there are many things monkeys can eat that we can't, so next time ask first, okay?"

She shrugged. "Okay."

"Oh, and in case I forgot earlier, thank you for the wonderful breakfast."

She blushed prettily. "You're welcome."

After eating, we went exploring, though we never wandered too far from the hollow. We found a few more pools containing trapped fish; most were too small to eat, but one pool had a good-sized eel in it that ended up tasting very good. At first Melodee wouldn't try it, saying it reminded her too much of a snake. I assured her that even some snakes were good to eat, but she wasn't convinced. Finally, she tried a bit, but didn't ask for more. We also found a few guavas, and I unearthed some wild yams that were very fibrous and difficult to eat, yet wonderfully filling.

Toward midafternoon, the sunlit mists rising from the rain forest floor were shaded out as thick, cumulous billows clotted into dense, foreboding masses in the sky. Melodee and I both knew we were in for another drenching. Luckily, we were able to make it back to the grotto before the deluge hit with a vengeance, another downpour reminiscent of the days of Noah. The rain continued throughout the night and all the next day. Once again, we found our hunger pains high and our spirits low.

"There'll be fish in the morning," Melodee said in a light-hearted tone.

"Probably," I said with little enthusiasm.

The fire had died out long ago, but I thought it best not to relight it until we actually had something to cook. That evening was especially dark, and doing anything except staring out at the perpetual rainfall proved impossible. Subdued flashes of lightning occasionally skittered across the inky sky, illuminating everything in stroboscopic pulses, somewhat like a discotheque's rhythmically syncopated light show.

I leaned against the mossy wall and sighed wearily. My thoughts ran forward to our prospects of survival. We could probably exist on sporadic meals, but the repetitively unnavigable days meant our progress toward civilization would be like measuring the daily growth of a redwood tree. I should have been encouraged by the fact we were both relatively healthy. The diseases that flourish in rain forests are the kind most physicians hope they never see in a lifetime. If Melodee became seriously injured, I could do little to help her, especially while recovering from a broken arm. If I became seriously injured, I doubted there was anything she could do for me.

I shook my head, chastising myself for such wandering and pessimistic thoughts. Melodee had already helped by splinting my arm, and had done much in the way of furthering our progress. Nevertheless, the longer we were lost in this jungle, the narrower our chances of survival became.

Another flicker of lightning momentarily lit the grotto. Melodee lay curled beside me, apparently sleeping. She still looked weak, hollow, gaunt. I leaned my head back and closed my eyes. I knew we had to get out of the rain forest soon.

Thoughts of Melodee's family again flooded my mind. The physical hardships we were going through were nothing compared to the emotional suffering they must be experiencing. An aching pit widened in my gut that was more painful than the emptiness in my stomach. Melodee's family was undoubtedly preparing for a somber funeral: receiving the attention of caring friends and relatives, thoughtful flower arrangements, mementos, and remembrances . . . and coping with an empty casket. My heart went out to them, ached for them. I wished there were some way to communicate the fact that she was alive, but I had no physical means of doing so.

Then an idea came to me—one that was foreign to my past, totally alien to my character, unknown to my expertise.

I bowed my head and softly whispered, "God, if you're really there, let Melodee's family know she's all right. And let my family know I'm safe too. Thanks."

It was the first honest prayer I could ever remember offering. Amazingly, a feeling of rightness seemed to take a portion of the bitterness from my soul. I didn't understand the strange feeling—I actually felt intimidated by it—but for once I didn't fight it or try to rationalize it away.

It felt good, so much so that I fell asleep smiling.

THIRTEEN

I awoke to Melodee singing. It was soft, lyrical, and quite beautiful. She had a tonal quality that was neither childlike nor adult. She had a slight vibrato and a subtle breathiness that softened the high-pitched range of her voice, giving it a depth uncharacteristic for one so young.

The rain had passed, leaving a warm, sunny day in its wake. Life had come again to the jungle, and Melodee seemed unaware she was adding an unusual—yet no less enchanting—voice to the resplendent symphony of animal life.

She was sitting just outside the grotto weaving some lengths of plant material together, singing mostly to herself. I was unfamiliar with the song, but found myself immediately captivated by its lyrics.

Whenever I hear the song of a bird or look at the blue, blue sky,
Whenever I feel the rain on my face or the wind as it rushes by,
Whenever I touch a velvet rose or walk by a lilac tree,
I'm glad that I live in this beautiful world Heav'nly Father created for me.

"Actually, the lilac is a shrub, not a tree," I said lightheartedly.

She flinched and blushed. "I didn't know you were listening."

"Well, please don't stop. It's a very pretty tune. And I like any song that talks about the bounties of nature."

"That's not really what it's about. It actually describes the ways Heavenly Father shows His love for us."

I opened my mouth to make a glib comment about my currently vacuous relationship with God, but Melodee cut me off before I could get a word out. "Yes, even you, Uncle David. I already told you Heavenly Father loves everyone. Just because you don't believe in God doesn't mean He doesn't believe in you."

The frankness in her rebuke took me by surprise. I cleared my throat, which was suddenly as dry as Death Valley, California. "I never said I *didn't* believe there was a God. All I'm saying is I'm not sure who God is, that's all."

"But if you understood who Heavenly Father really is, you'd want to get to know Him that much more."

"And how's that?"

"We believe God is an actual being, a person of flesh and bone, a loving Father."

"An actual person? You mean He's not a spirit that's everywhere and nowhere at the same time?"

"Come on, Uncle David, how much sense does that make? The Bible says we were created in the image of God, right? So He must look like us, right? I don't think He likes being thought of as some spooky ghost popping in and out of closets and people's souls. Have you ever seen anyone who can be everywhere and nowhere at the same time?"

"No." I had no additional rebuttal. I did believe in a higher being, but was unsure how to describe the characteristics of that person. I guess *God* was as good a title as any, but referring to Him as my *Father* in heaven was somewhat uncomfortable.

"Look at it this way: you like nature because you're a scientist, right?" Melodee asked pointedly. "You like the birds and the trees and plants because they are of use to you, right?"

I nodded. "Natural materials are what we make most of our medicines from."

"Okay, but did you ever stop to think *why* you appreciate them—beyond their usefulness to you?"

I thought hard but could not come up with a precise answer. "I guess not. I'm not sure what you mean."

"Okay. Listen to the song carefully and see if the lyrics help you understand what I'm talking about."

She sang the first verse again in her sweet, pure voice, only it was slightly tense this time, I guessed because she was now aware of an audience.

Then she added the next verse:

He gave me my eyes that I might see the color of butterfly wings.
He gave me my ears that I might hear the magical sound of things.

Of course! I instantly understood what she was trying to teach me. In fact, it made more sense than I cared to confess. Sure there was abundant beauty in the world, and I enjoyed it because of my physical senses—sight, sound, taste—but until now, I had never thought of *why*.

He gave me my life, my mind, my heart: I thank Him reverently . . .

My life. I knew I took many things for granted, but until that moment, I never realized how devastating that ambivalence could be. So many experiences missed because of apathy. So many memories left unmade because of willful neglect. It was terrifying.

My mind. I had always felt I had a gifted mind, but could it grasp the significance of the simple things and assign them as much importance as mathematics, scientific enlightenment, or miraculous inventions? What about the simple acknowledgment of a Creator and His gifts of sight and sound?

My heart. Was it merely a four-chambered pump that circulated blood throughout my body? No. I was certain the lyricist was referring to a more aesthetic definition of the heart: the ability to emotionally grasp things for what they are and acknowledge the rare privilege of experiencing them.

For all his creations of which I'm a part. Yes, I know Heavenly Father loves me.

Was I a part of His creation? Was I truly more than the result of evolution, as I had learned in school? Could I accept the creation story espoused in the Bible as literal?

No, definitely not. Too much was left to blind faith. However, that's not what Melodee's song was trying to convey. It wasn't so much about creation. It wasn't about proofs and evidence or scientific facts that confirmed there was a God. The senses Melodee sang about were given so we could enjoy the *beauty* of nature, not just the bounty. They were a gift to humankind. There was no doubt her song was about love. Why else would God have placed these things on earth? It was not solely to prove that He exists. It was to show that He loves us.

A tingling coursed through me and filled me with wonder. All my life I had been so caught up in determining the "how" that I had completely overlooked the "why."

"Now do you understand?" Melodee asked tenuously.

I opened my mouth to speak, but nothing came out; a curious tightness gripped my throat, making it hard for me to speak. I simply nodded and smiled sheepishly.

"Good. I hoped you would."

The awakening realization continued to fill my mind until it announced that I, David Kirkham, Ph.D., man of science, was now a "believer"—which was not at all true. I held up my index finger to emphasize the point. "That doesn't make me a Mormon, you know."

Melodee rolled her eyes. "Of course not, silly. You haven't done nearly enough to qualify for that. You need lots more study and prayer."

"I don't know if I'll ever study *that* much."

"But you're a scientist. That's all you do."

"Yes, but only things I don't understand or that merit scientific scrutiny."

She put her hand to her forehead in much the same way the mother of an unruly child does when frustrated beyond the ability to cope with the current crisis. "I think we've had this conversation before," she said.

"Yeah. It is somewhat of a dead horse, isn't it?" I admitted.

"Only because *you* keep shooting the horse."

That one caught me off guard. I had no argument, no rebuttal. She was to the point and very convincing in her logic. I again began wondering where all her intelligence came from. I knew she read a lot, but it had to be more than that.

Changing course, I asked, "What does your father do for a living?"

"He teaches seminary for the Church."

"Seminary? You mean like teaching Church doctrines and how to be a Mormon? Like stuff like in a convent or a monastery?"

"Kind of. He teaches high school kids. He loves it."

"With everything he's taught you, I thought he was a science professor or something."

"He has a degree in biology, but he wanted to be a teacher and didn't feel right teaching things he didn't believe in. So he went back and got a religious studies degree. My mom's got one too."

"So you've basically been brought up indoctrinated with a bunch of religionist thinking. No wonder you feel so strongly about—"

"I was brought up to R.S.P.P.," she said, cutting me off.

At first, I thought I had misunderstood her. "You mean R.S.V.P.?"

"No. R.S.*P*.*P*. Before you judge anything, you need to Read, Study, Ponder, and Pray. R.S.P.P."

"Oh, like it says in the Book of Mormon."

This time she was the one caught off guard. "How did you know that?"

I noticed a beetle crawling over my shoe and slowly flicked it away, trying to delay my answer. "I read the introduction," I admitted softly.

Smiling broadly, she said, "That's a start."

"Well, I hope you won't be disappointed if I read it and don't come to any real conclusions."

She snorted. "That's impossible."

I frowned. "Why?"

"You'll come to *some* conclusion; you have to. It might not be the one I'd like, but you'll have an opinion one way or the other about the book. Just like you do when studying a science paper."

"Okay, so I'll have an opinion, but how can you be certain I'll agree with what your book says or not?"

"Because you're smart. Very smart."

"What makes you think that?"

"Because you know a lot about things ordinary people don't—detailed things that most people find boring. It's kind of geeky, but in a good way."

"Gee, thanks."

Instantly, her demeanor changed. She was no longer on the attack but adopted a passive stance, as if suddenly embarrassed by the tone of what she was saying. I hadn't minded the exchange of opinions. Just the opposite, I was stimulated by it, especially coming from a smart little girl.

Melodee moved to the mouth of the grotto and stared out into the jungle.

"I'm sorry for calling you a geek just now."

I chuckled. "It's just another one of those truths you keep talking about. I can accept it."

She looked at me and smiled in appreciation of the way I brushed over her insult. I knew she hadn't meant to offend, and I thought nothing of forgetting the remark.

"Listen, I plan on reading your book. Honestly." I took on a serious demeanor of my own. "You have given me a challenge and I am rising to it. But let me decide things on my own time, okay? I promise to R.S.P. I'm not sure about the last *P*, though. You already know I'm not much of a pray-er."

She didn't answer me, but I felt it wasn't because she didn't have an answer; I believed she hadn't heard a word I'd just said. Her concentration seemed fixed on some point off in the jungle, and I guessed I could have said anything at that moment and it wouldn't have mattered. Her body was tense, and I could hear her breathing come in short, shallow gasps.

"What is it, Melodee?"

She didn't answer but continued to stare out into the jungle. I joined her and followed her line of sight out to the horizon. At the top of a rise to the north, behind an escarpment of enormous laurel trees, a thin line of blue-white smoke rose from the canopy. It climbed straight into the windless sky as if channeled through a towering chimney, diffusing to nothingness some twenty or thirty feet above the tree line.

It wasn't a forest fire or a wisp of dust. It was a deliberate, isolated campfire. Definitely man-made.

FOURTEEN

"Who could it be?" Melodee asked with edgy apprehension.

"Could be anyone: natives, lumber workers . . . "

"Or more drug runners."

"Yes. Or it could be a film crew from the National Geographic Society."

"Or from *Bill Nye the Science Guy,* or from Jeff Corwin's show."

I laughed. "Yes, even them."

"Well, there's only one way to find out," Melodee said, zipping up her backpack and getting ready to depart.

Although her actions were determined and frank, her face still displayed a weariness caused by inadequate rest and poor nutrition. She did her best to hide the fact that she was exhausted, but the darkness under her eyes and slow, labored movements told me she was near the end of her endurance. Still, even though her body was weak, her spirit remained as strong as ever.

After taking a compass bearing on the filigree of smoke, we headed out along the best trail we could find. Fatigued beyond description, we both hoped this would prove an end to this adventure. But we also harbored anxious feelings that we might encounter more drug manufacturers or other dangerous types.

The trail was ill defined and quite rough going. We stopped several times, sipping water trapped in the crooks of bromeliads, and foraging other foodstuffs whenever possible. It wasn't much.

We knew we had to push on, that a *Swiss Family Robinson* lifestyle in these jungles was something only seen in movies, and that our most important concerns were adequate nourishment, hydration, and sending word to our families regarding our whereabouts.

The smoke vanished after we'd hiked about two hours. We had the compass bearing, but found it nearly impossible to move in a direct course toward it. The trails and waterways we followed veered in directions inconsistent with our destination, and we had to blaze our own path more often than not. By the time the sun had reached its zenith, we were completely exhausted.

"Let's rest here," I croaked through parched lips.

"Okay," Melodee said in little more than a dry whisper.

We found a dry spot under a huge balsa tree choked with tangles of pathos and orchid tendrils. I knew that once my rear end hit the ground, the rest of me would be unable to remove it from that perch. It didn't matter. My muscles were so spent I simply didn't care. We lazed in some wonderfully cool, deep shade with our feet propped up for over an hour. I was tempted to remove my shoes and stockings but knew that would be a mistake. My feet had swollen substantially, and if I were to free them from my footwear, I would not get them back in again until later that evening when the edema had subsided.

After resting a while longer, I took out a piece of the white willow bark I had gathered some time earlier and began grinding it between two flat stones. The juice dripped from the stones into a leaf-cup I had fashioned. I then diluted the juice with fresh water I found trapped in a plant hollow. The resultant mixture was bitter and almost impossible to drink. Looking around, I spotted a stevia bush, a plant whose leaves produced a very sweet resin. I selected a few choice leaves, mashed them between the stones, and added them to my willow-water mix. I sipped it slowly. *Not too bad.* I knew the pain-killing mix was nowhere near the reliability of store-bought analgesics, but at least it was a palatable concoction. More importantly, it worked. Within minutes, the pain lessened, and I knew the swelling in my feet would soon diminish.

Melodee lay drifting in and out of sleep. Perspiration ran from her forehead and glued the longer portions of her blond hair to her temples. As stoic as she had been, she was now able to display only brief bouts of energy and enthusiasm. After hiking half a day through a muggy rain forest on trails that slowed rather than aided one's progress, the little girl was desperately in need of rest and nourishment.

"Here, sip this," I said, lifting the pain-deadening mixture to her mouth.

She took the proffered drink and gagged on its aftertaste, but kept it down.

"Sorry. I tried to make it taste like Gatorade but came up a bit short."

She smiled weakly. "Thank you."

I found a moss-covered area and stretched out for a rest. I closed my eyes for what only seemed a minute. It ended up being much longer.

* * *

I thought I heard something. Whispers—soft but determined.

At first, I thought I was dreaming again, painting images of times more pleasant. Or perhaps it was simply Melodee praying again. I concentrated on the gossamer sounds and concluded they were neither part of my mindless wanderings nor Melodee's spiritual entreaties. These whispers were from someone else.

I opened my eyes and discovered the day had slipped much closer to dusk. Even though my mind still drifted in a dreamy, cerebral fog, I felt genuinely refreshed. I hadn't slept that soundly in a long time, figuring I must have been out three to four hours. Then more whispers.

I tried to sit up, but my body refused to answer the commands from my brain. I took a few deep breaths and used every bit of strength I had to rise on one elbow.

The whispers immediately stopped.

I looked toward Melodee, who was still lying under a spray of ferns, sleeping peacefully. I half expected to see her singing to herself again, but no sound passed her lips that I could detect.

Then the whispers came again. From directly behind me.

I spun around and saw the eyes and forehead of a little girl. She was about nine years old and seemed an equal mix of Hispanic and . . . something else. I couldn't really tell because most of her body remained hidden behind a moss- and lichen-covered rock. Beside her, a little boy, not much older, poked his head up. They quickly ducked from my eye contact but didn't run away. I smiled and tried not to move, so as not to scare them off.

Only a few seconds passed before their faces peered over the stone again. I eased slowly onto my knees and began building a simple tower from random sticks and twigs. The children's curiosity was immediately piqued, as I knew it would be, and they cautiously crept from around the rock to get a better look at what I was doing. They were bronzed-skinned with riotous black hair and dark brown eyes. That surprised me. Expecting a rain forest native, I thought the children would exhibit the characteristic chocolate-brown skin, straight, jet-black hair, and anthracite eyes common to the tribes of these jungles. Yet these kids looked more Mexican than Indian. The boy wore only a pair of shorts and the girl a light tunic, both made of some homespun material I didn't recognize. No shoes. Their meager adornments and unkempt hair convinced me they were not the children of an affluent drug czar. Perhaps they were with the people whose fire we had sighted earlier.

I grinned openly, almost absurdly, and winked both eyes to show them they need not fear me. I slowly raised my good hand and gave them a whimsical little-finger wave.

They looked at each other before giggling and stepping closer. They kept looking from me to Melodee, then back again. A mix of caution and inquisitiveness filled their eyes, but youthful curiosity was overpowering their trepidation.

Then the little boy showed his inborn, masculine bravado by speaking first. Nodding toward Melodee he asked, "¿Está muerta?"

I don't know if it was my elementary Spanish or my scientific training that gave me the Latin root for the word *dead,* but I understood what he was asking just the same. The little girl shushed him sternly. He balked but kept eye contact with me, awaiting an answer.

"No. She's just sleeping," I said softly so as not to awaken Melodee. "Um, está dormiendo."

The two looked at each other and exchanged a string of Spanish mixed with some other gibberish from which I got nothing. I again cursed myself for having a brain capable of conquering the most intricate scientific processes and memorizing voluminous amounts of Latin and Greek taxonomy, but not having a better grasp of conversational linguistics.

I pointed to my mouth. "Hable despacio, por favor." I needed him to speak much slower.

"Hablas muy extraño," the little boy said without humor.

I shrugged. "Lo siento. Hable español muy poco. "

My mispronunciation of the language caused the children to giggle even more. My bilingual stumblings seemed to soften the tension they felt from our presence, and because of the frailty of our predicament, I didn't mind being the object of their laughter.

Melodee groaned, stretched her sore legs and flexed her back, but remained asleep. I reached over and gently brushed her hair from her face.

"She has hair of gold," the little girl said in Spanish with a tone of wonderment. "¿Ella es una de la gente elegida?"

Not understanding the last part of her sentence, I said, "No entiendo."

The boy grabbed a handful of his hair and then pointed at Melodee and said, "Pelo de oro."

He had just reiterated that her hair was golden. I nodded. "Si. Pelo bonita." Then, punctuating each word as if that would increase their comprehension, I said, "¿De—dónde—es—usted? Where—are—you—from?"

I had always scoffed at people who spoke to foreigners much slower and a lot louder in a ridiculous attempt to break the language barrier. Yet even though I realized the ludicrousness of such action, I found myself doing the same thing.

The children smiled but said nothing.

I cleared my throat. "¿Dónde está el . . . " My mind went blank. For some reason, I could not recall the word for *village* or anything that might indicate where they were from. *Casa* meant house, but what if they didn't have a house? Before I could form another sentence, I heard myself ask, "¿Dónde está el baño?"

The two children burst out with sidesplitting laughter. I didn't comprehend how odd my question was until I realized exactly what I had asked. In the middle of a primeval rain forest, the query seemed ridiculously stupid, even to me. I had just asked them where the bathroom was.

They were still leaning on each other, laughing as if some invisible personage was tickling them unmercifully, when I realized that laughter was coming from behind me as well.

"Why did you ask them that?" Melodee chuckled through a huge smile.

I didn't know when she had awakened, but apparently it was some time before I tried to communicate my last sentence with our guests.

I smiled weakly. "It's been a while since I've spoken any Spanish."

She continued to laugh with the other children. "Uncle David, you're too silly for words."

I shrugged. "I was hoping they could take us to their village. We might find help there."

"By asking them where the bathroom is?"

"I know, I know. I spoke before thinking."

Melodee smiled at the children and said, "Hola. Me llamo Melodee."

The children stopped laughing and gawked at Melodee with wonder. They slowly backed away, obviously frightened by Melodee's ability to speak their language. I too was staring at my blond companion. *Where'd this come from?*

"Wait—you speak Spanish?" I asked.

"Just a little," Melodee said, shaking her head.

"Who are you?" the boy asked in Spanish. The girl backed up even farther. Both children looked ready to bolt.

"Queda, por favor. Necesitamos ayuda," I stated with unfeigned urgency. We really needed their help.

The little girl continued to back away, but the little boy stayed put. He looked from Melodee to me and back again. "¿Él es tu padre?"

From the corner of her mouth, Melodee asked, "Did he say something about his father?"

To Melodee I said, "He wants to know if we're related." To the boy I said, in Spanish, "I am her friend. What is your name?"

"Andro."

"Good to meet you, Andro. We are . . . " I paused, again searching for the correct Spanish word.

"¿Perdidos?" the little girl offered.

"Yes, lost. Can you help us?" I asked in their language.

"Sure. Follow us."

The two children darted into the jungle with amazing speed. Melodee was quickly on their tail using one of her curious bursts of energy. I stumbled along, struggling to keep up. Fatigued muscles made my movements labored and awkward, and now I had a pounding headache from trying to remember all of my travel Spanish. It wasn't long before all three children were slipping from my view.

"Wait!" I hollered, but to no avail.

FIFTEEN

"Melodee!" I called to a seemingly empty jungle.

Having lost sight of Melodee and the children, I had to follow by sound alone. Luckily, their light banter and frequent laughter echoed through the forest and gave me some direction.

After about twenty minutes, I came to a clearing of velvety green grass. The children were sitting in a circle with a number of other children. With them were three women, one probably in her late seventies, one about thirty years of age, and one perhaps in her midtwenties. They had with them baskets for gathering fruits and berries. The women were all clothed in homemade dresses, and the children wore clothing similar to the little girl's tunic. The women wore simple jewelry, and one even had a wristwatch. Although they appeared to be mostly of Hispanic lineage, I guessed they had some North American Indian heritage because of their high cheekbones, deep-set eyes, and aquiline noses. But the dominant Hispanic blood seemed to soften the harsher lines of brow and nose into a look that was decidedly unique.

The women acted cautious but very friendly toward Melodee. The children took turns touching her blond hair, a hue they had undoubtedly seen little of before.

As I entered the clearing, my foot caught on a root, and I landed face-first in a puddle of mud churned up by numerous travelers. Surrounding me, the children laughed merrily and chanted, "David, David, David," putting my name to some unknown melody that delighted them to no end.

I struggled to my knees and choked down my embarrassment as I tried to brush the muck from my shirt and pants. My arm throbbed with new resolve, reminding me of my recent injury and that I still needed to take it easy.

"Hola," I said in as friendly a tone as I could through the pulses of pain.

Suddenly someone grabbed me under both arms and hauled me to my feet. I turned to see a surly-looking young man around twenty years old standing behind me. He had long, dark hair and powerful arms, which he slowly folded across his chest. He was wearing Levi's and a rather modern-looking canvas safari shirt with four sizable pockets on the front and epaulettes on the shoulders. His thick, black hair was pulled back into a tight ponytail and held in place by a flash of purple twine festooned with a few stunning Quetzal feathers. He was not smiling.

"Thank you. Gracias, I mean," I said, trying to lighten the tension he brought with his hard, even stare.

He didn't respond; he simply stood there eyeing me with minimal civility, zero friendliness, and a hint of contempt. I nodded and turned to the women who were approaching me with good-humored faces.

"¿Está bien?" one of the older women asked.

"¿Qué pasó con su brazo?" the younger one asked, pointing to my bandaged arm.

I answered, "Está roto. ¿Muy malo, sí? It's hurt bad."

I hoped they understood my words, and if not, at least felt good about my tone. Melodee came to my side and put an arm around my waist. She seemed somewhat uncomfortable not knowing the language better, but still exuded her *all is well* confidence. She had had plenty of time to introduce herself while waiting for me to catch up, but how much she was able to communicate remained a question.

"Can you help us?" I asked in Spanish.

The young man snapped, "No!" a word common to English and Spanish.

I had no idea why he said no, but I didn't want to argue with him. Even if my arm was healed and I was feeling fully rested, I doubted I could win a physical contest with him. The young man looked as solid as a granite statue of Atlas himself, though perhaps not quite as muscular. I wondered about his apparel in contrast to the others of his clan, but sensed that now was not the time to inquire. He obviously had some contact with the outside world, but to what extent I didn't know. Still, it was encouraging. This revelation meant they might have access to some modern accoutrements, such as a phone or radio or even an automobile. I decided to be as docile and meek as possible until we had further information.

The oldest woman stepped forward and gave me a stare-down that would have wilted the grandest oak tree to a dried-up twig in a matter of seconds. I smiled again, knowing it would do little good to challenge her stare. My egocentric machismo balked at showing such submissiveness in front of the brawny young man behind me, but I kept my temper in check.

"Si ha venido a causar problemas le rechazaremos más rápido que rechazaríamos una perra enferma," the old woman spat in a string of Spanish so rapid it sounded like one continuous word. I understood something about not causing trouble and a sick dog, but that was about it.

Assuming it was a warning of sorts, I simply smiled and said, "Okay," hoping the oft-used American colloquialism was familiar to these people.

The old woman nodded curtly then spun around and called the children after her. They immediately followed as if she were playing a tune on the Pied Piper's magic flute. The young man also followed, bumping his shoulder against mine, knocking me off balance as he walked past. He did it intentionally. The young woman in the group scowled at him. Looking fairly confused, Melodee stood apart from either group. The young woman gently took her hand and turned to face me.

"Do you need help walking?" she asked me in her language.

"No. No es problema."

The insufferable humidity of the day and the anxiety and confusion of the setting had my temper on a razor's edge. The fact that I had stumbled while entering the clearing did not mean I was incapable of walking on my own, as the young woman seemed to infer. I found myself strangely incensed at her condescending question while still feeling grateful for her willingness to help.

"What did you tell them about me?" I complained to Melodee.

"Nothing other than your name. I don't know much more Spanish than that."

"Why didn't you mention you spoke some Spanish?"

She shrugged. "You never asked."

The young woman looked from Melodee to me, clearly not understanding our conversation. "So . . . would you like me to help you walk to our village?" she again queried in Spanish.

I shook my head. Not understanding the young woman, Melodee looked to me with raised eyebrows.

"She seems to think I need some help walking," I said with an accusatory tone.

I don't know why it galled me to be offered help when it was obvious I could walk on my own, but it did. Maybe it was because I wasn't able to grasp every word the strangers spoke, which made me feel inferior. Perhaps it was because they seemed friendlier to Melodee than to me. Their favoritism didn't make sense, as I clearly spoke better Spanish than she did.

Up until this point, my ego had worn thin having Melodee do more for me than I had done for her. My male machismo mandated that I be the steady one on whom all others were dependent. The strong, silent type is what I thought my persona conveyed, maybe not as ruggedly confident as the Marlboro Man or the Old Spice Sailor, but certainly more self-assured than Gilligan or Forrest Gump.

Whatever the reason, when the woman repeated her question, I answered with a sharp, "¡Yo dija que no!"

The woman stiffened and a frown quickly creased her brow.

"No, *thank you*, would be a better answer," Melodee interjected in her peculiar nonaccusatory way, obviously understanding the tone of my negative outburst.

I sighed and tried to smile. The young woman did not smile back. She was somewhat plain looking but had rather striking, liquid brown-black eyes under sharply arched eyebrows.

In a much softer voice, I said in Spanish, "I am sorry, señora. Thank you, but I can walk by myself."

My words seemed to have the proper effect. She nodded, then led Melodee and me on a trail exiting the clearing.

"What's wrong, Uncle David?" Melodee asked.

"Nothing. I'm sorry for seeming a little angry, but—"

"You about bit her head off."

I sighed again, heavily this time, and tried to collect my thoughts and emotions. "Okay, fair enough. I did snap a bit, and I'm sorry. Really."

Melodee did not respond but continued to pierce me with her sapphire blue eyes.

"Look, I know I should be acting a lot happier," I went on. "I guess I was a bit . . . embarrassed."

"Well, they seem willing to help. Let's go with them. Maybe they'll give us something to eat."

My stomach grumbled as if on cue, and I patted it with my good hand. "Let's hope so, kiddo."

She nodded and quickened her pace.

"Hang on," I whispered sharply. "Let's keep in mind we still don't know anything about them. We should really be extra careful until we're more sure of their intentions."

"Okay."

"I mean it, Melodee. We're foreigners here. They might not like our kind."

"Well, we can't just stand around waiting until the time seems right, Uncle David. We really don't have much choice, do we?"

"No, I guess not."

"Heavenly Father still has His eye on us," Melodee said. Then she added in a whisper, "We'll just try to avoid the unfriendly ones."

Whatever that meant, Melodee seemed to have no apprehension about following the strangers into the jungle. I wasn't so sure. Her confidence was the antithesis of my trepidation, and I wondered if we were entering a situation more precarious than our previous trek through the rain forest.

SIXTEEN

The village was very small, but at least it wasn't simply a collection of drafty grass huts. Rusty sections of corrugated metal, terracotta shingles with green lichen patina, scraps of plywood and tree bark, and bamboo walls formed small dwellings which stood in uniform arrangement around an open courtyard and a central stone cistern. The scene was reminiscent of those adopt-a-Third-World-child-for-only-fifty-cents-a-day advertisements, where starving, sad-eyed, fly-swarmed waifs played in mud and filth outside of a hut made from old refrigerator boxes. The biggest difference was that even though these huts were of meager construct, the people and area around them seemed healthy and happy. There was very little debris or trash littering the paths and central courtyard, and the people, though dressed in fourth-generation hand-me-downs, were free from the swarms of flies that covered the children on television. *At least they look* somewhat *civilized*, I thought to myself.

As our little entourage entered the clearing, the fluid motion of the village froze as if caught in a Polaroid snapshot. A couple of cur dogs warily approached us with hackles raised and teeth bared. The old woman again barked out a string of Spanish that sounded like one long word. I caught very little of it. A few men came up to me and appraised me cautiously. As the village children grew bolder, so did the dogs, until one of the dogs came in for a quick nip at my leg. Before I could react, the old woman's foot moved faster than a rattlesnake strike, and in an instant, that same dog flew backwards some six feet in the air, its surprised yelp sounding a fraction after it reached midflight. Melodee took my hand and smiled at me. She seemed to have absolutely no fear of the situation.

"Hello. We are very pleased to meet you," I began nervously in Spanish.

The men looked at each other and smiled broadly. An elderly man knelt in front of Melodee and offered his hand. She took it without pause. "Buenos tardes, señor."

He asked her something and she responded, struggling with the words midsentence. "I'm sorry, sir. I speak very little Spanish," she explained in his language.

The old man's features softened as he nodded. More words were exchanged among the villagers as I stood by, trying my best to exude an air of friendliness and charm. I probably looked more like the idiot who had somehow lost his village, but I didn't care. I thought it best to wait for one of them to make the first move, because I didn't want to seem overbearing or rude. Besides, everyone's attention seemed focused on the old man and Melodee.

I took the opportunity to steal a better look around. I was hoping to find signs of modernization. Unfortunately, I saw no power lines or cables that would suggest a telephone. I listened for the static tinniness of a transistor radio or television set, but heard nothing of the sort. I acknowledged with devastating assuredness that, unless one of these people had a cell phone in their hut, the chance of a quick call to home was out of the question.

My heart sank further as I realized there were also no signs of contemporary transportation. No car or truck, no motorcycle, not even any tracks that indicated such machinery had recently visited this place. As I stood there lamenting my characteristically bad luck, the setting closed in on me like a fog, making the scene feel more and more primitive by the second. Everything within view smacked of a time when recorded history was nothing more than a few cave paintings. Everything, that is, but the people themselves.

Some of the villagers were dressed in modern clothing, such as old Levi's and tee shirts, but nothing as contemporary as the safari shirt worn by the gruff young man we had met earlier. The children were barefoot, and most of the adults wore handmade sandals. A couple of the villagers even sported wristwatches and baseball caps—one advertising the Astros ball club, the other, Bud Light. Their clothing demonstrated that they had some contact with the outside world. That fact alone allowed me to breathe again.

As I continued to appraise the area, I realized the huts weren't as ramshackle as I had first assumed. Each had a foundation of wood or bamboo raised on stacked-stone columns approximately fourteen inches off the ground. All had overhanging eaves, which I assumed channeled the ubiquitous rainwater away from the walls and doorsteps, and some even had extended verandas and awnings. A few additional evidences of the modern world hung from the bamboo-lath and plywood walls, including a number of copper-bottom pots and other cooking utensils.

But still no phones. No motor vehicles. The only mechanized conveyance was a rusted-out bicycle with metal rims but no tires. These people appeared to live in almost complete isolation. The simplicity of the village and the humble look and manner of its citizens revealed a lack of exposure to the modern marvels of advanced society. It was probably for the best. Along with modern conveniences came modern problems: Internet pornography, large-scale consumer debt, illegal drug use, and more.

After a short time, the old man gave up trying to converse with Melodee and gently cupped her cheeks in his gnarled hands. He stood and whispered something to another man standing next to him. Melodee looked confused and discernibly embarrassed.

"What did he say?" I asked her quietly.

"I don't know."

I frowned. "But you two were talking for fifteen minutes."

"Trying to. I only caught one or two words."

I raised my eyebrows in anticipation of further information, but she seemed unwilling to offer any. I persisted. "Melodee?"

After a moment, she shrugged and said, "I think he was asking about where we came from and what we're doing here. That kind of stuff."

"He thinks she's a chosen one," a caustic voice said from behind us—in English!

I turned to see the young man with the safari shirt glowering at me, his eyes menacing, his arms akimbo. "Her," he said, thrusting an accusatory finger at Melodee.

"You speak English?" I asked the already-answered question.

"Enough."

"Why didn't you say so earlier?"

"Why should I?"

"As a courtesy," I said a little too harshly. The impudence of this cocky young man irked me, and I felt my temper rising uncontrollably.

"Are you not in our land?" he spat. "Should not you speak our language as a courtesy to us?"

He almost seemed to imply we had intentionally intended on visiting this rain forest. But Melodee and I were neither hopeful immigrants nor sightseeing tourists. Our stay here wasn't by choice; we were accidental denizens.

"News flash, buddy: we didn't plan on coming to your lousy country in the first place," I grumbled. "Our plane crashed."

Melodee grabbed my arm and stepped in front of me. To the young man she said, "You speak English very well, señor. Where did you learn it?"

He continued to scowl at me, not answering Melodee.

"I do not care how you came to our land," he said, challenging me. "You are not welcome here, gringo."

Although I knew I should calm down, I scoffed. "Who would want to be?"

"I think your rain forest is beautiful," Melodee said, trying to ease the tension between the young man and myself.

"Its beauty is spoiled by too many strangers."

"You call this beautiful?" I smirked. "You couldn't pay me to live here."

"If you hate this land so much, then leave," he said between clenched teeth.

I wasn't about to cow to his disdain. He was impudent and spiteful and totally without manners. "That's exactly what we want to do, Tarzan. The sooner the better, as far as I'm concerned."

"That's true," Melodee interjected in her soft, pleasing voice. "But we are hopelessly lost. I bet you know this jungle inside out. Can you help us?"

The young man faltered a bit and flashed a brief glance in her direction. The tension between the two of us was palpable, and Melodee was doing her best to dispel it. Why I had suddenly let this young upstart irritate me so much I could not readily explain, but there was something about him that bothered me, that raised a warning voice in me, and I felt the only way to counter it was to be as abrasive as he was. Maybe it was that he was behaving just the opposite of everyone else in the village. Or maybe it was simply because I never could tolerate arrogant, smart-aleck, disrespectful young males whose overproduction of testosterone outweighed their maturity and made their presence unbearable. Whatever the reason, this young man seemed determined to get the best of me, and I was just as determined not to let him.

The rest of the villagers stood silently watching our exchange. Perhaps they were interested in seeing how it would all turn out. Or perhaps they were judging me, seeing how I would react to a difficult situation. If the latter were the case, I had to admit I was giving a rather poor showing of things.

"Even if you could just show us which trail to take, we'd be very appreciative," Melodee said happily, trying hard to mask her nervousness.

The young man paused before spitting on the ground and storming off through the small crowd that had gathered.

Melodee whirled on me and slapped my shoulder. "Why were you being so rude?"

"Me? He's the one who started it all."

"Oh, that's a mature answer: *He started it all*," she mimicked in a whiny tone, as if I were a child trying to explain his part in a school-yard brawl. "In case you haven't noticed, Dr. Kirkham, we're in serious need of help, and these people are probably our only hope of getting out of here."

Her reprimand irked me almost as much as the young man's gall, but at the same time, I knew she was right. Her maturity outshined mine, and I was not very proud of myself at that moment. The fact that she had dropped "Uncle David" and used my last name showed the intensity of her anger.

"I'm sorry, Melodee. I don't know what came over me. But there's something about that guy that's dangerous."

"I know. I felt the same from him, but that doesn't mean acting like a jerk will make things safer."

I smiled. "You have such a subtle way of putting things."

She maintained her stern tone. "My mom always told me not to beat around the bush. Just say what you mean—and that's exactly what I do. But I try to be tactful at the same time. You do know what tact is, don't you?"

I sighed heavily and nodded. I felt embarrassed and foolish. I hoped that no one within earshot of the earlier exchange spoke English. I glanced at the old man. He had a disapproving yet curious look on his face.

"Speaking of beating around the bush . . ." I said softly. I turned to the man and asked in Spanish, "Excuse me sir, but what did you ask this little girl?"

The old man spoke slowly and clearly, as if what he was about to divulge carried great importance. "There is a people, an *antiguo* people, who used to live in these lands. They were a people with fair skin, many with golden hair and light shining from their eyes. We call them the 'chosen people.' I thought she might be one of them."

Surprisingly, I understood most of his words, though I had no clue what he was talking about. An ancient, fair-skinned people? A *chosen people*?

"Melodee is an American. She is not from an ancient people," I tried to explain in Spanish.

The old guy was adamant. "No, she has the look. She has the spirit. She must be from the City of Gold."

"She could be worth a fortune," another man added.

City of Gold? She's worth a fortune? Now what were they talking about? "I am very sorry, but you are mistaken," I explained.

The men in the crowd began jabbering excitedly among themselves as they wandered toward a large, palm-thatched hut.

Melodee stayed by my side, looking very weary but still maintaining a smile.

"Pardon me. Are you hungry?" an older woman asked in Spanish. "Would you like something to eat?"

"Sí, sería mucho gusto. Gracias," I said for the two of us.

"Where did you learn Spanish?" Melodee asked me.

"My company gave me a crash course in Spanish and a tutor when they started sending me to South America. He was with me almost five months straight. I'm not fluent, but I can get by in most situations—as long as they don't speak too fast."

"That's way cool."

"It's part of the geek in me," I said with a teasing wink. "How about you? You seem to speak it pretty well."

"Corpus Christi is only a few miles from the Mexican border. Almost everyone there speaks Spanish. We moved there when I was seven, and I just sort of picked it up."

That made sense.

The old woman led us to a low table under a bowery of palm leaves draped over a framework of bamboo poles. The helpful woman from the clearing brought plates made from some ceramic material. Each plate had two strips of fried meat I did not recognize. The scent was intoxicating. A large plate in the center of the table contained piles of pole beans, leeks, and some kind of yam.

I admitted to Melodee that, when it came to foreign foods, ignorance was often better than a sure knowledge. In my many travels for BioCraft, I had learned that if I knew what the food was, its taste invariably suffered—as did I. Still, because of my famished condition, this meal looked delicious.

With a mouthful of food, I noticed that Melodee had paused to bow her head and pray before eating. The woman serving us also took note and seemed immensely pleased. I bowed my head and chewed as inconspicuously as possible. Prayer was still an uncomfortable undertaking for me. Probably always would be.

When Melodee finished her oblation, she lunged for her food, wolfing it down with reckless abandon, pausing only to wash down one mouthful after another with huge gulps of fruit juice. Luckily, the food tasted as delicious as it looked. With every bite, I felt my strength growing and could see the same effect in Melodee. Within minutes, a strong drowsiness washed over me, much like the triptophan rush one gets after a big Thanksgiving turkey dinner.

Thanksgiving. My mind flashed to what Dyana and Paige might be doing at that moment. Had they put out a request for a search party yet? Or had enough days passed without communication that they would question my absence? I wasn't even sure what day of the week it was. I checked my watch and only then discovered it had stopped working. *Figures.* Had November passed into December yet? If so, what was the precise date? I asked Melodee, but she was more interested in finishing her plate of food, and merely shrugged her shoulders.

As soon as our plates were empty, the woman pointed to an adjacent bowery under which hung two hammocks. A small stream next to the bowery tumbled over and around large, algae-coated stones, gurgling a lullaby that had me drifting into a restful slumber almost before I had fully stretched out in the hammock. The restfulness of my sleep, however, was short-lived. Dreams wracked my mind: haunting, disturbing visions of evil men chasing us through endless labyrinths of jungle-choked trails. Why they were chasing us I did not know, but I knew that Melodee was in grave danger, and it was up to me to protect her. Being caught meant sure death—for both of us. A few of the villagers were in my dreams too, but I could not tell whether they represented friends or foes. Somehow, I knew when I awoke that most would prove untrustworthy, but I didn't know how.

SEVENTEEN

It was well past midnight before consciousness wrested me from my nightmares. I opened my eyes quickly, nervously, but didn't move. A sticky breeze picked at my hair and found its way under my shirt. A distant thunderclap rumbled over the rain forest, deep, reverberant, menacing.

I could sense someone or something standing near me, staring at me in the darkness.

I opened my eyes as wide as possible to acclimate them to the darkness. Shifting only my line of sight, I tried to determine who—or what—was looking at me. There were shadows within shadows, vague amorphous shapes that didn't belong. I continued to move my eyes slowly from side to side while barely moving my head. My gaze stopped on a particularly deep pocket of darkness—an alcove behind a stand of snake grass, masked not only by the awning, but also by the walls of the adjacent hut. An encroaching web of vines creeping along a trellis added further camouflage. Such a nook would probably be dark even at noon on a cloudless day. I knew there was someone—or some*thing*—there, blended inside the shadow, a living, breathing part of the black gloom. I couldn't tell who or what it was, but I sensed that he/she/it was not friendly.

Melodee's soft breathing stuttered slightly as she wriggled into a more comfortable position. The fact that she was resting peacefully told me she was feeling better, which should have relaxed me somewhat, but didn't. My concern for her was stronger than I cared to admit. She had probably saved my life, and her insurmountable spirit and positive attitude held me in humble admiration. I felt a *duty* to protect Melodee. And I sensed this intruder within the shadows was more than a physical threat to her. It was almost as if the thing wanted her soul.

I decided that waiting for the entity to make the first move was foolish. I had read somewhere, *When confronted by something fierce, act fiercer.* I took a deep breath, sat up quickly, and turned to face the blackness. I heard a soft rustling of vegetation, but saw nothing move. It could have been a breeze pushing the foliage around.

"What do you want?" I asked the shadow.

I received no answer—but then, I didn't really expect one.

I'm not sure how long I sat in my hammock before the feeling of being watched went away. I lay back down but kept my ears tuned for anything untoward. The rest of the evening passed without incident, yet I found it difficult to obtain any refreshing sleep. My mind spent the remainder of the night trying to calm portentous anxieties and a troubled heart.

* * *

I awoke to the sound of children giggling. Opening my eyes, I found myself under the scrutinizing gaze of a dozen wide-eyed youngsters insatiably curious about the strange visitors to their village.

"Buenos días," I said with a half-hearted smile.

The children erupted in a burst of laughter that intensified a dull throb just behind my temples. I sat up very slowly. My entire body ached as if ten men twice my size had beaten me to a pulp. My mouth felt like pasty cotton, and my arm complained with renewed retribution. I managed to throw my feet over the edge of the hammock and sit upright. It was not a graceful maneuver. I must have resembled a newborn foal trying to stand for the first time, because the children's laughter increased with every move I made.

"Children, leave him in peace!" a voice commanded loudly in Spanish.

The children retreated a few paces but continued their ogling. A woman approached, squatted in front of me, and placed a gentle hand on my knee.

"Are you hungry, señor?" she asked slowly so I could understand.

"Yes. I mean, sí," I answered. She was the thirtyish woman who had helped us the day before. The woman stood and turned to go.

"Una momento," I said, struggling to rise from the wobbly hammock. While fairly easy to get into, a hammock is a challenging thing to dismount. Putting my feet in front of me instead of under myself, I pushed off. The hammock, not being a stationary object, instantly swung in the opposite direction, and I plopped heavily on the ground, bringing yet another uproarious din of laughter from the children. The woman smiled compassionately and helped me to my feet.

"Thank you—um, gracias," I stammered.

"You welcome," she said in English.

"Do you speak English?" I asked eagerly.

"No," she said with a coy smile. "Thank you. You welcome. Hello. Yes. No. Pero no más."

Speaking in her language, I said, "I understand. I don't speak much Spanish. Sí?"

She smiled. "Sí."

We stood in awkward silence for a moment while the children seemed to hold their breath to see what other slapstick humor I might provide. Extending my hand to the woman, I said, "Me llamo David Kirkham. What is your name?"

She lowered her eyes and said softly, "Emalia."

"Señora Emalia. Thank you for your kindness."

She nodded and left, chastening the children as she passed. They scattered in various directions, but I felt confident they'd be back soon, their wide, dark eyes gawking at me as if I had two heads with three eyes on each—like something that crawled out of a dark hole, waiting to spring forth . . .

Instantly, I recalled the skulker from the previous night. I turned to examine the alcove where I had felt the presence. It was still dark, but no longer exuded evil. I moved closer to inspect it, dreading what I might find, and at the same time chiding myself for being so fraught with flighty emotion. The alcove was only a few feet deep and was completely empty. But I *knew* someone had been there last night. I wondered if Melodee had sensed it too. I then noticed that a shoe print dimpled the moist floor of the alcove. The imprint, made by a rather large foot, displayed a modern waffle-tread pattern like that found on high-end hiking boots.

Another chorus of laughter erupted, distracting me from my sleuthing. I turned to see the cause of this new outburst and only then noticed Melodee was not in her hammock.

As the foggy remnants of a restless sleep dissipated from my head, I focused on a scene that was equally chaotic and tranquil. The village was alive with activity. Women bustled around cook fires and wash tubs, and performed a dozen other tasks in fluid choreography. The day was clear and bright and a gentle breeze kept the humidity at a tolerable level. Sitting in a circle under a veranda a few yards from mine, a gaggle of children was anxiously engaged in a game using small polished stones, laughing at each play. I half expected Melodee to be the center of their excitement, but she was nowhere to be seen.

"Where is Melodee?" I asked the children in Spanish.

They uniformly pointed across the compound. "She's with the old ones," one of them volunteered.

Looking across the plaza, I saw Melodee sitting with a half dozen older villagers. She appeared comfortable in her efforts to converse with them. Feeling she was okay, I moved to a table and sat down, breathing heavily from that simple exertion. I found it curious how a night of rest seemed to amplify my ailments rather than ameliorate them. But I knew it was simply part of the healing process.

The woman who identified herself as Emalia brought me a plate of food: fried plantains, mashed breadfruit, and two strips of sinewy meat. Foolishly, I asked what animal it came from.

"Capybara," she answered.

Great. The capybara is the world's largest rodent. I put into my mind it was freshly jerked beef from a prime, corn-fed Nebraska steer. It helped—a little. Looking up, I saw that a number of the children had quietly joined me.

"Hola," I said pleasantly. They fled as if I had threatened them with their lives.

I finished my breakfast in peace, then stood and stretched luxuriously. Melodee was no longer in sight. I assumed she was still entertaining questions from the village elders, although just how much they'd get from her made me smirk. Nevertheless, I hated the idea of her being out of my sight. As friendly as some of the villagers were, I still felt an uneasy portent about most of them.

I wandered over to the hut where I had last seen her and heard Melodee's voice coming from inside. Although she struggled with her Spanish, she sounded fine, and her tone didn't indicate that she might be in danger. I poked my head inside the hut and smiled. Filtered sunlight illuminated the space enough for me to see Melodee wave at me, a big smile painting her face. Remembering my poor showing yesterday, I decided not to interrupt.

With a full belly, my body felt suddenly tired again. I rationalized a return to the hammock, arguing that I really hadn't slept very well the night before, and with my recent adventures in the rain forest and bones still in need of knitting, I deserved an early morning nap. I walked back to our veranda, smiling at everyone along the way. Only a few smiled back.

Using my hands to support myself, I backed into the hammock, but owing to the design of the thing, instead of providing any support, the hammock again swung away, and I landed hard on my rear end, under the hammock instead of on it. While pretending to concentrate on their game, the children had kept a constant eye on me, and their efforts paid off as they again broke into laughter. My head again pounded, and my arm twitched with sharp flashes of pain.

"Are you okay, Uncle David?" Melodee was ambling toward me, a slight limp slowing her pace.

"Just dandy," I grumbled. "How about you? You seem to have a hurt foot or something."

"My legs and back are really sore, but a bit of stretching usually makes it go away. Do you need some help getting up?"

"No," I snapped, unable to control the anger that arose from pain as well as embarrassment. "What I need is a stiff drink."

I rolled to my feet and attempted to mount the hammock again. This time, instead of sitting, I fell into it, which apparently was the right thing to do. The children seemed disappointed. Melodee took the hammock next to mine.

"You still got that mini-bottle?" I asked, hoping for a chemical reprieve from the pain in my head and arm.

She gave me another of her matronly scowls and said, "You really shouldn't drink that stuff, you know."

I knew this topic would come up eventually. "Why, because your Mormon health code says not to?"

"The Word of Wisdom, as it's called, is more than a health code. The eighty-ninth section of the Doctrine and Covenants says—"

"The what and who?"

"The Doctrine and Covenants. It's a collection of revelations that give specific instructions and messages and warnings to the Saints in the latter days."

"Oh, okay. Thanks," I said conclusively, hoping to avoid a lecture. It didn't work.

"Anyway, the Word of Wisdom is more than just counsel on what food and drinks to avoid and such; it also tells what foods are good for you and—more importantly—gives promises to those who follow it. You wanna hear it?"

"You've got a copy with you?" I asked, somewhat astonished.

"I wish," she chuckled. "No, but I think I can quote the important parts."

"Good for you," I said none too pleasantly. I wasn't much in the mood for this sermon.

She sat on the edge of her hammock and looked at me with profound intensity. "'All saints—that means everyone—who remember to keep and do these sayings, walking in obedience . . . shall receive health in their navel and marrow to their bones; And shall find wisdom and great treasures of knowledge, even hidden treasures.' There's more, before and after, but that's the part I like."

"What, the 'healthy navel' part?" I chided.

She pouted at me. Obviously, she didn't find humor in my flippant remark. "No, Uncle David, my favorite part is the one you of all people would be interested in." When I didn't respond, she continued, "Your career is spent looking for information about new plants and drugs, right?"

"For the most part."

"You could call new information a 'treasure of knowledge,' couldn't you?"

I nodded as a dim light of understanding began to glow in the back of my mind.

"How would you like to find some *hidden* treasures?" she asked in a voice dripping with promises of marvelous potential.

"I'd like that very much."

"Then I'll make you a promise. If you don't drink the alcohol in that little bottle, if you follow the Word of Wisdom to the letter and continue reading the Book of Mormon, then I testify you will someday find hidden treasures of knowledge—both temporal *and* spiritual."

It was a dubious promise; I had some pretty lofty and ambitious dreams of success. Nevertheless, there was an intensity in her stare that convinced me she might be onto something, that said she knew beyond any doubt the promises in her Word of Wisdom were true, and that she would be proven right.

By then the throbbing in my head and arm had diminished a bit, negating the need for medication, and I decided to buoy her spirits and go along with her challenge. "Okay, kiddo. I'll stop drinking for now."

She frowned. "It's more than just not drinking, Uncle David. You have to do it for the right reasons. You have to *believe* you will be blessed by following the commandments, and *then* you'll find your hidden treasures of knowledge."

Have a positive mental attitude. Yeah, I had heard that before and concluded it couldn't hurt. "Okay, I'll do my best."

"And finish reading the Book of Mormon?"

"Yeah, I promise."

"Great," she said as she left her hammock and slowly walked over to the group of children.

I marveled at her optimism in light of such adversity, and actually felt strengthened by the promise I had just made.

I stretched languidly and put my hands behind my head. My eyes eased shut as I listened to the soothing sounds of the gurgling stream, the harmonic banter of Melodee and the children playing, and the chorus of women performing daily chores. I don't remember the exact moment I drifted off.

EIGHTEEN

"¿Señor?"

I awoke slowly.

"Venga conmigo, por favor."

The day had all but passed, and the warm ambience of late afternoon hues painted a hush over the small village. A man stood over me, beseeching.

"Come, please."

"Sí," I said, struggling to my feet. I am a quick learner and managed to exit the hammock without incident this time.

As we walked across the compound, I caught several worried glances from the womenfolk and the saddened faces of youths at their sides.

"What's wrong?" I asked my guide. He did not respond.

An air of foreboding enshrouded me as I followed the man across the strangely hushed compound. We entered a thatched hut tucked into a hollow between two huge queen palms. Vines and tendrils framed the doorway, which created a gloomy entrance dappled with jagged flecks of sunlight. It was quiet and dark inside the hut.

I stood in silence, sensing that any attempt at communication would be frowned upon. A feeling of dread filled the small room. Something was definitely wrong.

It took some time before my eyes adjusted to the darkness. I almost wished they hadn't.

Melodee lay on a straw mat in the middle of the floor. She looked ashen, gray, sickly. Beads of sweat glistened on her skin, giving it an unhealthy sheen. Her shallow breathing was coarse and ragged. Her eyes were closed.

An obese man loomed over her. He was dressed in what I took to be the ornamental garb of a headhunter: beads and bones dangled from his thick neck and puffy earlobes; multicolored strips of raffia bound around his biceps hung down his fleshy arms; and a luxuriously feathered headdress, complete with the skull of some long-dead animal, crowned his bald head. Bizarre, colorful tattoos completely covered his flabby chest and rotund belly. A thick, black band of dye traced a broad stripe from temple to temple, making his eyes look like two phantom orbs in a starless night—one intensely piercing in its gaze, the other offset and milky. He was the local shaman, or so I gathered. It surprised me that these villagers had a witch doctor. They seemed much more civilized. Nevertheless, this medicine man was currently performing some ritualistic voodoo on Melodee, using his terrifying appearance to convince those present of his magical abilities and omnipotent mojo.

Apparently, they had called on him to help Melodee. She indeed looked sick, but I could not readily ascertain why. As I moved toward her, the man who had escorted me there held me back. He shook his head, then nodded toward the shaman. A sharp pang of concern gripped my heart. If Melodee had contracted some latent jungle fever, I knew she needed medical help immediately.

A low gurgle churned deep in the shaman's throat as he waved his huge arms over the unconscious girl, shaking a rattle made from a large rodent's skull in one hand while sprinkling some glittering flakes over her body with the other. Pungent filigrees of incense moved throughout the small hut like spectral apparitions.

Several men and a few women were present to witness this spectacle. None of them looked like they were enjoying it. Except for the grunting shaman, all remained silent.

Pointing at Melodee, I asked a woman next to me, "How long has she been like this?"

The woman blanched and shook her head as the shaman let out a guttural bark and glared at us with his good eye. He spat some vile oath in my direction and went back to chanting and perspiring over

Melodee. I found the whole scenario frightening . . . and somewhat humorous. I knew his incantations and spells would have zero effect on Melodee, but I also recognized that something was truly wrong with her.

Ignoring the protests around me, I slowly moved toward Melodee to examine her. When the shaman hissed again, I knelt slowly, abjectly, which seemed to appease him temporarily.

The little girl was definitely suffering from some kind of fever. I had no idea what was causing it, but I knew she needed to be cooled immediately. I had seen a few plants that had antipyretic properties just outside the village boundaries, and figured I could gather some quickly enough to help break my little friend's fever.

I began to shuffle backwards when the shaman pulled out a wicked-looking dagger, complete with a crooked horn haft and a gleaming, serrated edge. He raised it high over Melodee with one hand as he continued to rattle the rodent skull with the other. My heart nearly stopped. Was he planning to stab the defenseless child? My muscles were as rigid as a tightly wound spring. I didn't know if I had the strength to overcome a downward blow from his massive arm, but I was ready to deflect it as best I could. The horrifying gleam in the shaman's eye mirrored that of the dagger and created a terrible, nightmarish tension. Chills skittered up and down my spine. I was quivering, ready to explode. The shaman held this pose for a moment before an eerie, bone-chilling mewl issued from between his puffy lips. Holding the dagger with malicious intent, the huge man ceremoniously set the rodent skull on Melodee's forehead. Then, before I could blink, he grabbed a chicken from somewhere behind him and held the dagger to its throat. The shaman began a disturbing ululation that sounded like something from a realm of lost and tortured souls. He positioned the chicken over Melodee's unconscious form, apparently ready to slice the bird open.

I had seen enough. "Stop!" I yelled, taking a bold step forward.

The shaman's horrid cry caught in his throat, and he staggered back, gagging on his own breath. His eye bulged with disbelief at my temerity as a pinched wheeze leaked from his throat. Ignoring the dagger in his hand, I knelt beside Melodee, tossed the rodent skull to one side, and began wiping the sweat from her face. She was hot to the touch, burning up with fever. The shaman screeched something to everyone in the hut while shaking the unfortunate chicken at me. I was expecting the sharp point of the dagger to enter my back, but instead, the shaman suddenly clamped his mouth shut and stormed from the hut.

"I need some water," I said in Spanish to no one in particular. When no one answered, I yelled. "Water, now!"

A woman nodded and ran from the hut. She quickly returned with a gourd of cool water and a piece of cloth. I soaked the cloth well, then washed Melodee's face. Her breathing was still coarse, her heartbeat rampant.

"Melodee, can you hear me?" I asked as I continued to wipe the sweat from her face and neck.

She did not respond. I recognized the signs of febrile dehydration and knew I had to get water into her quickly. Without it, she would go into seizures and possibly develop dangerously low blood pressure and even brain damage. But to do so now would be risky. With her unconscious, I could accidentally drown her.

"Melodee, wake up and drink this," I commanded.

No response.

A man knelt beside me and gently raised her into a sitting position. I held the gourd to her lips. "Melodee, I'm going to pour some water into your mouth. Swallow as much as you can."

I poured slowly. The first few ounces washed past her lips and down her face and neck. I repositioned the gourd and pinched her mouth open a crack. Water entered and I saw her neck muscles contract in a lifesaving swallow. She gagged and spit up most of the water, but didn't lose it all. She then let out a soft moan and coughed. I held the gourd to her mouth again and watched her swallow several times. Putting the gourd aside, I again wiped her face with the moistened cloth. The man laid her back down, and a woman helped wipe Melodee's arms and legs with another wet cloth.

Sudden tears burned my eyes as I realized just how sick Melodee was. When did this come about? And why so suddenly? Other than her sore legs, she seemed fine just hours ago.

Choked with emotion, I said to those around me, "Gracias. Muchas gracias."

Feeling somewhat assured that Melodee was in safe hands, I decided to search for plants I could use to make a fever reducer. Upon exiting the hut, I had to pause with my hand over my eyes as the evening sun shone directly into my face, temporarily blinding me. Suddenly, a wailing screech sounded not ten feet from me, causing me to jump.

The shaman was standing there, a long spear in one hand, a creepy-looking bamboo and raffia talisman in the other. He began to chant and gesticulate, glaring at me with his good eye while the milky one stared off to one side. A crowd quickly gathered to watch. Buoyed by an audience, the shaman's mantra increased in volume until I thought he was going to lose a tonsil if he didn't back down.

But he didn't. Instead, he began a dance of sorts, much like a fire dance one would expect from a Cherokee Indian, only he encircled *me* instead of a roaring pyre. As the obese shaman weaved and jumped, so did his rubbery excess of skin and multiple folds of fat. With his flabby arms flapping against his girth and his grossly disproportionate belly bouncing atop his waist, he quickly ran out of breath and began wheezing instead of screaming. A florid ruddiness colored his face a crimson hue. Sweat poured from his brow as if from an open faucet. The sound of flesh slapping against flesh; the feathered headdress bobbing atop his glistening, rosy head; and the squeaky wheeze that issued from his constricted throat all combined to make the shaman look like a large, hideous, exotic bird—one that, with any luck, would never be discovered.

After only one or two minutes of this spectacle, the shaman collapsed in a gasping, gelatinous mound of adipose tissue and feathers. I shook my head, tried unsuccessfully to suppress a smile, and walked over to the veranda where I had napped. Locating Melodee's backpack, I opened the front pouch to retrieve her Swiss Army knife. I hoped the villagers had left her things alone, knowing they would covet such a useful tool. Luckily, they had.

Finding the knife, I paused, wondering if she had anything else that might come in handy. I doubted it. If she had, she would have offered it to me already. I pocketed the knife and headed into the jungle to find the plants I had seen earlier.

I wondered if the shaman might come after me seeking vengeance, but dismissed the thought almost as quickly as it came. Even with one arm in a splint, I was fairly certain I could win a fight with him and positive I could outrun him if necessary.

I followed a path that wound its way through the underbrush. Despite the encumbrance of my splint, the going was not difficult. Obviously well-used by the villagers, the path led directly to a river.

At the river's edge, I searched for the plants I needed: willow, arnica, wild tobacco, guarana, and others. Climbing over some large roots, I lost my footing and fell into a muddy pool. I stood slowly, gasping in pain and wiping away the sweat that was stinging my eyes. Stepping beyond the mud, I reached into a clear pocket of water and splashed my face several times. I wiped my eyes again, turned around, and stared into the muzzle of a double-bore shotgun.

NINETEEN

I didn't recognize the gunman, but the smile on his face gave me hope that he was friendlier than the shotgun suggested. He was clean shaven, and his shirt, although sweaty, looked brand new. Additionally, he wore a straw hat tilted jauntily to one side.

"Come with me," he said softly in Spanish.

I rose slowly. His gun pointed to one side as he offered his hand to help me from the pool.

Not knowing what else to say, I mumbled, "Thanks."

The man nodded. "Come," he said in English.

We moved onto the trail. When the trail forked, my captor indicated that we should take the path to the left. I thought I had come down the one on the right to reach the river, but as I had done so in a blind run, I knew I could be mistaken.

"Where are we going?" I asked urgently in Spanish. "To the village?"

"No," was his calm reply.

"But the little girl is sick. Understand? Sick? Enfermedad? I've got to help her."

I wasn't sure whether to speak in English or Spanish, but it didn't matter. He smiled as if he comprehended exactly what I was saying and then encouraged me with the barrel of his shotgun to keep moving—away from the village.

I had no idea where we were going, but knew it couldn't be good. Furthermore, we were heading away from Melodee, and she needed my help right away. She was terribly ill and might not survive if she did not receive the proper medicines. But I didn't know how to communicate this to my captor.

My mind began buzzing as disjointed thoughts burst in my brain like a thousand random camera flashes. Who was this man? Was he a drug runner? Where was he taking me? What was wrong with Melodee? Why did she become ill so suddenly?

I considered making a run for it, taking my chances and sprinting helter-skelter into the jungle. If the man held a handgun I might have had a chance, but a shotgun was too much to risk. I was taller than the gunman and outweighed him by about fifty pounds. But none of that mattered as long as the barrel of his gun was pointed at my back.

We continued walking. And walking. *When will we get there?* I wondered, not knowing where "there" was. As the sun set behind the western mountains, a buzzing swarm of mosquitoes came upon us with a vengeance. (Since this was our first encounter with mosquitoes, I knew my captor had until this point avoided the boggy, lowland areas.) I swatted a mosquito on my neck and then examined the carcass in my hand. It was enormous. I tried not to think about the myriad of diseases these pests could transmit with each bite. Another one landed on my right arm, and I swatted it with my left. Although my fracture seemed to be healing well, it still flared with pain, and I let loose a string of expletives that would have made a sailor blush.

The gunman chuckled. "Mosquito bad, sí?"

"Sí," I responded, and swatted another one. I didn't know why the bloodsuckers hadn't bothered us in the village. Perhaps the cooking fires kept them away. Or perhaps we were constantly upwind. Whatever the reason, it seemed like I had just walked into the biggest swarm of *Anopheles* in the world, with a sign on my back advertising, Eat Here, Good Food.

I swatted again and again. It occurred to me that while Melodee and I were lost in the forest, we were always drenched with rain when night fell. Perhaps that is why the mosquitoes didn't pester us. I looked heavenward and saw a gloomy, gray sky, with no stars or moon, which meant there was ample cloud cover. But would it bring rain? I scoffed at the thought. I couldn't believe I actually wanted *more* precipitation.

Another mosquito pierced my neck. I killed it.

"Señor," the gunman said. "Take."

Although it was getting dark very quickly, I could see in his hand a few glossy, forest-green leaves. He pantomimed rubbing the leaves between his palms and then running his hands over his arms and face. The gunman then plucked a branch that had more of the small, glossy leaves on it. The tree from which it came resembled an ash—but not exactly. I couldn't identify it in the darkness, but I reasoned that the locals would have many home remedies from the indigenous plant life, and trusted that my companion knew what he was doing. The gunman pinched his shotgun between his knees, stripped the branch of leaves, and ground the leaves between his palms. He applied the resultant sticky substance to his arms as if he were slathering on lotion. I followed his example. The resin had an extremely bitter smell that reminded me of quinine. A botanic name came to mind: *Simaroubaceae*, the Jamaica Quassia tree. I knew of its antiparasitic properties but had never heard of its use as an insect repellent. I ground more leaves and applied the sap liberally to my face and neck. It worked instantly. The mosquitoes buzzed around and harassed me, but they no longer tried to land on my exposed skin. "Gracias," I said with a smile.

The gunman smiled back and gave me a playful slap on the shoulder, as if I was his best friend and all was right with the world. He then retrieved his shotgun and pointed it at my chest.

"Vámonos," he said while still smiling. So much for best friends.

We marched for hours along a faint trail until my legs felt like they would give out any second. Just as I was about to collapse, we rounded a bend and came upon a modern-looking building made of gray cinder block and corrugated tin roofing. A single yellow lamp illuminated a doorway near one corner of the building, and a mind-boggling collection of insects swarmed around the lamp. The pulsing, churning mass buzzed, clicked, chattered, flittered, and hissed as if it were a single mutant entity.

I pointed at the door. "In there?"

"Sí, rápido."

I swatted as many bugs as I could while reaching for the door-knob. The door groaned open as if the hinges had never once seen a drop of oil. The gunman and I entered a large room full of materials I wish I didn't recognize, but I was all too familiar with the fraction-ators, distilleries, and desiccators used to process plant material into consumable chemicals—in this case, illegal chemicals. This was obviously a well-equipped, well-designed, and well-stocked drug lab. Judging from the random samplings of plant material lying around, the lab's chief products were cocaine, opium, and their many illicit derivatives.

There were also a half dozen men in the room, each looking at me with hatred and disdain. I quickly surmised my only hope of survival was to play dumb and not let these surly characters know what I knew about their operation. If they found out, I'd be shot without hesitation.

TWENTY

The gunman led me to a small back room. As my eyes adjusted to the dim setting, I saw a table strewn with paperwork; I also saw a few empty bottles; two chairs; some rubber hose; a single, low-wattage, incandescent bulb dangling from a wire; a locker; a few boxes; some baskets filled with rotting plant material; and an old man tied up in one corner.

He appeared to be asleep. Or dead.

As the gunman shoved me into the room, I tripped over a coil of hose and fell, hitting my head on one of the chairs. My eyes instantly watered and my ears began to ring. Two other drug men entered the room and went straight to the old man. One of them delivered a brutal kick to the old guy's ribs; the other crouched in front of him and, using a club, forced the old man's eyes to meet his. The second drug man began regaling the prisoner with questions. Because my head was swimming and my ears wouldn't stop ringing, I only caught a word or two.

"¿Dónde está el toro?" the drug man asked.

"Sabemos que sabes," the other one sneered.

"¡Dínos o morirás!"

The old man did not answer but simply returned the drug man's stare without blinking. The other man kicked him again. He didn't flinch.

Admittedly, I was confused at the few words I had understood. It seemed they were willing to brutalize and kill an old man over a bull, but why? After a few more acid-laced questions and a couple of hard slaps, the drug men decided to leave. I was grateful they didn't see fit to interrogate me, but I figured my turn would come soon enough.

As the light bulb clicked off and the door slammed shut, the room plunged into darkness. With the small window as the only source of light, I felt drawn to it in the same way the multitude of insects swarmed around the lamp at the front of the building. I staggered toward the muted light and stared up at it, gaping like a thirsty man in a desert gazes longingly at a mirage.

When my eyes grew more accustomed to the darkness, I glanced toward my cell mate. He was nothing more than a vague, shadowy form in the corner, but I could make out his shape: his bound feet drawn up in front of him, his bare arms pinned behind his back and secured to a timber, his glossy eyes staring at me intently.

I flinched. His stare startled me so much that I fell backward against the wall. My breath caught for a moment, and I began coughing violently. I could not tell whether the old man was smiling or frowning, but his eyes registered mistrust, a scrutiny of who I was and what I was doing there. When my coughing fit ended, I swallowed hard and tried to smile.

"Hola," I whispered. I wasn't sure if we should talk. After seeing the number of guns and churlish men in the adjoining room, I didn't want to draw attention to myself and, therefore, kept my voice low.

The old man didn't answer. He continued to stare at me from the darkened corner, his eyes unblinking, penetrating. I avoided his stare, unsure of what to do. Surely a man of his advanced years wouldn't present much of a physical threat to the men in the other room, but his stare conveyed a power that was intimidating to say the least. I eased from the wall and moved around, trying to appear confident.

A light breeze stirred outside the window, pressing against the foliage and whistling through the screen. Distant thunder rumbled over the treetops, followed by the angry cries of birds startled from their roosts. I glanced toward the window, waiting for more nocturnal sounds to paint a picture of the outside weather. When none followed, I climbed onto a crate. I was just tall enough to look outside, but I could see nothing in the darkness. I pushed against the screen. Being solidly grouted into the cinder block, it wouldn't budge. It didn't matter. The window looked too small for me to squeeze through anyway.

The old man continued to stare at me as if appraising my actions while passing silent judgment.

"Are you okay?" I whispered to my cell mate. He said nothing. Perhaps he didn't speak Spanish. "You all right, buddy?" I repeated in English.

Silence.

I hopped off the crate and eased through the darkness until I was at his side. I began tugging at the rope that bound his feet. It was tight and his feet had turned an ugly shade of gray. I could not loosen the knot. I squatted back and placed my hands on my thighs. It was then that I felt Melodee's Swiss Army knife. I had forgotten all about it. Why the drug men hadn't searched me before shutting me in I didn't know, but the advantage was temporarily mine, and I was going to use it to the fullest.

I pulled the knife from my pocket and sliced quickly through the rope. The old man breathed a soft gasp of relief. I massaged his ankles and feet, trying to encourage circulation. He grimaced but didn't cry out. I then went to work on the bands securing his hands to the timber in the wall. As soon as he was free, the old man rolled onto his knees and clasped his hands in an attitude of prayer. In the darkness, he looked somewhat like a North American Indian, not at all like the Amazonian Indian one would expect to find in this jungle. Rather, he had refined, dignified lines, a strong brow, deep-set eyes, a chiseled jawline, and a hard, lean frame that bespoke years of physical labor. His hair was silvery and thick, his clothing humble and modest.

The old man's prayer was brief. He was unsteady as he rose to his feet, but he quickly regained his balance. I guessed he had been bound for some time.

"Hola," I said again.

He put a finger to his lips—quieting me—pointed to the door, and shook his head. I figured he didn't want the men on the other side to know we were up to something.

The old man moved catlike to the table and began removing the items from it. He jerked his head, indicating he needed my help, and together we moved the table against the wall below the window. This seemed futile to me because the opening did not look large enough for a person to crawl through. But this was not his intent. Instead, he led me to a dark corner where a large, vented locker stood with its door slightly ajar. He motioned for me to enter. I hesitated, positive I would fit inside, but wanting to know first what he had in mind.

I opened my mouth to ask, but he silenced me again with a finger to his lips. He thumped his chest and mine and pointed to the window. He shook his head slowly, knowingly, and grinned. He then pointed inside the locker and nodded with the same grin. I instantly understood his plan. It seemed too simple to be effective, but I could not think of an alternative. I had resigned myself to simply lie down and get some much-needed rest for the remainder of the night—if I could sleep. My thoughts were still clouded with images of Melodee lying on her deathbed. Still, I was certain the drug men didn't have a cheerful wake-up call or continental breakfast planned for me in the morning; therefore, I decided to go along with the old guy's plan. He motioned for me to hand him my watch and the Swiss Army knife. I did.

I slid into the locker and watched as the old man climbed onto the table and pushed against the screen. It would not budge. He used the Swiss Army knife to cut around the edge of the screen. When he pushed again, it gave way with a fairly loud screech. He placed my watch on the sill then jumped from the table with the finesse of a gymnast. He put his ear to the door and held that position for a long time, then scowled and shook his head. He grabbed one of the empty bottles and hurled it against the cinder block wall. It exploded loudly.

Chairs skidded against the floor in the adjoining room, and angry voices erupted. The old man joined me in the locker just as the door to the room flew open. Through the locker door, we heard the men cursing and glimpsed snapshots of movement as they discovered my watch on the windowsill. Seeing the room now empty, they cursed again and ran out, assuming we had escaped through the window. I heard the entrance door groan open and their voices fade into the night.

We eased from the locker and peered cautiously into the large manufacturing lab. No drug men had remained behind, but I knew they'd be back soon. I followed the old man across the main chamber to a small door I assumed opened to the outside. I paused briefly, drawn by the need to do something before we escaped. I returned to the center of the room and looked around. I loved a well-organized laboratory: the mathematical perfection of chemical processes, the precise interactions between substrate and reagent, the thrill of successful experimentation. But the products manufactured in this lab were purposely insidious, intentionally addictive. And it was all for profit—it didn't matter how many countless lives would be ruined. I wondered how many innocents would fall to the entice-ments concocted in this very lab. This was only one lab, but that didn't matter. If any illicit drug left this room when I had had the chance to do something about it, I would never forgive myself. I was already angry. Now I was furious.

I went to a shelving unit lined with glass and plastic bottles. I could read a little Spanish, but soon found I didn't have to. Labeled according to chemical ingredients, the reagent liquids lined the shelves alphabetically. I found a number of large containers identi-fied as C_3H_8O (isopropyl alcohol) and a few others labeled C_3H_6O (acetone), both highly flammable solvents. Very dangerous but very useful.

Although encumbered by my splinted arm, I managed to open a large bottle and began to slosh it over everything in the room. The old man followed my example and emptied several bottles himself. I was surprised that he would so readily mimic my actions, but his demonstration of trust encouraged me.

Noxious vapors quickly saturated the room. The pungent fumes made my eyes water, and I suddenly felt woozy and somewhat disoriented. I pointed to the door at the far end of the room. The old man nodded and moved toward it as I picked up a butane lighter from a table strewn with playing cards and cigarette butts. I took a rag from a shelf and soaked it in alcohol, then rammed half

of it into a partially full kerosene bottle, creating a makeshift
Molotov cocktail. Looking up, I saw that the back door was open
and the old man was gone. I moved to the doorway but could see
little in the darkness outside. Thunder rumbled across the lowering
sky. I lit the rag and threw the bottle into the room. I turned to
run—but not fast enough. The place exploded with a horrific
whumph, knocking the wind from me and hurling me a dozen yards
into the dank rain forest.

For a moment, I could see nothing, hear nothing. The intensity
of the explosion had rendered me temporarily blind and deaf. I
rolled to my knees and tried to remain calm. A throb in my skull
pulsed so fiercely that I forgot about the pain in my arm. The faint
tinnitus in my ears quickly grew to a brassy din, and waves of nausea
began to rise from deep in my throat. I leaned forward and vomited
with such force that it felt as if I might literally turn inside out. I
gagged and drew shallow breaths, struggling to remain upright and
lucid. Then I felt a gentle hand massage the back of my neck and
shoulders, and another support my cramped abdominal muscles.
After a few minutes, I lifted my head and saw a fuzzy image. It was
the old man smiling at me. I tried to smile back, but it probably
looked more like a grimace.

Before long, I was able to stand. When I was sure of my balance,
the old man motioned for me to follow him into the darkness of the
jungle. I fought to keep up with him, but the earlier shock to my
muscles and the ringing in my skull made it difficult to match his
pace. He slowed down and allowed frequent but brief stops so I
could regain my equilibrium. Although I had no idea where we were
headed, I decided now was not the time to ask. We simply needed
to put distance between ourselves and the drug runners.

I was amazed at how easily my guide navigated through the
pitch-black underbrush. The old man moved as if he had night
vision equal to that of an owl.

We marched at a brisk pace for a long time before deciding to
stop for a longer respite. The sky was still very overcast, but rain had
yet to fall. The fire from the drug factory had long since disappeared
behind a thick curtain of rain forest. I was concerned the drug men

might follow our trail to seek revenge, but the old man didn't seem the least bit nervous as he sat on his haunches eating a plantain he'd grabbed along the way. I still felt too nauseous to eat, so I watched him and tried to figure out how he fit into the drug runners' scenario. I assumed they would have simply killed a native if he got in their way. They must have wanted something from him to have kept him alive and tied up. But what? Certainly not some old bull. I must have misunderstood their brief interrogation. And they couldn't have cared about him having knowledge of their drug operations; after all, he was just an old man.

"My name is David," I said slowly, pointing to my chest.

He patted his chest. "Helam."

I frowned. What kind of a name was that? "Your name is He-lam?" I enunciated.

I saw his head nod in the darkness. It dawned on me I was speaking in English, yet he seemed to comprehend everything I said. Encouraged I asked, "Do you speak English?"

"No."

"But . . . you understand what I am saying?"

The old man held out his hands in an *I don't know* gesture. It was still too dark to make out most of his facial features and body language, but I felt at ease in his presence. He pointed off in the distance and vocalized a string of words I did not recognize. They didn't sound Spanish or like any of the native Indian dialects I had heard before. His words had an almost Semitic timbre to them, like something from the Middle East—maybe Arabic or Egyptian.

I pointed to my ear and shook my head. "Sorry."

Helam shrugged, then stood and motioned for me to follow. I struggled to my feet and tagged along like a sick dog following his master. I tried to get a bearing on our direction of travel, but as there were no stars visible, I didn't have a clue. I hoped we were heading back to the village, but somehow felt we weren't. I wished I had grabbed Melodee's compass, but then realized I didn't know in which direction the village lay anyway.

It was a good three to four hours before we stopped again. I was exhausted.

"Where are we going?" I asked with a weak, scratchy voice.

Helam pointed in a direction that had absolutely no meaning to me. I rolled my eyes. "Sorry I asked."

He laughed and slapped me on the shoulder. I was baffled. *Does he understand my English?* Perhaps it was simply my tone. I felt a strong surge of frustration well within me, but choked it down. It didn't matter right then. I was simply too worn out to pursue that line of questioning. Instead, I leaned against a huge oleander and closed my eyes, just for a second.

* * *

I swear I hadn't rested for more than a minute or two, but when Helam shook my shoulder, I opened my eyes and found it was morning. The storm had passed, and the large patch of sky I could see was a soft, robin-egg blue—and amazingly cloudless.

I rolled to my knees and stretched before attempting to stand. Helam moved directly in front of me, probably to help me to my feet. The old man was wearing handmade leather sandals, and I was immediately impressed with the tool-worked patterns stamped into the sandals and the very fine stitching that held the upper portion to the sole.

I stood and appraised the rest of his attire. Helam's clothing reminded me of something out of *The Ten Commandments*, only much simpler. He wore a neat tunic and belt and an animal-skin vest laced together with strips of leather. His silver hair was resplendent and flowing, and his teeth were surprisingly white and straight. All he was missing was a Hebrew headdress and a jewel-encrusted sword. He certainly cut a noble figure, but what shocked me more than anything were his eyes. They were the same color as the morning sky: a pure, pale, robin-egg blue.

TWENTY-ONE

I followed Helam with blind faith, a term I had never before ascribed to myself. But I had no choice. The old man seemed to know exactly what he was about and glided along the jungle trails as smoothly as if he were wearing roller blades on a concrete sidewalk. As I struggled to keep pace, I tried to imagine the lineage that would create Helam's eclectic blend of characteristics. In better circumstances, I would have been happy to follow him home and delve into the mystery—if his home was indeed our destination. But I knew that my help was needed elsewhere, if it was not already too late. I curbed my curiosity and my physical and emotional miseries, all of which vied for my attention, and tried to figure a way to get back to Melodee.

A sharp sorrow pierced my heart as my thoughts focused on the little girl. Though a thousand questions ricocheted through my mind, no answers rang true. I ached inside knowing she was ill and I was not able to help. I again wondered what was making her so sick and what kind of medicine she needed to recover. Had she even made it through the night? I dreaded the possibility of the obese shaman returning, bringing with him a cornucopia of snake oils and witchcraft. Once again, I felt that I had failed her, that I had not done all I could to protect her and keep her well.

I silently begged God to show me how to help Melodee. My eyes began to burn from emotions I had never experienced— poignant, deep emotions. A welling of sadness blurred my vision and tightened my throat, making it hard to swallow. Feelings of ineptitude, hopelessness, guilt, and inability to resolve these bizarre circumstances amplified my woes, making each second pass by painfully slowly. I felt I wasn't actively doing something to help Melodee, and it was killing me.

"Excuse me, Helam?" I began as politely as possible.

The old man paused and favored me with a wearisome glance.

"I need to get back to the village."

He frowned.

"There's a little girl there, a friend of mine who is very sick."

He said nothing but continued to frown at me as if I had asked him to do something utterly repugnant to his moral character. I pressed on.

"She's American, like me. Can you help me?"

Helam didn't show the least inclination that he understood me, let alone that he wanted to assist me. It frustrated me but didn't diminish my determination to find Melodee. I repeated my plea in Spanish. It didn't help.

"Fine. If you can understand even a little of what I say, then listen closely. I am going back to find Melodee. She needs help. You can come if you like, but I'm leaving now."

A heavy sigh filled his chest as resignation softened the hard edges of his expression. A crinkle of weathered skin pulled at the corners of his mouth, and sadness filled his eyes. He looked to the sky and pointed at the sun, then traced its path east to west with a finger. He next pointed at a mountain peak some distance away, but I felt certain that was not the direction of the village. He pointed at his chest and then held up three fingers.

"Three days?" I huffed. "For what? Are you saying your home is three days away or it'll take three days to get to the village?"

He shrugged and held his palms up. Whatever that meant, I simply did not have time for these charades.

"You're no help at all, old man," I spat. "The little girl might die in three days!"

This was ridiculous. *Three days!* It had only taken one day to get from the village to the drug lab. Helam knew this jungle inside out, and I had no doubt he could take me straight to the village without missing a step. Did he plan to take the scenic route?

I decided that although this old man might be a unique individual with curiously intriguing characteristics, he was completely
useless. What looked like sadness filled Helam's blue eyes as he
picked up a small stick and began twiddling it aimlessly. It made me
angry. How could he deny me this single request? I felt he understood at least *some* of what I had said. What gave him the right to
decide Melodee's fate? Did some mystic clairvoyance give him all
power, all knowledge—or did he simply not care?

My blood was suddenly at full boil. I closed my eyes and gritted
my teeth. Melodee had looked like she was on her deathbed. The
gray pallor of her skin, the shallowness of her breathing, the spiked
fever and tremulous chills all added up to a malady beyond a simple
flu or temporary viral infection. It was deeper, more sinister.

Angered by the fact that I could not communicate the serious-
ness of the situation to the old man, I wanted to scream. Because he
seemed to understand some of what I said but would not acknowledge it, I wanted to hit something, someone. Overwhelmingly
embittered because I could do nothing when I knew I had the
ability to do *something*, I wanted to cry.

My hands clenched into white-knuckled fists of rage. My arms
twitched with emotions barely held in check. I opened my eyes and
found I was on my knees. How I had gotten there, I couldn't
remember. Helam was kneeling in front of me, his hand resting
gently on my shoulder, a placating smile on his face. I wanted to
smash that face with all my might.

I brushed his hand away, struggled to my feet, and stormed back in
the direction we had come from, not caring if he was accompanying
me or not. I had little idea where I was heading, but I was certain I
could find my way back in less than three days.

I paused at a crossroads on the trail. *Right or left?* I looked at the
sky. The sun was heading west, the direction of the path to the left.
Just as I took a step on that path, Helam's solid grip latched onto my
shoulder, startling me and halting my progress. I spun around, ready
for a fight. He smiled and pointed to the right fork, then said something in his cryptic language. Clearly, he wanted me to go down
that path.

"Why? What's down that way?" I snapped.

"Melodee," he said.

I gasped. "You know her name?"

Helam nodded, then turned down the trail.

I didn't move. "What's going on here?"

A look of complete innocence shone from his face as he cocked his head twice, indicating the direction we were to travel.

"No. I want to know how you know Melodee's name," I insisted, not remembering I had mentioned it once before.

He smiled softly and placed a hand over my heart, then moved it slowly to his head and nodded. *What is that supposed to mean?* Helam repeated this action a few times, concluding each performance with a questioning look on his face as if he were asking me if I understood. I didn't.

Frustrated, I snapped at him, "Just forget it, old man."

For a brief moment, a hurt expression darkened his face. I pushed by him and stormed down the trail he had indicated would lead to Melodee. I hoped there would be no other forks in our path, which would necessitate me asking directions.

We walked for some time before stopping at a fern-laden seep for a drink. My throat was parched. The cool of the hollow from which the seep trickled was so refreshing that I was tempted to stretch out and take a nap. But Helam seemed intent on continuing immediately, and, taking the lead, hiked at a much quicker pace than the one I had set.

It was late afternoon before we stopped again. Helam disappeared for a short time before returning with some papaya and mushrooms. I ate the fruit without question. It was the sweetest I had ever tried. But I was more leery of the fungus. Despite my extensive training in botanical sciences, fungi were always something I hesitated to eat straight from the field. While fairly easy to identify, fungi had so many varieties and subspecies that you could never be sure if the one on your plate would nourish you, give you incapacitating stomach cramps and diarrhea, or kill you with acute liver failure. The mushrooms Helam had found did not look like the classic death cap, *Amanita phalloides,* nor did they resemble any of

Amanita's equally toxic varieties, *A. virosa* or *A. muscaria*. These fungi were small buttons with a dull orange hue around the edge of the cap, a yellow crown and stem, and pale red gills under the cap. I scolded myself for not remembering their Latin name, yet I was pacified when it occurred to me that the old man probably didn't know either. In fact, I couldn't remember this particular species being catalogued yet. It looked like a cross between *Hygrophorus* and *Peziza,* but I couldn't be sure. Helam popped a few mushrooms in his mouth and chewed with obvious pleasure. I continued to scrutinize the half-dozen buttons in my hand but did not ingest them. Helam noticed my hesitation and encouraged me with hand gestures to try them. When I flashed him a weak smile, he reached over, nabbed one of my mushrooms, and tossed it in his mouth. He made an "mmm" sound and rubbed his belly joyfully. I had to chuckle at the universality of that sound, and concluded that if he could eat these mushrooms, so could I. As I bit one in half and chewed, an amazingly rich, woodsy flavor burst in my mouth. These small fungi—fresh from the field—tasted almost as if they had been sautéed in butter and lightly seasoned with basil and thyme. I chewed with pleasure, and tried again to place the family from which this species hailed. The market potential of these new mushrooms was astronomical. *If only I had my collection gear . . .*

Seeing my delight, Helam patted my shoulder and winked.

* * *

It was nearly evening when we reached the crest of a plateau that looked down onto the village. My heart leaped with joy as I watched the bustle and activity that had been so cathartic only a few days before. I was about to call out to the villagers I recognized when Helam stopped me with a finger to his lips, indicating the need for silence. He crouched down and tugged at my pant leg for me to do the same.

"What's wrong?" I whispered.

He pointed to the south of the village, but I couldn't see anything of significance. Helam moved about fifty yards farther along the path and pointed again. Through a break in the foliage, I saw a flicker of light from a small campfire about a half-mile from the village.

"Who is it?" I whispered.

The old man pantomimed sifting something in his open palm, then brought it to his nose and sniffed forcefully. I understood immediately—he was demonstrating the common way to inhale cocaine. Obviously, the drug runners were back—perhaps waiting for my return. My mind began to whirl as I thought of the implications of their presence. They figured I would come back to the village because of Melodee, and they were using her as bait to recapture me. But why? Of what significance was I to them? Did they intend to kill us or hold us for ransom? Was Melodee being held prisoner, or worse, subjected to something more insidious? Was she still sick or—heaven forbid—dead?

I began to head toward the village, but Helam stopped me. He pointed to the drug runners' camp and then to the village, then clasped his hands, indicating they were friends. I was appalled and confused. Did the villagers know all along that the drug men were looking for us? Most of the villagers seemed fairly accommodating and willing to help. Melodee had caused a stir among them, but I had assumed it was because of her guileless aura and innocent demeanor. There was the notion about her being a "chosen one," but who knew what that meant. A noxious lump of betrayal filled the base of my throat as I pondered the heartless deception of those seemingly humble villagers. Once again, I was at a loss as to what to do, feeling totally helpless.

Helam correctly discerned my angst as he smiled and crossed his hands over his chest. He nodded slowly, as if he were trying to tell me everything was going to be all right. Curiously, how and when my problems would be resolved didn't seem to matter right then. Somehow, I took comfort in the fact that he was sure of himself and the situation at hand. We sat there for almost an hour as the old man continued to evaluate the lay of the land, the location of the drug men, and whatever else caught his sharp eyes.

The sky was a deep purplish black when we finally wrested ourselves from our hiding place and descended into the valley. The stars twinkled brightly, but no moon shone yet.

We made our way as silently as possible. Helam went directly to the hut where I had last seen Melodee. For some reason, I felt I should trust his instincts more than my own, so I followed. We made our way to the back of the hut and eased around the side in deepest shadow. He motioned for me to stay there while he crept inside. I scanned the area for the village dogs and fortunately saw none. It seemed an eternity before Helam came back to me—alone. I held my hands out in a questioning manner and frowned. He shook his head and shrugged.

"Where's Melodee?" I whispered urgently.

Again he shrugged.

I cautiously moved to the front of the hut and stepped through the doorway. It was pitch black inside. I began feeling my way around, moving according to my memory of the interior's layout. Time seemed to drag, as if I were moving in slow motion, making my ability to search frustratingly sluggish. I could sense no movement anywhere, no sounds, no body odors. I moved to the center of the room and felt the thatch mats on which Melodee had lain. At length, I located a bundle with shoulder straps and zippers. It was Melodee's backpack.

It only took a few more minutes to search the entire hut. Melodee was no longer there.

TWENTY-TWO

The weight of Melodee's backpack convinced me that most of her belongings were missing, but it was too dark to check. I took the backpack anyway and left the hut.

Luckily, the village courtyard remained deserted as I skirted into the shadows. Helam was waiting for me behind the hut. I found him scratching the belly of one of the local dogs, as if he had no concerns or worries. We could be caught at any moment, and there he was playing with a smelly cur. The dog leaped up and snarled loudly at my appearance. Helam shushed the animal and it scampered away into the night. The old man signaled for me to follow him, and we entered the darkness of the rain forest.

The going was painfully slow but steady. Helam moved like a shadow, and I stumbled after him as silently as I could. Many times, I lost sight of him and simply stood motionless until I either heard him whisper or felt him tug at my clothing. I got the impression we were traveling in a wide circle around the village; our destination was anyone's guess. Occasionally, Helam would stop and listen, staring at the ground in front of him as if to focus his ability to detect signals, clues, and warnings in the darkness. Once, he dropped into a crouch, his legs cocked, quivering like tightly wound springs poised for release. I copied his every move—or at least tried to. After a moment we moved on.

At one point Helam paused, sat on his haunches, and looked at the sky. The stars were brilliantly clear, but there was still no moon. I sat next to the old man and watched the heavens. I didn't know what we were looking for, but I tried to concentrate with the same intensity my companion was showing. It was only a few minutes before a breeze began to stir the trees above us. The *tick-tapping* of leaves striking against each other and the soft groaning of branches bending to the will of the elements filled the moist air. Before long, the wind picked up and a perceptible heaviness thickened the atmosphere. Helam grunted softly and nodded. He rose to his feet and continued into the dense, dark underbrush. I followed at his heels.

It wasn't hard to figure out why Helam had waited for the wind to come up before moving on. The noise created by leaves fluttering and branches creaking masked our progress, and we were able to move more quickly and remain undetected. How he knew the wind would come up was another question on which I chose not to dwell.

At length, I began to hear voices: men and women speaking Spanish, not in causal conversation but in debate. Bitter arguments and curses. I could also smell smoke. I knew that we must be approaching the drug runners' campfire. We crept up on the perimeter of a clearing in which a small fire danced and whipped about with the rising wind. Two drug men sat on a log on one side of the fire. Both were holding rifles. The arrogant young man I had argued with in the village was also there, standing next to the drug men with his arms folded powerfully across his chest. In his hand rose a large, pointed machete. The campfire reflected from its sharply honed edge. Across the fire was Emalia, the helpful, kind woman from the village. She was also standing, her fists on her hips, as if challenging the young man across the flames. At her feet lay Melodee.

My heart skipped a beat—then stopped cold. Melodee didn't appear to be awake or breathing. She lay motionless next to the fire in a fetal position. The only movement I could see was the stroboscopic flicker and pulse of firelight and shadow across her static form.

Helam pointed to Melodee and raised his eyebrows, as if asking if she were the object of my concern. I nodded. He indicated I should stay there while he circled around. I didn't know his plan, but I was confident it was better than any I could have conjured up.

The agile old man silently disappeared into the darkness while I sat where he'd left me—feeling utterly useless.

Eventually, I crept a little closer to hear the argument more clearly, but Emalia and the young man spoke so quickly that it was difficult to interpret their Spanish. They continued to yell at each other, although they now had to raise their voices against the building wind. They repeatedly pointed at Melodee—Emalia using her finger, the young man, his machete. The gist of the altercation was clear, even without understanding more than a word or two of their Spanish. The drug men wanted to take Melodee for some reason, and Emalia was trying to prevent that from happening.

Without warning, a fist-sized rock was hurled from nowhere and landed in the fire. Shards of flaming wood bounced into the air. Fireflylike embers whirled around the young man and Emalia. Nearly extinguished, the campfire fluttered low.

The drug men jumped to their feet, their guns at the ready. They looked beyond the clearing, obviously searching for the intruder. However, I doubted they could see anything; it was much too dark. One man told the other to go look around, and he disappeared into the underbrush. The remaining drug man and the younger man began circling the perimeter of the camp. The drug man passed within a few feet of my position but didn't see me. An angry grumble of thunder sounded in the distance. A storm was coming. A big one.

When he was a few yards away from me, the drug man called out in Spanish: "Jorge. ¿Dónde estás?"

The only answer was the keening of the wind and the rustle of vegetation.

"Jorge!" the young man hollered.

Again no answer.

Way to go, Helam, I thought.

The young man quickly surmised what had happened and stormed over to Emalia and Melodee. He shoved the young woman aside and knelt next to Melodee. He yanked her head back by her short hair and held his machete to her throat. Luckily, she was still unconscious. Emalia screamed.

"Come out or I kill her," the young man yelled into the darkness. He knew I was there.

"No!" Emalia cried as she clambered to her feet and rushed at the young man.

A brief struggle ensued as Emalia leapt onto the young man's back and tried to wrest the machete from his hand. He twisted and threw her to the ground. Even from where I sat, I could hear the air burst from her lungs. Lightning flashed overhead, followed by a bone-jarring clap of thunder. The young man knelt next to Melodee again and poised his machete point over her back, ready for a quick plunge into her vital organs.

"Show yourself now, gringo!"

Emalia struggled to her feet and approached the young man, her hands clasped in a beseeching manner. "Gilberto, no."

Another burst of lightning showed the remaining drug man standing directly in front of me, watching the confrontation by the low fire.

"I count to three, Norteamericano," Gilberto announced.

I tried to calculate the odds of my overwhelming the drug man, securing his rifle, and shooting the young man named Gilberto before he could thrust his machete into my helpless little friend. They were not good odds.

"One!"

A wave of thunder hit the clearing like a tsunami. Everything trembled from the deep, reverberating noise. It sounded much like an earthquake, and the way the ground shook, I wasn't certain there hadn't been one.

"Two!"

Another flash of lightning revealed Emalia creeping up behind Gilberto, a large club of wood gripped in her hands.

"I am not joking you, gringo," the young man warned.

The drug man raised his rifle and took aim. I was frozen, unable to move, unable to do anything. Emalia lifted the club over her head.

"Look out, Gilberto!" the drug man called out.

Finally forcing myself into action, I grabbed a stick, stood, and cocked my arms back.

"Three!"

Emalia wound up and swung.

A rifle shot rang out. Thunder boomed from the angry sky.

The woman faltered, never finishing her swing. Gilberto stood as Emalia collapsed. I took a step forward—and tripped over an unseen root. I let out a grunt of pain as I landed directly on my splinted arm. The drug man whipped around and pointed his rifle at my head.

"Wait. Don't shoot," I called out from the muddy ground.

Gilberto ran up and knelt on one knee in front of me. His smile was condescending, filled with malice. "Buenas noches, amigo."

I said nothing. I was as infuriated at myself as I was at them. These men were cold-blooded murderers. I knew for certain that Gilberto would have cut Melodee severely, perhaps even killed her. Emalia was probably dead. I could have saved that brave young woman if I had acted quicker. I was seething at my delay in action— and at my cowardice. A fiery rage unlike any I had ever felt before welled inside me.

The young man sensed my anger. He held his machete to my throat. "Do not be foolish, gringo. Relax, or something bad happens."

The drug man kept his rifle pointed at me. Shaking with anger, I knew there was nothing I could do. I stood slowly and held my hands up, signaling my surrender.

"Bueno," Gilberto said. "Come."

I entered the clearing and stopped short after two steps. Behind me, Gilberto and the drug man also halted, but I knew they weren't looking at my back. Like me, they were staring into the clearing.

Emalia was lying next to the fading fire—motionless and, sadly, very much dead. Melodee was gone.

I started snickering.

"Why you smiling, gringo? You think this funny?"

With my hands still held in surrender, I said, "Immensely."

"You won't be laughing when I am through with you, I promise," Gilberto said with convincing intensity.

"Look, I don't know what it is you want with us. We have no money. We barely survived a plane crash. Can't you just let us leave?"

Gilberto grinned. "The girl, she may be of use to us. And you. The States often pay good to have their citizens returned."

Gilberto and I stood by the fluttering campfire awaiting the return of the other drug man. He had gone in search of Melodee. I'm sure they figured she had crawled off into the jungle to hide, since they apparently had no idea Helam was with me. Even if the old man had to carry her—which was probably the case—I knew his nocturnal familiarity with the rain forest would have them both hundreds of yards away by now. My respect for the old guy grew by the second.

A light rain began to pelt Gilberto and me as we stared into the dark foliage surrounding us. The wind was still keening, and periodic flashes of lightning continued to illuminate the clearing. I was no expert, but already I could discern the various weather signals in this region. I knew the light sprinkles would soon be a torrential soak-fest.

"Miguel. ¡Más rápido!" Gilberto shouted.

Miguel did not answer.

"We'd better find shelter," I suggested.

"Miguel!"

"I think he's lost."

Gilberto whirled on me and hit me hard in the gut with the butt of his rifle. "I do not care what you think. Do not speak again unless I tell you."

With the wind knocked out of me, I had no choice but to obey. Inwardly, I wanted to excoriate him with curses and vulgarities, but I held my tongue. Gilberto grew increasingly agitated the longer we waited. My stomach pains passed, but I still held my gut tightly so I would not have to raise my hands over my head again.

Suddenly the clouds opened up with a sheet of water. Huge drops of precipitation slapped against the tropical broadleaves that encircled the clearing and instantly doused the campfire. Gilberto jerked his head and said something to me, but I couldn't hear him over the downpour. He cupped his hand to his mouth and shouted into my ear. "Follow me. If you try anything, I will kill you. ¿Comprendes?"

I nodded.

Our progress through the rain forest was dismally slow. I was soaked to the bone, and my clothes chaffed against my skin like sandpaper. Many times, I lost sight of my captor and was tempted to simply step off the trail into the blackness of the night. But I knew the young man was at a flash point, and if he found my hiding place, I would be a dead man—ransom or not.

As the night wore thin, so did my stamina. I wasn't even watching the back of Gilberto anymore; I simply put one foot in front of the other and tried not to stumble over any roots or vines. I coughed and choked on the intense deluge that seemed to thicken with each step. If I were a fish, I couldn't have been happier.

The rain finally softened as we made our way under a dense copse of enormous ficus trees. In the center of the copse, a limestone abutment formed a snug, semi-dry grotto. Gilberto hunched into the grotto and leaned heavily against the back wall, visibly exhausted. I crouched to enter but stopped short as the muzzle of his rifle appeared before my face.

"You stay out there," he called over the noise of the rain snapping against the vegetation.

"What? You're kidding, right?" I exclaimed.

"Sit in the mud where you belong."

"Come on, Gilberto. I won't try anything, I swear."

"No."

"Look, I don't know what you think I did, but I just want to get home. I mean you no harm."

"You and the little girl are all trouble. My people think she is a 'chosen one,' but I say she is not."

"I know that."

"The chosen ones do not get sick. They have strange medicines, strange ways. They disappear in the forest, and no one knows where to find them. Some go looking and never return."

A clap of thunder accentuated his cryptic tale-telling with an eerie overtone. I had no idea what he was babbling about but was intrigued by the fervency in his speech.

"If you know we're not chosen ones, why are you holding us captive?"

"My friends in the city have an interest in the little girl."

What interest? What city? I didn't want to entertain the first question. The second gave me some hope. "What city are you talking about?"

"That is not your concern."

"Have you told your friends she's not a chosen one?" I asked urgently.

"Sí. But they have other plans," he said, looking out into the soggy night with no interest.

"So what do you want with me?" I hesitated to ask.

"The little one, she said she is your . . . *enfermera,* your nurse?" he struggled with the word. "She is helping you because you are sick. She says she will do nothing—say nothing—if anything happens to you."

I'm the one who's sick? Melodee was near death when I last saw her in the village, and I wasn't so certain she hadn't been dead in the clearing a few hours ago.

"She said if we help you then she will do what we ask."

No! My legs instantly lost their strength, and I fell to my knees. A profound sorrow pressed on my shoulders and wrenched my heart. Bitter tears burned my eyes, and mixed with the rain on my face. The little girl barely knew me, barely knew anything about my past, and knew nothing of the kind of man I was. Yet she was willing to sacrifice her life for mine. What manner of child was this?

Tears fell from my eyes as I thought of how selfish I had been. Sure, I had told myself many times that I should be caring for her, that I should be her protector. But what had I done for her up until that moment? Nothing.

"Amigo," Gilberto said over the droning rain. "Perhaps the little one is worth more than you say. No?"

I looked into his smirking face. He was laughing, totally pleased with himself and the situation. Melodee, the most innocent, caring person I had ever met, was the crux of his desire for money. He could care less about her health and safety, or her innocence. My anger peaked, and suddenly I went mad with rage.

Before I could think, I was on my feet, lunging toward him. He whipped his rifle around and fired. The blast ruptured my eardrum, sending a white-hot spike of pain through my skull. My vision went totally out of focus as I grabbed the rifle and hurled it out of reach. I clenched his throat, squeezing hard. Choking with all my might, my fingers gouged deep into his flesh. Then his knee found my ribs and knocked me to one side. I rolled into the rain and staggered to my feet. Gilberto was standing with his machete drawn, glaring at me like a rabid, half-crazed animal, drawing raspy breaths through his bruised throat. As I took a step back, my foot landed on the rifle. I dropped to grab it. The angry young man lunged at me, his machete poised for a kill. I twisted the rifle up in time to deflect the point of his blade but could not stop the force of his thrust. I landed heavily on my backside with the rifle pinned behind me. Gilberto lay beside me, having fallen in the mud from the energy of his attack. I slid the rifle around and tried to find the trigger. Caked with muck, it was temporarily inoperable. Gilberto twisted, flailed, and managed to thrust the point of his machete deep into my left thigh. The jolt of pain stung like an electric shock, and my leg twitched uncontrollably. I rolled away and tried to stand, but my left leg would not respond to my brain's command. I flopped around like a freshly landed salmon.

Gilberto stood slowly and glowered at me. I felt a warmth coat my leg around the wound. Using a tree root, I pulled myself upright. Standing on one leg, I wielded the rifle like a club. Hot blood poured down my thigh, washing away the coolness of the heavy rain. I knew it was not a simple flesh wound. The machete had bit clean through to the other side. I could see a throbbing press from inside my pant leg as blood pulsed from the laceration. My head grew light as the young man walked toward me. My vision began to darken around the edges in a glaucoma-like fog. I was losing blood—and consciousness— quickly. A fierce bark of thunder rumbled over the canopy and echoed down among the branches. It sounded a million miles away.

"Now I kill you," Gilberto croaked, an ugly, red bruise already forming on his neck.

I was still livid, angrier than I had ever been in my life. I was also helpless, but I didn't care. "Bring it on, Tarzan."

Without warning, my vision blackened. I staggered and blindly swung the rifle in front of me. Not connecting with anything, I stumbled forward. I shook my head, and my vision cleared for a brief moment. I saw an object sail out of the shadows—a rock. It hit Gilberto squarely in the head.

Again, my vision narrowed to a pinpoint of gray, then blackness. I felt myself falling, but I don't remember hitting the ground.

TWENTY-THREE

Fog. Inside my head as well as out. Thick, pasty fog.

All around me was dull and white. Moisture stuck to my face and matted my hair. I felt myself carried as if on a litter. The sky above was only slightly brighter than the misty nothingness on either side of me. I did not recognize the man at my head or the one at my feet. Both were middle-aged, and both wore simple clothing.

I could smell the dank odor of wet vegetation and sodden earth. I could hear the faint, laboring puffs of my escorts. I felt a hot burning in my thigh and a sharp throbbing behind my temples.

I could not see Melodee or anyone else. I lifted my head with the intent to look around. The world spun. Then blackness.

* * *

A white flash of pain seared up my leg and settled in my gut. I sat up and heard myself yell some obscenity. I was indoors, lying on a bed of sorts. The small room was semidark but not gloomy. The walls were masonry—hand-cut stone fitted together with amazing precision, seemingly without mortar. A cheerful oil lamp dangled from a timber-and-plaster ceiling. Woven tapestries hung from the walls, and gentle sunlight filtered in through a bamboo latticework that filled a large window. To my right, a curtain of woven material hung from the ceiling, dividing the room in two. I couldn't tell what was on the other side. More importantly, I had no idea where Melodee was.

A young woman, probably in her midtwenties, was changing the dressing on my injured thigh. She regarded me with a furrowed brow, probably offended at my foul outburst. I found myself shirtless and in my boxers. My legs were embarrassingly white—especially the wounded one—either from a loss of blood or from the fact that they had not seen direct sunlight for many years. The woman said something in a language I did not recognize, but the look on her face told me she was offering an apology for hurting me. I gave a halfhearted smile and nodded an acceptance. To reciprocate, I apologized for cursing so crudely in front of her. She smiled and nodded.

I watched the young woman gingerly poke about the laceration in my thigh. It was deep, swollen, and hot. The tissue adjacent to the cut protruded painfully, apparently due to extreme internal pressure. All signs indicated a severe infection. *Great! And I'm in the middle of who knows where without antibiotics! Hello, sepsis.*

The young woman moved to a table on which lay an assortment of plant leaves, roots, rhizomes, powders, crystals, liquids, and other paraphernalia. She selected a few materials and ground them in a stone mortar and pestle, which looked as if carved from pure jade. I did not recognize the ingredients the young woman used, but promised myself a close inspection of everything on the table before the day was through. She added a yellowish powder and a few milliliters of clear oil, and mixed everything together. She poured the mixture into my wound and covered it with a very fine moss—probably a *Sphagnum* or some other bryophyte. She wrapped the wound with a meshlike cloth and tucked the end under the top layer. Overall, a very neat dressing.

I assumed the oil-herb mix had some antiseptic properties, but I doubted it would stop infection. I was correct earlier when I thought things had gone from bad to worse to hopeless, but now they were life threatening. Imminent foreboding settled over me with such vivid assuredness that I felt like simply giving up and resigning myself to complete doom.

The young woman indicated that I should lie back down, which I did. Her bedside manner was so calming and assuring that I didn't need to see a framed diploma on the wall or a starched white coat and stethoscope to know I was in the hands of a skilled healer. I was intrigued not only with her manner, but also with her age and gender. A tribal healer or shaman was typically male, and usually quite old. This young woman was quite the opposite and quite beautiful. She had waist-long strawberry blond hair pulled back in a ponytail, a delicate nose, and a wide, full mouth. But her most striking feature was her eyes: they were large and round, a vibrant green color that hinted of an Irish-Celtic heritage rather than Hispanic. Conversely, her olive skin and high cheekbones hinted that her ancestry included Native American blood. It was an intriguing combination.

Her tactile fingers felt around my jaw and throat, neck and collarbone. She placed a hand over my heart and felt the regularity of its beat. Her fingers probed my armpits, probably searching for swollen lymph glands. The healer tapped my sternum a few times and gingerly examined my ribs. She leaned close and squinted inside my mouth. She next held open each of my eyes, gazed intently into them, and grunted knowingly, as if she could see into my brain and read my thoughts. Having removed my splint, she probed my arm and sniffed the flesh surrounding my broken bones. She wrapped the area with mesh soaked in a sweet-smelling substance, but didn't replace the splint. To my surprise, the break was not as sore as it had been earlier. I knew the knitted bone was still fragile, but felt confident I could use my arm in any non-weight-bearing task. She finished her examination by placing her ear to my abdomen, listening to various sections as if she could hear how well each organ functioned.

With the exam concluded, she covered me with a blanket that was surprisingly cool and soft. She gave me a small, shallow dish, filled with about ten milliliters of opaque liquid and indicated I should swallow the stuff. I bravely gulped it down as if it were a shot of whisky. It was horrible. I gagged and coughed. My eyes watered as if blasted with pepper spray. I felt my face flush and perspiration bead on my forehead.

"Thanks," I said in a voice rasping with hoarseness.

The young woman nodded and tried unsuccessfully to hide a smile. She put her palms together, raised them to her cheek, tilted her

head, and closed her eyes, indicating that I should get some sleep. I
didn't feel like sleeping but didn't know how to convey that. So I drew
a deep breath and closed my eyes to show I was a good, obedient
patient, eager to comply with my doctor's every instruction.

I wanted to ask a million questions: Where in the world was I?
Where was Melodee? And was she all right? But a calming sensation
immediately began seeping through me, washing away any anxiety,
apprehension, and immediacy of action. I felt myself drift off as a
weightless cloak of warmth oozed into every muscle and relaxed me
to the point of transcendental oblivion. That was the last thing I
remembered.

* * *

A monotonous drone pierced a painful haze. I was suffering from
severe muscle spasms. My leg twitched violently, uncontrollably. The
muscles in my lower torso contracted to the point that my body
arched backwards in a continual spasm. My neck was rigid and my
jaw clenched so fiercely that my teeth hurt. My mouth pulled back
in a tight grimace, and I found it increasingly difficult to breathe.
Drenched in sweat and panting, I felt my heart race as if injected
with pure adrenalin.

My mind searched for the cause of this affliction and pinpointed
an immediate answer: Gilberto's machete. While the point and edge
were honed to surgical sharpness, the rest of the blade was cankered
with rust. Horrified, I concluded that I had contracted acute blood
poisoning brought on by the *Clostridium tetani* bacterium.

But that can't be, my mind argued.

I had received my first tetanus inoculation as a child—along
with diphtheria and pertussis vaccines—and continued the regimen
to adulthood. Then, as a field analyst for BioCraft, I routinely had
tetanus boosters for protection. I shouldn't be suffering from
lockjaw or any other symptom of neurotoxin poisoning.

The pain in my leg shot up my back and landed brutally inside
my abdomen, causing me to double up and tremble. I knew this was
the end. If I had contracted tetanus in the middle of a Mexican rain

forest, with no antitoxin, antibiotics, or muscle relaxants to combat the symptoms, I was a dead man.

The haze in my head thinned a bit as I continued to argue with myself. *But the effects of tetanus poisoning usually don't exhibit for two to three days. Why am I going through this so suddenly? Could it be something other than tetanus?*

A cool cloth daubed my forehead, and a delicate hand tenderly rubbed my shoulders, as if to assure me I was not alone. Someone was humming a soft tune, an ethereal melody that was both haunting and heavenly. My body alternated between chills and fever, but each time I was given relief in the form of a blanket or a gentle swabbing from a moistened cloth.

The haze continued to clear. I could hear rain now—a heavy, steady downpour. I couldn't recall where I was or how I got there. I remembered fighting with Gilberto and falling to his machete blade. A flying rock. Then oblivion. There was a dream about a young woman who was tending to my wounds. A sip of some drink that knocked me out cold. My body was wracked with tetanus poisoning. *Was it all a dream?*

A low peal of thunder rumbled its way into the room. I opened my eyes and recognized the place from the dream yesterday. Only it was not a dream.

The room was dark. Sunlight no longer filtered through the latticed window. It was late at night. A single oil lamp bathed the room with warm, amber hues. The stone walls and ornate tapestries were still there. The table littered with herbs and medicines stood off to one side. The curtain partition to my right stirred almost imperceptibly. My beautiful physician was swabbing my neck, chest, and belly with a cool cloth that smelled lightly of alcohol. She was the one humming the bittersweet melody.

I sat up quickly and stayed her hand as my head swam from the sudden change in cranial blood pressure. I forced my mind to focus enough to speak.

"Where . . . ?" was all that croaked out.

The young healer smiled softly and put a finger to my lips to shush me. She propped a few pillows behind me and gently settled me back into a reclining position, then pulled a blanket up to my chest. She went to her table and returned with an animal-skin flask. She held it to my lips, and I found it contained a juice that tasted a lot like mango. I wanted to drink deeply, but she allowed me only a sip. It seared down my throat as if I had not had anything to drink in days.

"Where am I?" I asked with a small, raspy voice.

The healer pointed to her ear and shook her head. With a wave of my hand, I indicated the room and window. "Where is here?"

"Cumorah," the young woman answered.

And where exactly is Cumorah? I wondered. Was that the name of the drug men's village? Or was this a bigger city in which their cartel was the governing power? The room was definitely not of primitive construct, like the village we were in a few days ago. Skilled engineers had built this room. It was modern yet archaic. I concluded it had to be some pseudo-Aztec architecture commissioned by a wealthy drug czar.

I was apprehensive, and the questions still plagued me: Why did they bring me here? What had they done with Melodee? Gilberto had mentioned something about using me to coerce Melodee . . . Was that why I was being nursed back to health?

"How did I get here?" I asked tentatively, pointing to my chest then indicating the room again.

"Helam."

Ah! So I wasn't in the lair of drug lords. *Good.*

"Where is Melodee?"

The young physician moved to the curtain partition and drew it back. The other side of the room was even darker. Melodee lay in a second bed—more like an elevated cot, actually, similar to mine—and was fast asleep.

She did not look well. But at least she was alive.

I tried to swing my legs from my cot, but they would not respond. The young physician shook her head slowly and eased me back onto the pillows. The concern on my face must have shown plainly.

The doctor quietly whispered something, but of course I didn't understand a word of it. She drew the curtain so I could no longer see Melodee, yet continued to smile as if to say everything was all right. But it wasn't. Not until I knew exactly what was going on.

"How is she doing?"

The young woman nodded. She whispered another string of verbiage that sounded almost like Farsi, much like the syntax Helam had used. I still got nothing from it. As she spoke, she pointed to her torso and pinpointed various organ systems. I guessed she was explaining what was wrong with Melodee.

A serious expression painted her face as she moved to the table and returned with a metal goblet filled with a black, viscous liquid. It looked like coal tar, a substance sometimes used to treat severe eczema and psoriasis, yet it didn't exude the sharp, pungent odor characteristic of that medicine. Instead, I detected an acrid, sulfurous tang that burned my sinuses and made my eyes water. I hoped she didn't expect me to drink the stuff. I wanted to get a better look at the mysterious liquid, but it was still night, and the sparse light from the oil lamp didn't afford much illumination. The healer returned the medicine (I assumed that's what it was) to the table and brought back the shallow cup I had drunk from the night before. She motioned for me to drink again.

"No way. That stuff knocked me out last time. I don't want to sleep until I get some answers. Where's Helam?"

I guess my voice had risen to a level higher than she approved of because she quickly brought a finger to her lips and flashed an angry frown. But I was getting upset again. All this Alice-in-Wonderland stuff was honing my temper, giving it an edge with which I was too eager to slice. She put her hands to her tilted head and closed her eyes.

Asleep? Who, Helam or Melodee? She pointed out the window at the nocturnal sky. *Of course they'd be asleep,* I chided myself. It felt like the middle of the night.

I took a few deep breaths and tried to calm my nerves. I smiled inanely and said, "Sorry. My name is David, by the way."

She smiled back and resumed daubing my forehead with her cloth. I persisted, poking my chest with my index finger. "I am David."

"David," she echoed.

"That's right. My name—David." I pointed to her. "You?"

Even in the dim light of the room, I detected a slight blush color her cheeks. "Ester," she answered.

"Are you the only doctor here?"

She smiled and shrugged. It was stupid of me to ask, knowing she didn't understand a word I spoke. Neither Helam nor this physician seemed able to grasp much of what I said. I fought down my frustration and asked, "¿Hable español?"

Ester pointed to her ear and shook her head.

I pointed at Melodee's side of the room. "Is she okay?"

Another shrug.

I pointed my thumb toward the ceiling and smiled broadly. "Good." Then I pointed it to the floor and gave an exaggerated frown. "Bad."

A burst of laughter escaped the physician's lips. She quickly covered her mouth to quell the volume of her mirth, but she had difficulty restraining the light that shined from her amused eyes. She mimicked my actions and words. Thumb up: "Good." Thumb down: "Bad."

I smiled and nodded encouragingly. "Yes, that's it. Good. Bad. You understand these signs, right?"

She responded by pointing her thumb up. "Good."

Great! Again, I pointed at Melodee. Thumb up: "Good?"

The laughter immediately left the young woman's eyes. Slowly she raised her hand and pointed her thumb toward the floor.

TWENTY-FOUR

I was frustrated—and angry. The number of whys that filled my head were daunting. Scientific reason and deduction did little to help answer any of them.

My eyes searched the dark room without purpose. The young healer sat next to my bed under a candle sconce, reading from a leather-bound booklet. The pages looked to be made of parchment or foolscap and were hand-lettered in sepia tone ink. The written font was one I had not seen before but appeared to be block characters, as in Chinese calligraphy or Egyptian cuneiform text. Or perhaps it was simply the darkness playing tricks on my weary eyesight.

My gaze continued to wander. A shadow here, a vague shape there meant nothing to me. I was as lost as ever and didn't have much hope of clarifying my situation. At least I was being cared for. But to what end? My eyes rested on a bundle nestled in shadow under the medicine table. I hadn't noticed it before, but as I stared at it with forced concentration, the thing took shape as if by magic. I sat up straight.

It couldn't be . . .

"Excuse me, miss," I whispered urgently.

The young doctor's head snapped up. Her eyes swam with disorientation. She had fallen asleep while reading.

"Could you bring me that?" I asked, pointing to the bundle.

She rubbed her eyes and yawned, then favored me with a questioning glare.

"Please. Por favor. I need that backpack—under the table there."

The healer got to her feet and retrieved the backpack. Melodee's backpack. How she had come to acquire it, I had no idea. I examined it greedily. It seemed in perfect order. I opened it. While I had never dissected its contents, the backpack was now mostly empty. I rifled through Melodee's remaining things, itemizing each in my head as I did: the compass, a torn copy of Laura Ingalls Wilder's *The Long Winter,* some tissues, my mini-bottle of vodka (hidden in a side pouch), a pencil tin, the hardcover Book of Mormon, an empty coin purse, and an amber prescription vial—pills rattling within.

I removed the prescription bottle and examined the label. What I expected to find was a prescription for an allergy medicine, a fluoride supplement, or something else rather benign. What I found almost stopped my heart.

Instant comprehension flashed in my mind, a disturbing perception that was both enlightening and devastating. I am not a medical doctor, but owing to my ties with pharmaceutical research and development, I am familiar with numerous drugs. At that moment, I almost wished I wasn't.

The label on the vial read:

Rx # 7100342 Melodee Braithwaite
Gleevex 400mg tablet
Take one tablet by mouth twice daily as directed

I closed my eyes and shook my head, hoping the label would somehow read differently when I opened my eyes. Of course, it didn't.

All the clues I had missed previously suddenly fell into place with shocking clarity. On our flight from Phoenix to Corpus Christi, when Melodee told me she had been visiting her grandfather because an imminent sickness would make it the last time she would see him, I had assumed that the old man was terminally ill—not the sweet little girl sitting next to me. Melodee's short, ragged haircut was not a fashion statement—it was a side effect. Her sunken eyes and hollow cheeks were not simply from malnutrition or dehydration. Her nausea and stomach cramping were not solely the consequences of days of starvation. Her occasional "sore legs and back" and lack of endurance were not the stress-induced results of surviving a terrifying plane crash. These were all classic symptoms of her condition and the side effects of modern medicinal treatment.

A tight burning welled in my throat as hot tears brimmed in my eyes. *Why hadn't I seen it?* I felt like an idiot. *Why did she not tell me?*

Gleevex, the medication in Melodee's prescription vial, was the latest in antineoplastic chemotherapy. It was used to treat cancer.

TWENTY-FIVE

Ester read the forlorn, helpless look on my face perfectly. Her eyes softened as she sat on the edge of my cot and put a consoling arm around my shoulders. I was not sobbing, but tears flowed freely from my vacant eyes. I was completely numb. I felt empty, vacuous, as if the substantive something that had once occupied my body had suddenly vanished, leaving a hollowed-out exterior. Nothing inside me seemed of value, at least not compared to Melodee. I was in a state of total humility.

"Is she alive?" I heard myself ask in a voice barely more than a whisper.

Ester nodded.

That was good news, but my thoughts were preoccupied with why Melodee hadn't said something—anything. And why was a young girl like her, who had such indomitable faith in her God, burdened with such a grievous malady? Why would an all-loving God allow such an innocent child to contract cancer? Suddenly my tenuous faith in a compassionate Father above took a precipitous dive. Melodee's condition didn't make sense; it wasn't fair.

I heard my voice again. "How long does she have?"

The healer said nothing, but showed me a thumbs-up.

I blinked hard as it registered she was answering my questions . . . sort of. "You understand what I'm saying?"

Ester held her thumb and forefinger close together, but left a small gap in between. *A little bit.*

"Why didn't you say so earlier?"

She shrugged.

If this was some kind of sick game, I wasn't in the mood. "Look, Ester, it would be nice to get some straight answers here."

Ester faced me and placed her hand over my heart. She then moved her hand to her ear and smiled.

"I'm sorry, but you've already lost me," I sighed.

She patted my shoulder and returned to her reading.

I tried to work through her signs and body language, but didn't get very far. Rather than try to figure out that mystery, I decided to absorb as much information as I could in other ways, beginning with what I already knew.

"So this is Cumorah?"

She wearily marked her place in her book and favored me with a half smile.

I raised my knees, forming a peak with my kneecaps. Pointing, I said, "Mountain."

Ester cocked her head but did not look like she fully understood.

I indicated the area by my ankle and moved my hand in an undulating motion. "River. There is a river at the base of this mountain?"

No response.

Using my fingers, I mimicked a person walking up my leg—up the mountain. Her eyes brightened. She gave me a thumbs-up. Pointing to my knee, shin, and ankle respectively, I said, "Cumorah? Cumorah? Cumorah?" asking where on the mountain her village was located.

She understood. Setting her book aside, the physician used her fingers to walk up the "mountain" from my ankle, over my knee, and halfway down my thigh. "Cumorah."

"Okay, great. So we are here?" I asked, pointing to the same spot.

A nod.

"And the village? The place where Helam found us?" I said, gesturing to Melodee and myself.

She looked at my bent leg as if trying to determine its topography. Then she turned up her palms and shrugged.

"Come on, you've got to know. It can't be that far away," I said, trying to keep my voice at an even tone, trying harder to contain my rising temper.

She gave me an apologetic smile, then moved to the window to stare out at the soft rain.

I bit my tongue and willed my frustrations to subside. It didn't work. Try as I might, a bitter acid roiled inside me, turning my remorse and humility of a moment ago to anger.

"Listen, Ester—doctor—healer—whatever you are, I want some answers and I want them right now!"

Her demeanor wilted as she favored me with a sorrowful glance. She shook her head and sat in the chair beside my bed where she began to read her book again.

I was relentless. "Don't ignore me like some smug physician tired of answering banal questions. I'm not some ignorant hick, you know."

She nodded and said something in her native dialect. I didn't understand a word of it. It made me furious. These charades were getting us nowhere.

Melodee was in serious need of medical attention—*modern* medical attention—and I wasn't getting that across to this woman. Did she simply not care? No, that couldn't be it. As her patient, I had seen and felt her altruistic concern. And she seemed to know what she was doing. My arm no longer ached, and my leg felt weak but not as if infected by a life-threatening bacteria. My muscles were sore, like I had just finished a good workout at the gym, but they didn't feel knotted with lactic acid buildup, or paralyzed as they would be had I actually contracted tetanus poisoning. The symptoms I had felt earlier were gone. This young physician obviously had skills beyond any Third World healer I had ever heard of.

Was Ester working her medical wonders on Melodee too? I couldn't tell until I got a closer look at my little friend. But doubts flooded my mind, inundating my optimism about Melodee's chances with a tide of pessimism. If she was on chemotherapy, then her cancer was very advanced. She needed her prescription.

I shook the amber vial, rattling the pills within, and said, "Ester, we need to give this to Melodee. It's her medicine. She's very sick."

Ester looked up from her reading and gave the vial a curious appraisal. She stood and took the bottle from my hand. She rattled the vial and tried to get the childproof lid off, but couldn't. I opened the safety cap for her. She dumped a few of the off-white tablets into her hand and held them to the candlelight. Her brow furrowed. She sniffed them, and her brow creased even deeper. She touched one of the tablets to her tongue and her whole face wrinkled into a grimace of pure disdain. She spat into a wastebasket and rinsed her mouth from the flask. She then dumped the pills into the wastebasket.

I jumped from the bed. My feet landed solidly but my legs, having no strength, failed me, and I crumpled to the stone floor. Lying prostrate I cried, "She needs those pills!"

Ester knelt in front of me and offered a hand to aid me to my feet. I brushed it away. Even though the blanket had stayed on the bed and I was splayed helpless on the cold floor, I was too angry to care.

"Melodee needs those, you imbecile! It's her cancer medicine. Don't you understand?" I swore, using one hand to point to the wastebasket, the other to the curtain separating Melodee from us. "She'll die without those pills."

Ester looked at me quizzically for a moment before returning to the wastebasket and retrieving the prescription vial. She again took one of the tablets and examined it closely, first by sight, then by smell, then by taste. Coming to the same conclusion as before, she shook her head forcefully and said something I took for *bad medicine.*

My temper flared. "What do you know of modern chemistry?" I spat. "Intellectually I could run circles around you. You don't know squat. Who's to say you're even a real doctor? What proof is there you even know what you're doing?" I pointed at her, then forcefully turned my thumb down. "Ester, bad doctor."

I could tell I struck a nerve as Ester marched up to me and began removing the bandage from my leg. She wasn't smiling—or being very gentle. I don't know how she knew what I said, but she certainly got the gist of my tone. When the bandage was gone, she held a candle to the wound. My eyes widened. The tissue around the laceration wasn't red or swollen anymore. It was smooth and fleshy and looked like nothing more than an old scratch. I couldn't believe my eyes. I knew Gilberto's rusty machete had penetrated clear through and had left a gaping wound. How could it have healed so quickly? And so cleanly?

I gazed up at Ester, who returned my look with a scowl. "This is amazing," I said in a reverent tone. In time, I doubted I would even be able to discern the scar from the surrounding tissue. It would probably look like no more than an age crease.

As I struggled to climb back onto the cot, the young physician helped me from behind. I cautiously massaged the wound on my leg. It was tender but not to an extreme. I was fully confident the tissues below were healing as well as the skin on the surface. Such healing could not have taken place over a matter of hours. It simply wasn't possible.

Ester snapped the blanket and let it float gently over my waist and legs. I continued to gawk at her with newfound respect. As my harsh words echoed in my mind, I felt stupid, childish. "I'm sorry for doubting you."

She nodded and gave a half-hearted smile as if to say, *Okay, but I'm still mad at you.*

Pointing to my leg wound, I asked, "How did this heal so fast?"

Ester indicated the table littered with medicines.

"Yes, but how did they work so quickly?"

She obviously didn't understand my meaning. I tried another tack.

"How long have I been here?" I pointed at the window then held up one hand with my fingers splayed and mimicked the path of the sun, rising and setting. "How many days?"

She caught on and mimicked the sun's path five times.

Five days? That couldn't be right. But I sensed I could trust Ester, so I finally decided it must be true. If five days had lapsed since I was brought to Helam's village, I felt confident in assuming these people were friends to Melodee and me. The people in the other village had the drug men at our doorstep within a matter of hours.

I looked over at Melodee. The steady rise and fall of her blanket, such slow breathing, was indicative of deep sleep. To see her in such a peaceful slumber did my heart good. But my stomach still churned with remorse, knowing her ailment was incurable. I wanted to wake her, to console her, but I decided sleep was more healing than anything I could do for her. I sighed bitterly and rubbed my weary eyes.

As I looked around the room, the stone architecture impressed me as thoughtfully planned and constructed. This room was completely different from the hodge-podge assemblage of bamboo lattice, corrugated tin, and random sections of plywood I'd seen in the other village. This building had substance, permanence, pride. My anthropologic curiosity stirred in me as I wondered what the rest of this village and its people were like.

Our young physician was orderly and methodical, the antithesis of the shaman with whom I'd had the bizarre encounter. My wounds were healing remarkably fast. After my minimal communication with the physician, I could only assume Melodee's sickness was not abating. No one could cure cancer.

Ester had returned to her chair and resumed her reading. I knew I would get scant information about anything else until morning. As I was not terribly sleepy, I decided to follow the young doctor's example. I took Melodee's Book of Mormon and opened to the first book of Nephi. I noticed that each chapter began with a synopsis. If I were still in college, I might be tempted to simply read the synopses and breeze my way through the entire book. But a few key words immediately jumped from the first two verses—*parents, taught, language*—and I was impressed with a feeling that this was not a volume to skim through.

I recalled the title page explaining the historical and spiritual nature of the text, and decided to treat each verse with the same respect Melodee would show it. Besides, I had made her a promise. I was determined to see it through.

It began: "I, Nephi, having been born of goodly parents, therefore I was taught somewhat in all the learning of my father . . ."

I had always felt that learning begins in the home. Dyana felt the same way; hence, she opted to forgo a full-time career to raise our daughter. For the most part, I thought it was working out just fine.

Rehearsing Dyana's ultimatum in my mind, I grimaced. Apparently, I was wrong.

A feeling of remorse washed over me as I thought of the countless hours Dyana spent with Paige, usually without a father. Dyana's favorite pastime was reading to Paige. I tried to get involved, but I could never seem to put the same life into the words. Dyana was a natural at emphasizing exactly the right words or concepts to let Paige know what was important to remember. I tried but could never distill my graduate-school methods down to a grade-school level of teaching. Would I ever have the chance to try again?

I pushed that worry from my mind and continued reading. ". . . And having seen many afflictions in the course of my days . . ."

Afflictions? Take a look this way, buddy. My mind briefly flashed over everything I had been through to this point.

". . . Nevertheless, having been highly favored of the Lord in all my days . . ." *That makes* one *of us.* ". . . Yea, having had a great knowledge of the goodness and the mysteries of God, therefore I make a record of my proceedings in my days. Yea, I make a record in the language of my father, which consists of the learning of the Jews and the language of the Egyptians."

Interesting. Jewish knowledge and Egyptian writing. Both had Semitic origins. It would make sense to meld the two together, especially if one were more descriptive than the other or had a more concise writing style. If this record were scrawled on plates of gold, I'm sure the engraver would certainly prefer a condensed form of inscription.

I continued to read. The tone of the narrative took some getting used to, but before long, I was more involved in the story than the mode of writing. Lehi was old and wise. Nephi was the good kid. Laman and Lemuel did a lot of murmuring and complaining. I was annoyed with them right away. Disobedience by children at any age was something that had always irked me.

I got so absorbed in reading that I lost all track of time. I read chapter 8 twice and still didn't understand the dream Lehi shared with his family. Luckily, Nephi explained it all a few chapters later. Chapter 13 was interesting because it talked a lot about books—one of my favorite topics. I guessed that the book that came from the Jews to the Gentiles was the Bible. Although I had never read it, I had always assumed the modern Bible was complete. Apparently, Nephi felt otherwise. The second book mentioned was supposed to clear up the things lost from the first. I wasn't aware of a Bible II— the sequel. I made a mental note to ask Melodee about those books.

In chapter 16, something unusual caught my eye. Nephi said they were traveling in a "south-southeast" direction. How did he know that? I suppose they could have had compasses back then. Or perhaps there were *N, S, E,* and *W* markings on the Liahona. The verses simply said that one of the spindles pointed in the direction they *should* go, so the other one must have been a control or reference point of some kind. *Cool—a GPS tracker from God. You could never get lost with one of those,* I mused.

I was about to finish the first book of Nephi when a rooster announced the arrival of dawn. I noticed a pale graying of the sky through the lattice, and my anticipation of the coming day grew sharply. My stomach growled; it had been a while since I had had a good meal. Nevertheless, I felt surprisingly fit and awake. My arm had stopped complaining, and the dull fog in my head had completely cleared. I felt like getting dressed and going for a walk to find some breakfast.

I noticed that my healer-companion was asleep again. She was still quite a mystery to me. I wondered how long she had been attending to our needs. Had she been treating our wounds without any rest for the five days we'd been there? It occurred to me that I had seen no one else the times I'd been lucid. I would have thought someone might have come to give her a break. If she had been with Melodee and me the entire five days, she must be utterly exhausted.

I cleared my throat loudly to ease her from her slumber, but she didn't stir. I dropped my legs over the side of the cot and gingerly rose to my feet. My wounded leg was weak, but it could support my weight as long as I didn't move too quickly. I noticed a walking stick of sorts leaning against the medicine table and inched my way to it. It was a solid, stout piece of ironwood, intricately carved with what looked like hieroglyphics. At first, I wondered if it might be a decorative piece, but the top portion was clearly worn smooth from continued use, so I reasoned it was okay to use it as a cane.

I hobbled over to the curtain dividing the room and drew it fully open. I breathed a sigh of relief seeing Melodee still sleeping. She lay curled on one side with her back to me. As I approached her bed, my empty stomach growled noisily. Melodee turned her head and opened her puffy eyes.

"Morning," she said in a raspy whisper.

It was one of the sweetest sounds I had ever heard.

TWENTY-SIX

Melodee's cheeks were still hollow, her skin pale and waxy, her hair matted and lackluster. She was obviously weak, unable to move without concerted, painful effort. She had been without solid food and adequate fluids for a long time, as evident in her sunken eyes and sagging skin. Her voice was barely more than an uttered breath. Her skin beaded with oily perspiration that exuded a strange odor. But her eyes twinkled. There was a definite life in them, a sparkle that refused to dim.

She forced a smile. "How is your arm?"

I couldn't believe it! Here she lay, in all likelihood on her deathbed, and she was more concerned about my well-being than she was her own. My eyes burned with a strange mix of joy, admiration, and sorrow.

"Fine," I whispered, not out of a need for quiet but because it was all the voice I could summon. "How about you, kiddo?"

"Never better."

"Liar."

She smiled ever so slightly. "Okay. A little tired, then. And a bit sore." She looked around the shadowy room. "Where are we?"

"I don't know, but I think we're in good hands."

"The village?" she forced out between clenched teeth, pain worrying her features.

I shook my head. "My premonitions about that place were right. Those people were not our friends."

"Too bad. The kids were nice." She coughed spasmodically and closed her eyes.

I said, "You know, when they told me what they called that village, I thought it was just a fancy name: Salsipuedes."

Melodee licked her lips and tried to swallow. I then noticed a cup of water at her bedside. "Here, sip this water," I said as I raised her head to the cup.

She sipped and swallowed with a grimace. "You sure that's water?"

I sniffed the liquid and found a sharp tang to its odor, somewhat familiar but unrecognizable. I tried a sip, and tasted a distinct bitterness. It was definitely water, perhaps just a little old.

"Yeah, it's okay, just a bit stale. I'll get you some fresh water later."

She nodded slightly. "Okay. More, please."

I helped her sip again, then set the cup aside. "Salsipuedes?" she whispered.

I snorted in self-ridicule. "Yeah. I guess I wasn't thinking."

"What do you mean?" She took a couple of sharp breaths, as if trying to quell a deep-seated pain. I waited patiently, wishing there were more I could do to alleviate her suffering.

"It's a command form in Spanish," I explained. "It basically means 'leave if you can.'"

"Really?" She smacked her lips and tried to stretch. The attempt looked agonizing. I gave her more water.

"Remember Andro, the little boy in the jungle? He told me the village had lots of flooding, and the ground got so muddy that you'd get stuck if you stepped in it. That's probably why most of the huts were raised on stilts."

I figured it also explained why the mosquitoes weren't too bad there. Mosquitoes normally bred in swampy areas, places where standing water sat for long periods. If the floods in the village caused mud pots instead of waterholes, the pests wouldn't frequent the area. The constant floods and resulting mud pots were the reason for the village's unusual and foreboding title. *Leave if you can.* To foreigners such as us, the name of the village carried a sinister double entendre.

"I think I'll rest now," Melodee said as she curled back into a ball and drew a long, ragged breath.

I gently stroked her hair. "Good idea."

She was out immediately. I pulled a blanket up to her neck and tucked it around her frail form. I turned and flinched. Ester was standing at the curtain, watching. I expected to receive a stern scowl from the young doctor, but instead, she rewarded me with a warm, approving smile.

"She's resting now," I whispered.

Ester nodded.

I took the cup and sniffed it again. "What is in here?"

The young physician bade me follow her. At the medicine table, she handed me a strip of bark. It had the same sharp odor as the water in the cup. I recognized it as cinchona bark, a natural source of quinine, one of the medicines used to treat malaria. South Americans had utilized its antimalarial properties since before recorded history, but its first mention in European medical literature wasn't until the mid-1600s from a Belgian physician named Herman van der Heyden.

"But Melodee doesn't have malaria," I said to Ester. "She has cancer. Do you know that word, *cancer?*"

The healer pointed to her ear and frowned.

"Does this help?" I asked, indicating the cinchona bark, then pointing to Melodee.

She nodded.

"How?"

She tilted her head and favored me with a look similar to Melodee's *Duh!* Did that mean I should already know the answer? Or that Ester would not be able to explain because of our language barrier? Whichever the answer, I knew I wouldn't learn the biochemical process the young doctor employed with this natural medicament until we first breached our communication roadblock.

I held up my hands in a defensive gesture. "Okay, sorry I asked."

She smiled.

My stomach growled again and I rubbed it vigorously. "It's empty."

She tossed her head back and laughed, then motioned for me to follow. We exited the stonewalled room into a hallway of similar construct. Curious petroglyphs carved into the limestone—much like an Egyptian hieroglyphic relief—told a story of which I could

only guess the meaning. If only I had an English translation of
Champollion's Rosetta Stone . . . and a lot more time.

At the end of the hall, we rounded a corner and pushed through
a wooden door. The sunlight was almost blinding. We were standing
on a raised veranda of stone that overlooked a large clearing
surrounded by other stone structures and bordered by tall, ultradense vegetation. It reminded me of the ancient ruins of Tikal in
Guatemala, Machu Picchu in Peru, or Teotihuacan in Mexico, only
these buildings were in excellent repair. The small village was located
in a deep valley, nestled between two verdant mountains of such
steep terrain that traveling up or down them would be a feat best
accomplished by birds.

The air was fresh and cool but very humid, and the sky was a
clear, brilliant blue. A small stream meandered through a mani-
cured, grassy courtyard in the center of the village and fed several
small pools along the way. Tall queen palms and Indian laurels lined
the courtyard, and numerous ferns and flowering vines planted
randomly along the terraced facades of the buildings gave the setting
an almost surreal, resort-style ambience.

My wandering gaze stopped on a number of people milling
about, performing daily tasks, unaware of my scrutiny. Most were
dressed in tunics and skirts adorned with colorful ribbons, shells,
baubles, and feathers. Some wore headdresses, others simple pony-
tails. Most wore sandals or moccasins. A few men wore homemade
pants, but I also saw the odd pair of Levi's, too. What struck me
almost immediately was the curious mix of nationalities. Most
resembled South American Indians with a trace of Hispanic blood.
But there was an equal amount of people with lighter-colored hair
and fair skin—not American Caucasian, but something else I could
not place.

"David!" I jumped when a seasoned voice bellowed at me, inter-
rupting my observations.

It was Helam. I don't know why I felt so happy to see him, but
Helam's smiling face made me feel as if I were greeting a friend from
long ago. He stepped up and embraced me, then pointed to my leg
and asked something in his foreign tongue.

"It's fine," I answered, even though I didn't understand his exact words. "A bit weak, but I can use it. I'm just worried about a secondary infection."

Helam's expression turned to one of apology for not understanding what I said. I again indicated my leg, then gave a thumbs-up turning to a thumbs-down, and shrugged my shoulders. Ester gave a huff of exasperation and rolled her eyes, telling me *she* understood everything I had pantomimed. She folded her arms stiffly across her chest and marched back into the building.

Helam chuckled and clasped my shoulder warmly. He jerked his head to one side and carefully led me down some steps to a large bowery of thick bamboo poles supporting an awning of palm-frond thatch and fragrant trumpet vines. The going was slow, but the walking stick helped. Several tables made of slate stone stood at one end of the bowery, and a cooking section with a sizeable cobblestone fire pit and several preparation tables filled the other end. It appeared to be a communal cafeteria, well organized and surprisingly clean. The musty tang of roasting meat and the sharp sweetness of sliced citrus fruit mixed wonderfully with the trumpet-vine perfume, making me all the more cognizant of how hungry I was.

A few people paused from eating their meals to gawk at me, and for the first time since the plane crash, I felt somewhat self-conscious about my appearance. Everything about these people looked orderly and clean. I assumed I must have looked like a drowned rat recently used as a chew toy by a pack of rottweilers. I had several days' growth of beard, and my hair was in such disarray it would have been easier to shave it off rather than try to comb through it. I dropped my face to my shoulder and tried covertly to sniff my underarm odor. Not detecting the expected pungent, sour sweatiness, I tried the other armpit. Still nothing. I raised a forearm to my nose and inhaled. A clean, soapy smell filled my nostrils, and I suddenly realized Ester—or someone assisting her—must have bathed me while I was unconscious. I felt my face redden at the thought. Touching my face and head, I discovered that my hair felt quite clean and my beard was freshly trimmed. Perhaps I didn't look so bad after all.

Helam led me to an empty place where we took a seat. A young girl, probably about six or seven years old, brought us two metal plates, one loaded with strips of glazed meat, the other with slices of papaya, kiwi, and star fruit. I wasn't certain, but the plates had the look and feel of real gold.

I was about to reach for a kiwi when I noticed Helam bowing his head as Melodee had before she ate. I lowered my eyes and waited. After a time, the old man nodded and reached for a strip of meat. I did the same. The glazing on the meat was some sort of sweet sauce seasoned with ginger and a spice tasting somewhat like paprika. I didn't care what animal the meat came from—the combination of flavors was fantastic, and I ate with unashamed voracity. Before long, a small group of villagers surrounded me, watching my every move. Somewhat self-conscious, I made a concerted effort to slow my epicurean gluttony to a more civilized tempo. A low whispering of voices buzzed around me, and I could only guess what they were saying. Their conversation centered on the stranger in their midst, yet I didn't feel any animosity or contempt from the group. Where the people of Salsipuedes had eyed me with suspicion, these people displayed nothing more than curiosity and genuine concern for their injured guest. Their faces were all friendly, caring, even compassionate.

I was amazed at the variety of eye color: blue, green, various shades of brown, and some nearly black. Some wore intricate jewelry of turquoise, amethyst, and jade. Others sported vests of leopard skin, snakeskin, or other types of leather. Almost without exception, all wore beautiful feathers from the plentiful birdlife indigenous to this area.

I swallowed a cupful of crystal clear water and wiped my mouth with the back of my hand. "Thank you," I said to no one in particular. When no one responded, I tried "Muchas gracias."

"They understood your meaning," a deep, soothing voice said from the crowd. A few individuals parted, and a man of undeterminable years hobbled forward using a cane. He stood directly across from me as we evaluated each other. His face belied an age of at least eighty or ninety years, but his physique was that of a much younger man, very trim and well muscled. His smile was soft and pleasing. His eyes were much like Helam's, a very pale blue. "May I join you?"

"Y—yes, please," I stammered.

"Thank you." He extended his right hand in a very modern gesture. "I am Shemnon."

I took his hand and tried to match his powerful grip. "David Kirkham."

"David—a noble name. Helam told me about you and the little girl, Melodee. Tell me, my friend, how is it you came to our land?"

"Wait," I said, trying to organize the thoughts racing through my mind. "You speak English." It was a statement, not a question.

He nodded. "A little."

"How?" I asked. Then before he could answer I heard myself ramble in rapid-fire succession all of the questions that had been addling my brain. "Where is this place? Who are you people? Is there a phone I can use or some way to communicate with the United States?"

Holding up his hands, Shemnon chuckled deeply, his eyes twinkling with amusement. "Wait, wait. Slow down, my friend. All of your questions will be answered in time. Right now, it is important for you to rest and regain your strength. Melodee too. She is still very sick."

"She's got cancer. I think it's leukemia."

He nodded again. "Yes. Our physicians are helping as best they can."

"Ester. Is she a physician?"

"Yes. One of our best. She has a gift for healing."

"I need to talk with her. Can you interpret for me?"

"In time."

My temper began to rise uncontrollably. "You people don't understand—there isn't any time!"

A low murmur buzzed through the crowd. The looks of friendly curiosity morphed into steely glances of uncertainty. I didn't care. I had had enough mysteries to last a lifetime, and I needed some solid information right then.

"Listen, Shemnon. I appreciate all you've done for us, but I don't think you realize how serious her illness is."

"We understand perfectly. You need not worry. Melodee has a strong spirit about her. God is looking out for her."

God? What kind of religious nonsense was this? "Look, old man, if it's all the same to you, I'd rather put my trust in modern medicine, not some Third World rain forest witchcraft."

Shemnon lowered his eyes and sighed. "David, I know it is asking much of you, but you need to be patient and trusting. We are a humble people, but our knowledge of healing is more advanced than you may think."

My anxieties were on a razor's edge. The suspicious stares from those around me did not help. One little boy in particular scowled at me with fierce resolve. I closed my eyes and forced my mind and temper to settle down. "I'm sorry for my outburst," I said softly and with all the sincerity I could muster. "There is so much that confuses me lately."

"If you are patient, we will try to answer all of your questions," Shemnon promised.

"Thank you." I took another gulp of water before continuing. "May I ask one question right now?"

"You want to know how I can speak your language."

"Yes. But more important, I want to know how soon we can leave."

Shemnon shared a concerned look with Helam. He exchanged a few words with him in their language. A soft murmur washed through the crowd. He then cleared his throat and aimlessly traced a random pattern on the surface of the table with his finger. His brow arched in an apologetic crease as he said, "I don't know if that will be possible."

I blinked. "What do you mean? You have no idea how soon?"

Helam said something to Shemnon, and the old man responded with a grunt, a furrowed brow, and a shake of the head. An older woman in the crowd voiced an opinion, and a silent chorus of nods followed.

"What?" I asked, again perturbed at my inability to understand.

Shemnon again cleared his throat. "We are a secret people. We know of the outside world, but we choose not to let them know of us."

"Okay . . ." I said with a somewhat leery reticence. "So . . . what does that mean?"

His piercing blue eyes met my gaze with a profound intensity. "I am not sure we can ever let you leave."

TWENTY-SEVEN

I sat on my bed watching Melodee sleep. Ester, having excused herself, was replaced by a powerfully built man who appeared to be nineteen or twenty years old. He had clear, pale green eyes and wavy, dark hair. His name was Zeniff. I found the new-age sound of his name a strange contrast to his Old World appearance. But despite his formidable size, he seemed a likeable fellow, with an easy smile of enviably straight teeth.

Earlier, I had tried to pry more information from Shemnon but to no avail. He claimed I wasn't ready for the depth of what he had to tell me. He said his forefathers explained it as giving milk before meat. I had heard that expression before and mostly agreed with it. In any kind of knowledge, you have to grasp the basics before you fully understand the intricacies of more complex concepts. In this case, however, being a highly educated man, I felt confident I could digest whatever "meat" he chose to give me. Shemnon promised to share more later on. In fact, I was now awaiting his visit to the hospital, as I called it.

Melodee coughed and stirred. Zeniff was immediately at her side, gently daubing her forehead with a moistened cloth. The look of genuine concern on his face was moving.

"Are you a physician too?" I asked.

He shook his head. I wasn't sure if that meant he wasn't or that he simply did not understand my question.

"Are you a hunter?"

Again a shake. I mimicked a bow and arrow action, then pantomimed shooting a running animal with the arrow. "Hunter," I indicated.

He smiled and nodded.

"You? Hunter?"

A shake. No.

"A stone mason?"

No.

"A warrior?"

No.

"A butcher, a baker, a candlestick maker?"

He tilted his head to one side and favored me with a quizzical look.

"A bodybuilder, then?"

He went back to daubing Melodee's face and neck, ignoring my banal questions. I couldn't blame him, but I felt compelled to ask. One question led to the next, none of which the young man could answer. Shemnon had promised answers in exchange for patience. If that were the case, I expected very little information. I had zero patience.

Melodee stirred again and opened her eyes. Zeniff smiled broadly at her as a loving father would. I hobbled over to her and said hello.

"Hi," she whispered.

"How are you feeling?"

"Fine." A difficult swallow. "You?"

"Better than I deserve," I quipped. "Are you hungry?"

"A little. Mostly thirsty."

"You have to eat something. It's important to maintain your strength, especially when battling cancer."

Her brow wrinkled. "How did you know? I know I never told you."

"No, you didn't," I said in a mild tone of reprimand.

"I rarely tell anyone." She closed her eyes as if ashamed, embarrassed. "I don't want people feeling sorry for me," she added weakly.

What a remarkable little girl. Just when I thought my admiration for her could not grow any stronger, it took another leap to uncharted heights. "You're taking Gleevex. I know what that's used for."

She sighed. "Got me."

All this time, Zeniff remained silent but observant, scrutinizing our conversation as if reading its tone. Melodee turned to him and touched his arm. "Thank you," she said in a fatigued voice.

The large man's eyes began to shine as he bit his lower lip and nodded quickly. A small tear escaped and ran down the length of his cheek and jaw. This gentle giant definitely wore his heart on his sleeve. I found my own eyes burning just watching him and feeling the love he had for my little friend. "Yes," he said softly.

My breath caught short. "Wait a minute, Zeniff. I thought you couldn't speak English."

Melodee's eyes narrowed. "What did you call him?"

"His name is Zeniff. He's one of the bigger guys in this village. I think they've assigned him to be your bodyguard," I teased.

"What village? Where are we?"

I squinted at her. "You mean no one has told you? You've been out this whole time?"

"I guess. I don't remember much of anything since arriving in Salsip—whatever the name of that village was—and when I woke up this morning. I think—" She stopped short as a coughing fit overcame her. Zeniff fetched her some more water and gently rubbed her back until the fit subsided.

"You okay?" I asked.

She sipped the water and nodded. "These people seem different from the others we've met. Do you know who they are?"

I shrugged. "I'm barely beginning to figure things out myself. Why were you so surprised at Zeniff's name?"

Melodee took a long drink of water before answering. "Zeniff was an important leader from the scriptures—a king, I believe. It's strange to hear a name like that in the middle of nowhere, don't you think?"

"I don't know. Lots of South Americans name their children after biblical people."

"It's not biblical. It's from the Book of Mormon."

"Really," I chuckled. "Well, I don't know who these people are but . . ." I paused and glanced at Zeniff. "Could you give us a moment?"

The big guy gave a half smile. I pointed to the other side of the room and waved him in that direction. He nodded and moved away. I continued in a whisper, "But they may not be as friendly as they seem. One of them, an old guy named Shemnon, can speak English. He told me we may never leave this place because they want to keep their society a secret."

Just then, Ester came in carrying a large satchel. Helam and Shemnon, who were both carrying satchels of their own, followed her. They approached and smiled affectionately.

"Hello," Melodee said before they had a chance to speak first. "My name is Melodee."

"We know," said Shemnon, grinning warmly. "Your friend David has told us. This is your physician, Ester."

"Wow. You're much too pretty to be a doctor," Melodee said, her voice still scratchy and weak.

I don't know if the physician understood all the words, but Melodee's tone was plain to read. Ester lowered her eyes, blushed brightly, and began rummaging through her satchel.

Shemnon continued, "And this is Helam. He's the one who brought you here."

"Helam?" Melodee said with an astonished breath. "That's really interesting . . . and kinda strange, too. What's going on here?"

Shemnon and I exchanged confused glances but didn't know what she meant. The old man moved to the little girl's side and took her hand.

"Melodee, we are going to try to help you. I hope you can be strong."

She nodded and forced a huge smile. I could see she was in a lot of discomfort but was being her usual stoic self. "Sure. But I don't think there's much you can do. All my doctors back home said there's little hope. I have advanced myelogenous *and* lymphocytic leukemia. My radiation and chemotherapy don't seem to be working. They said I won't live past this Christmas."

She exhaled roughly and her body drooped, as if the exertion of her last remarks had sapped all her strength.

Zeniff returned to his chore of wiping Melodee's forehead as Shemnon helped her with another sip of water. Ester was busy removing all sorts of gourds, ceramic vessels, metal goblets, and other materials from her satchel and placing them on a table adjacent to Melodee's cot.

Still holding Melodee's hand, Shemnon said, "I do not recognize the names of your sickness, but I assume it is not a pleasant illness to have."

"It's an incurable kind of cancer," I stated, wishing I had something better to add to the conversation.

"I see."

"Great," I said, a little too harshly. "Now, what I *don't* see is how you speak English, and who you people are, and why I can't get any real answers around here."

"God has blessed me with the ability to speak many languages," Shemnon began. "Not only have I learned from my many travels, but also from strangers who come to our valley."

"It's probably the gift of tongues," Melodee said tentatively, "or something close to it."

When I gave her a look of total confusion, she continued, "Our church teaches us to believe in spiritual gifts: healings, visions, prophecies, stuff like that."

"What's that got to do with speaking a foreign language?" I huffed.

Shemnon faced me. "David, you could learn much from this little one. She is right; I am blessed with the gift of tongues—although I never expected to hear it called that from strangers such as yourselves. If the need is just, I can understand and speak several languages. They come easy to me." He looked down at Melodee, admiration glowing in his eyes. "These *are* gifts from God. Yours is the gift of faith. Did you know that?"

Melodee's eyes misted as she softly whispered, "No. But thank you."

The old man's gaze returned to me. "We follow ancient ways and believe in an ancient religion."

"Some tribal mumbo jumbo?" I said under my breath, not meaning for the others to hear.

"If you choose to call it that. We believe in God, as do many religions in the world."

"And just how do you know what other religions believe?" None of this was making sense to me.

"As I mentioned, we know of the outside world. There are many wonders we know of, but there are many evils, too. I do not have all the answers to what lies beyond our mountains, but such knowledge is not necessary to our way of life."

My thoughts focused on the Amish and Mennonite cultures. Although they lived in and were aware of the modern world, they chose to live a simpler lifestyle. Like the Amish, it was reasonable to assume that the people of Cumorah would know of different religions, different beliefs, and even understand different languages. But that still did not answer any of my questions—at least not to my satisfaction.

"The gift of tongues? The gift of faith?" I wasn't sure what to make of all this religious talk.

"When you are humble, you can experience many wonderful things," Shemnon said.

Melodee took my hand in hers. Her skin was clammy but her grip was strong. "Uncle David," she whispered, "just give it a chance."

I closed my eyes in resignation and forced the bitter emotions from my heart. If it would help Melodee, I would do anything. "Okay."

"You promise?"

"I'll try. Cross my heart."

Suddenly, a tingling pinpoint of acceptance began to penetrate my impenetrable arrogance and began to grow within me. It was a warmth, a glow, a comfort that filled me in a way I had never been filled. My emotions flowed uncontrollably to the surface. My heart pounded and my throat tightened. What was this feeling?

All this talk of spiritual gifts had my skeptical nature as tight as a mousetrap, but it was nowhere near springing. The feeling I now experienced was of such magnitude that I could not find words to express it. It was strange, marvelous, and confusing. But, as Melodee had asked, instead of fighting it, I opened my heart to it and basked in it. To ignore my analytical disposition was definitely an un-David-like thing to do, but it felt so right. This foreign emotion was something real, something tangible. I had no idea what it was, but I knew I wanted more. Much more.

TWENTY-EIGHT

Melodee's little burst of energy didn't last long. Ester brought her some thick porridge that looked like coarse-ground barley and some other grain. The young physician also had Melodee drink some broth and eat some mashed fruit.

While Melodee ate her meal, she asked how I was doing with my reading in the Book of Mormon. I told her that I hadn't read as much as I should have, but that I was making progress. I didn't tell her of my adventures since she had lapsed into her comalike state back in the old village. She smiled approvingly and closed her eyes. Her small frame slowly curled into a ball, and her breathing slowed.

As Melodee's eyes began to twitch back and forth in REM sleep, my emotions played havoc with my heart. I hoped that her dreams were pleasant and not the stuff of nightmares. I hoped that her strength would return and that she would find happiness. And I hoped beyond hope that she would be cured of her cancer.

Helam and Zeniff had left the room. I asked a few questions of Shemnon, but he remained frustratingly vague with his answers. I pushed on, my need for information gnawing at me like an addiction.

"Your village is called Cumorah?"

He nodded. "Yes."

"How many people live here?"

"It varies. A few leave now and then, most stay. As I said, we are a people who choose to remain separate, hidden from the world as much as possible. Too many modern influences corrupt our ways."

I had heard that argument before. A number of purists felt the United States was Americanizing traditional cultures right out of many Third World lands, causing an irreparable loss of language, art, tradition, etc. To some extent, I had to agree. But modern advances such as medicine, horticulture, and sanitation were things that would not degrade but improve—even save—lives. A professor of mine had spent four years in the Philippines with the American Red Cross. He told me how much trouble they had simply getting the men and children to stop urinating in the streets. If Shemnon knew so much about the modern world, how could he deny his people such beneficial improvements as sanitation and medicine?

"But advanced civilizations have so much to offer," I argued.

"And we have much to offer them," he countered. "Fear not. We are content in our simplicity. Tell me, do all your modern discoveries always bring your people true happiness?"

I was about to voice a definitive yes, but my mind conjured up images of discoveries that should never have been made: cigarettes, atomic weapons, chemical weapons, harmful pesticides, drugs which were commonly misused or were linked to devastating side effects and death, and a few genetically engineered human viruses that scientists now wished they could uninvent.

"I guess not," I admitted. "But it's pure isolationist ignorance to assume all modernization is bad."

Shemnon's eyes hooded with a look of mild reprimand. "I did not say they were all bad. I asked if they all brought true happiness. Consider your modern ways—do they bring people closer to the happiness of God, or do they make life more frantic?"

It amazed me that he knew so much about my world. And yet he was right. What things brought true joy to me and my family? How many times had I asked myself that very question? Was it the expensive trips they remembered? Was it the extravagant gifts they cherished? I used to think so. Now I wasn't so sure.

I thought of Orson Wells' classic film, *Citizen Kane*. Here was a man who had everything money could buy, but he was never truly happy. On his deathbed, his last words spoke of his only joyous memory: tobogganing on a sled named Rosebud. It didn't matter that that memory took place during an impoverished childhood where he lived in a humble shack with barely any clothes on his back and little food on the table.

I thought of how many times my own daughter seemed to have more fun playing with the box that had contained a large toy, rather than with the toy itself. Dyana's note also came to mind. What was she really asking for? Was I mistaken in thinking our happiness together depended on monetary rewards? Did she sense that the instability in our family resulted from a lack of time together? Or something deeper? Perhaps even a lack of God in our lives?

"There are some things worth protecting, even if it means not experiencing others," the old man continued. "The joy of community, of family, of a relationship with your Maker cannot be matched by anything else on Earth."

I couldn't let it go. "But to not allow each person their own choice is tantamount to dictatorship."

"Everyone has the right to choose—when they reach the age of accountability. As I said, some do wish for a different life and decide to leave. At the right time, however, God will call on everyone to give an account of his or her life. If we continue to live righteously, we will be looked upon with favor at that time."

"That's a lofty claim to make for yourself," I warned, concluding that Shemnon was more vain than he admitted.

"Like the Jews of old, we feel we are a chosen people."

A chosen people. A memory flashed into my mind. "When we were taken to Salsipuedes, we were asked if we were among the chosen people. I assume they meant you."

Again, Shemnon nodded. "But they are not interested in *why* we are chosen. We feel we are blessed of God. As I said before, too many others are interested only in riches and things of the world that bring fleeting happiness."

As the hour grew late, Shemnon excused himself and left me alone with Melodee and the young physician. I picked up the Book of Mormon and began skimming the pages, but I became distracted by Ester's fussing about. She was in a constant state of motion, moving here and there, organizing the materials she and Helam had brought in, setting the items in a precise, uniform order. I quickly became more interested in watching her than in reading Melodee's book, or in exchanging enigmatic ideology with Shemnon. It would have been fascinating to have the old man interpret everything she was doing, but he had explained earlier that he held little knowledge of the healer's arts. Also, he didn't want to ask many questions because the young physician needed to concentrate on her itinerary rather than answer a curious observer's incessant queries.

* * *

Night came quickly to the valley. An orchestra of nocturnal rain forest creatures tuned up and began its cacophonous symphony. A gentle, cooling breeze picked up, blowing in from the west, opposite of the rising crescent moon. In addition to the flickering wall sconces, Ester lit some candles to brighten the darkening chamber. She next lit a stick of incense, which gave off a faint, peculiar aroma, and placed it at Melodee's feet. Watching the lazy tendril of smoke, a brief twinge of anxiety knotted my stomach as I recalled the shaman's bizarre style of medical practice. Nevertheless, Ester had yet to reveal any rodent skulls or wicked-looking blades, for which I was greatly relieved. The scent from the incense was familiar, but I couldn't place it: somewhat spicy, almost a nutmeg scent mixed with lavender, but not quite. It was an aroma that had me feeling tranquil, relaxed. The young physician then began mixing powders and grinding leaves and roots in her jade mortar and pestle. These she placed in organized piles along the table. She next opened a book whose pages were made of a metal resembling copper. Characters embossed into the leaves lay in even, horizontal rows. She scanned a few of these thin plates before returning to her tasks. After a few hours, she seemed content with her preparations, blew out the candles, and left the room.

I wanted to take the opportunity to more closely examine what she had done, but as it was very dark where Melodee was sleeping, I chose instead to read under the sconce by my bed.

I opened the Book of Mormon, and read that Nephi had built a ship. It must have been fairly large to accommodate all of Lehi's and

Ishmael's families. The ancients used oceangoing vessels from as early as 2000 BC, but they were mostly coastal ships. I wondered what Nephi's boat looked like. The families had a rough voyage because Laman and Lemuel kept complaining, but they eventually made it to a place they called the Promised Land. I came across a passage or two referring to other plates, other records being kept, and remembered Ester's copper book. Again, my curiosity was piqued. Where were these other records now? Had they been destroyed, or were they still hidden? If they still existed, would they be discovered and translated in my lifetime? I glanced at Ester's medicine table. A flicker from a candle reflected off one of the metal pages from the open book. It made sense to record things of lasting importance on metal plates, as they would be less likely to deteriorate over time. I was strangely comforted that Ester was using a textbook of a similar kind. *What I wouldn't give for an English translation of its contents!*

I continued to read throughout the night. Even though I was tired, I found myself enthralled with the details of the Book of Mormon. In 2 Nephi, I read a passage that I didn't fully appreciate at first, but something told me I was personally witnessing its fruition. In chapter 5, when Lehi's family split into two main groups, the Lord cursed the evil people with a darker skin. I immediately thought of African Americans, but then concluded that that wasn't quite right. My mind toyed with the differences in skin types I had seen during my travels for BioCraft, but I didn't feel all dark skin was a result of living corrupt lives, as the Lamanites' dark skin in the Book of Mormon had been. I knew too many Caucasians who would be the color of India ink if that were the case. The curse mentioned in the book had to have been a one-time event, which had diffused over the years to a variety of skin tones. Today's Latin Americans were not as brown as the rain-forest Indians, who were not as dark as native Brazilians, and so on. And currently there were countless shades of people in between.

I remembered hearing how the early Spanish explorers were mistaken for white gods when they first landed in the Americas. I wondered how that tied in with what I was now reading. Not all of the people of Cumorah were as white skinned as Melodee and me, but many were a much lighter shade than the other people we had encountered since the plane crash.

As my thoughts wandered, my mind began to spin. The introduction to the Book of Mormon stated that the record was an account of the ancient inhabitants of the Americas. Did that mean the Incas, the Aztecs, the Mayans, and others south of the border were actually descendants of the Lamanites? The possibilities seemed to ricochet around my head. A marvelous enlightening swelled within me, filling me with a clear understanding, as if I was part of a great discovery to which not many were privy.

Then a second thought focused in my mind. If there were still remnants of the Lamanite people, what about the Nephites? Thus far, the books of Nephi referred to the righteous Nephites as a people *chosen* of the Lord, fair-skinned, intelligent, and peaceable.

A tremor of astonishment rippled through me as I realized those characteristics described the people of Cumorah to a *T*.

* * *

I spent the next few days helping Ester care for Melodee. We had very little interaction with anyone else in Cumorah. It was encouraging to see Melodee waking and eating on a regular schedule, but I could tell how draining each session was for her. Ester seemed to want to encourage this, often pushing Melodee to the point of exhaustion instead of letting her rest. The young physician ignored my protests and suggestions, and continued her relentless regimen of waking times and eating, and she even had Melodee stretching and exercising a little when her strength allowed. Each day I could see the pain and fatigue on Melodee's face, yet she stoically bore each session without complaint. (I, on the other hand, complained all the time.) Each night I feared that Melodee would not wake the following day, because she had often literally collapsed in bed and would not respond to anyone or anything. But each morning she would open her eyes and smile at me in her endearing way and ask how I was doing.

Our conversations were limited to a few minutes. Her mental fatigue matched her physical weariness, and I felt guilty each time I asked more than a couple of questions. I continually tried to do things that would buoy her up and make her happy. She seemed particularly interested in what I knew of this village. I described the Mesoamerican architecture and the look of the people, and the things I had learned from Shemnon.

"They call this place Cumorah," I said.

Melodee smiled weakly. "That's way cool."

"What, the name?"

"The place. Everything."

"Why?"

She paused, a fiery sparkle glowing in her eyes. "How far are you in the Book of Mormon?"

"About the middle of Nephi's second book. I haven't felt much like reading lately."

"Oh, Uncle David, you have to keep going. There is so much to learn and not very much time left."

My heart skipped a beat when she spoke those words. She knew she was dying, and yet she still seemed more concerned about the salvation of my soul than her own life. She wanted me to finish the book before she passed on. She trusted I would hold my end of our bargain to share my opinion about the Book of Mormon, but it scared me to think what that opinion might be. I certainly didn't want to disappoint her on her deathbed. Still, I knew she wouldn't judge me for whatever conclusion I came to, and I vowed to read as much as possible before it was too late.

"I'll read as fast as I can, sweetie," I promised her.

"Great."

She smiled, then turned over and fell asleep.

TWENTY-NINE

After a few more days, Ester communicated through Shemnon that she wanted to step up Melodee's and my exercise routine. I protested. Melodee agreed. We spent the next morning working up a sweat. Ester led us to a templelike structure at the far end of the central plaza. It reminded me of the Temple of Kukulcan in Chichen Itza on the Yucatan Peninsula. It was a terraced pyramid with about 100 extremely steep steps leading up to a small platform and building at the top. Ester wanted us to walk up and down the first few steps several times, but Melodee was drenched with perspiration and collapsed just after beginning the first ascent. For safety's sake, we never pushed higher than about twenty feet. I was astounded that my injured leg had almost totally healed, although it did feel plenty sore with such exertion. I couldn't imagine how painful the exercise was for Melodee.

When my little friend's strength gave out, she landed with a grunt. Ester was immediately kneeling at her side. The young physician used a piece of lamb's wool to wipe Melodee's forehead and neck, and then sniffed the gathered perspiration with scientific intensity. I couldn't fathom why she would do this, but she seemed to glean some information from the scent of Melodee's sweat, and, more importantly, seemed pleased with the odor. To me, it smelled a bit like turpentine. She next used a thin piece of bamboo to gather a large bead of Melodee's perspiration and then held it to the sky—I assumed to get a better estimate of its color and clarity. Again, she seemed pleased with the results.

She next led Melodee and me to two wonderfully clear pools fed by the central stream. Each was no bigger than a small hot tub, but they were clean and inviting. We bathed in separate pools for privacy, although anyone making a minimal effort could have seen either of us in full glory. Melodee seemed to take it in stride as part of her therapy; I was much more self-conscious. I had to admit, however, that the many days of reduced caloric intake and constant hiking—and running—through the jungle had trimmed my waistline considerably. Dyana would be impressed. She was always after me for not exercising enough. Because of my busy schedule, I usually didn't have time. Her philosophy was that if I saw the importance of it, I would make the time.

My heart again went out to my wife and daughter. I wondered if they had given up all hope of ever seeing me again. Had Melodee's family begun to heal from the grief of losing her? They may have been somewhat prepared because of her leukemia, but the loss of a child is never something one can totally plan for, or quickly recover from—if ever. Again, my thoughts triggered a resolve to get her home before it was too late. Had we still been in the old village, *too late* might have already come. Here in Cumorah, however, the slightest glimmer of hope was just beginning to surface in my quagmire of doubt. Melodee was not only still alive, but seemed to inch toward better health each day.

After the refreshing rinse in the pools, Ester led us to a small, stone sauna where heated rocks under a steady drip of water created a thick steam that opened the pores and cleared the lungs. The sweat we generated by climbing the few temple steps was nothing compared to the copious amounts of fluid that poured from our skin as we sat in the claustrophobic room, struggling to breathe and yet wallowing luxuriously in the purgative atmosphere. After ten or fifteen minutes, we again dipped in the pools and then began the walk back to our hospital room. Because we felt totally drained of energy, Ester and a few others almost had to carry us to where our beds awaited—begging us to fall into them as if each had an actual voice. We immediately fell into deep, exhaustive slumber.

* * *

I awoke the next morning to find that Ester had wrapped Melodee's abdomen and torso with a gauzelike material that gave off a horrific odor. Fortunately, Melodee was still asleep. As Ester was not present at the moment, I eased out of bed and crept over to examine this latest treatment. The odor that wafted from the gauze smelled of a mix of so many odors that I had trouble isolating any single scent. Sulfur, ginger, arnica, balsam, eucalyptus, lavender, and even something kind of fishy. It wasn't a pleasing combination, but because no one odor overpowered the other, the mix created a strangely pungent, medicinal-smelling potpourri.

I could only guess how those substances would help Melodee's condition. I decided to leave well enough alone, picked up the Book of Mormon, and ventured outside for a bit of reading.

Clouds covered the sky with a solid patchwork of gray and white. Moisture beyond the ambient humidity saturated the air. It was going to storm again. I found a palm-thatched arbor covered in wisteria and sat on a cut-log bench to read. A breeze picked up, but it did nothing more than sporadically flutter my shirt and keep the humidity from beading on my skin. A soft rain began to tap against the fronds above me, creating a pleasing, tranquil background to match the mood of what I was reading.

Yet in spite of the cathartic environment, I found it difficult to get into the tone of the scripture. I noticed in the chapter headings that Nephi was quoting a lot of Isaiah. I had never actually read the Old Testament, but I knew the sound of it when I heard it. I felt guilty about skimming a bit, but it was the only way I could cover those chapters without becoming totally confused. The books of Jacob, Enos, Jarom, and Omni were better. Words of Mormon seemed a bit out of place until I noticed the timeline indications at the bottom of the page and realized it was not a contiguous part of the narrative. Then I came to the book of Mosiah and things really began to take off. Immediately caught up in the story, I began reading not from a didactic standpoint, but as if the book were more of a historical fiction novel. I read until nightfall.

* * *

A man cleared his throat, startling me. I hadn't noticed him arrive, but suddenly, there stood Zeniff, holding a torch. His handsome face wore an apologetic smile. He motioned for me to follow him, which I did. We went to the eating bower where a woman served a meal similar to what I had the night before. It was as delicious as I remembered, and I didn't complain about the repetition. Again, the plates and goblets looked to be made of gold. I asked if they were, but of course got nothing more than a confused smile for an answer.

When I got back to our room, I saw Ester administering a substance to Melodee from a shallow dish. I wondered if it was the same sedative I had taken. When I asked to see it, I found it was something completely different. Melodee gagged but kept down the amber-colored liquid. A rush of concern filled me as I struggled to determine what she had just swallowed. The odor was very strong, similar to that of turpentine yet not as sharp; the odor alone left an almost sweet aftertaste in the mouth. When I asked what the liquid contained, Ester simply shook her head. That I had to trust her without question irked me to no end, but I had no choice. To date, her other treatment modalities had been within the parameters of logic. But I couldn't help but think that this one would be too drastic for Melodee's already compromised system. If the Cumoran physician had just given the little girl any derivative of turpentine, it went against everything I knew about the volatile product. Even in a mildly concentrated form, turpentine was very toxic. Bottom line: Melodee would be dead by daybreak.

Over the past twenty-four hours, it was obvious Melodee had taken another turn for the worse. Was Ester administering some sort of euthanasia? Had she suddenly given up trying to cure Melodee of her cancer and started intentionally putting an end to her pain and suffering?

I got no further answers from the healer and spent a restless night wondering what the morning would bring.

* * *

Thunder shook me awake, not a bone-jarring, deafening clap, but a deep, resonant rumble that felt more like a passing train than an atmospheric discharge. Torchlight glowed from behind the curtain. Voices whispered.

I swung my legs from the cot and cleared my throat. The curtain parted and Helam peeked through. He waved me in.

Propped up in bed with a bunch of pillows, with her head bowed and eyes closed, Melodee sat in reverent repose. Shemnon was standing behind her, lighting a candle in a brazier of highly polished silver. He nodded to me, his face solemn. Another elderly man I did not recognize was at Shemnon's side, equally solemn. Ester, who had been standing off to one side, took my arm and led me to the foot of the bed.

"What's going on here?" I asked, a bit more harshly than I meant to.

Melodee opened her eyes. She looked at me with a glazed expression, as if not sure I was actually standing in the same room with her. When her eyes cleared, she said, "It's okay," in a sticky whisper.

"What's okay?"

She swallowed painfully and held her stomach tightly, clearly hurting. "I think I'm getting close," she said without remorse. "They're here to pray with me."

I pulled away from Ester's embrace. "Listen," I said, dreading an encounter reminiscent to the one with the old village's shaman. "This isn't some kind of tribal witchcraft, is it?"

"Uncle David, please." There was an intensity in her small voice that conveyed a power I didn't understand but with which I felt incapable of arguing. "I don't want any unhappiness or anger in this room. Not when I'm so close to meeting my Heavenly Father."

I refused to acknowledge the implications of what Melodee was saying. Again, I was astounded at her calmness, her courage in accepting the inescapable conclusion of her disease.

"I'm so sorry," I said, duly humbled. "I guess I don't know what to say."

"You will. Give it time."

Her confidence overwhelmed me. "Sure, sweetheart. If you say so."

"Please continue," she said to Shemnon.

The old leader knelt next to Melodee. The others in the room followed his example and knelt around Melodee's cot. It was a moment before I realized they were all staring expectantly at me. I nodded and dropped to my knees.

To me Shemnon said, "If you keep an open heart and remain humble, you will understand everything that God wants to convey."

"Okay," I whispered reverently.

There was something tingling within me, a warmth of sorts that was calming, revealing, and comforting. It was very much like the sensation I had experienced a few days before. I did not try to fight it, to assign a logical explanation to it. Instead, I let it wash over me and through me. I did as Shemnon instructed and allowed the feeling to give me understanding without rationalizing it in my mind. It astounded me how soothing the sensation was, how utterly enlightening everything became. What Shemnon and the others were doing was something profound, something powerful, something true. I smiled as the gentle warmth in my heart filled my entire body. My eyes burned as pooling tears blurred my vision. I hoped no one had seen my sudden display of emotion.

Looking up, I saw the old man smile at me with a notable measure of pride. Shemnon then began to speak softly, but with such power that I *felt* the words more than heard them.

"Father, God of all, we approach Thee in behalf of this little one . . ."

I wasn't sure if he spoke in English or if I simply understood in English, but the others around me seemed to comprehend everything the village leader said, so I didn't question it.

"Thy daughter lies sick from a grievous illness and longs to rejoin Thee . . ."

I closed my eyes and felt my body trembling. I wrapped my arms protectively around myself, as if I were in the midst of a winter blizzard, yet inwardly I was glowing with an unseen fire. Tears ran freely down my face—something that was happening rather frequently lately. I felt Ester's arm wrap around my shoulders.

Shemnon continued, asking God for guidance and help in understanding Melodee's illness. He then asked to bring an end to her suffering, and that she would soon feel the love of God's embrace. What he didn't ask for was her recovery, her cure. Then he said, "Father, Give us strength to accept Thy will."

As deeply as I was basking in the peculiar warmth of the moment, my mind still tripped on those words. If he had *any* influence with God, he should be asking that Melodee be made whole. It sounded as if Shemnon had already consigned her to the grave. I shook the thought from my mind and tried to concentrate on the rest of the prayer, but found it difficult. Shemnon said a few more words and then ended his entreaty by invoking the power of the name of Jesus Christ.

These people are Christians? I thought the Aztecs, Incas, and Mayans—whom I assumed these people were descended from— were pagan-idol devotees who reveled in the worship of Quetzalcoatl and in bloody human sacrifice.

Melodee was crying, but not from sadness. Her waxy skin had a ghostly, cadaverous pallor, yet she smiled as if Shemnon had just promised a total remission of her cancer. Her sunken eyes shone with a light that revealed a trust in everything pronounced at her bedside. Try as I might, I could not understand her apparent gladness over Shemnon's words. I had no doubt that Melodee believed everything the old man had said. But to not promise her she was going to live was beyond any sense of tact or decorum. Still, I smiled and tried not to appear worried as she gazed at the faces of those surrounding her. She held her arms out to me, and I gladly accepted her embrace. She turned her head and kissed me on my cheek.

"Thank you for bringing me here, Uncle David," she whispered.

But I hadn't brought her here. Helam had. I think. I couldn't remember much of what happened after my fight with Gilberto. Then Melodee turned my face to meet hers and added, "Everything will be all right now. Don't worry; I'm not afraid."

But I was! I was nervous, mortified, downright scared. I chastised myself and felt ashamed. If I had even a particle of her faith, I would be a much better man. As it stood, while I appreciated the positive feelings these people were giving my sweet Mormon friend,

I still put my trust in the abilities of the young physician in the room—and even then held little hope for Melodee's survival.

"How can you not be afraid?" I said in barely more than a breath.

"I know there is something better on the other side." Her eyes misted over, but that did not diminish the sparkle within. "I will see Grandma Braithwaite again, and I will get to meet Heavenly Father and Jesus."

"But you will be . . . dead." It hurt physically to say those words.

"Only my body will be, Uncle David. In the Resurrection, everyone will live again. Don't you believe that?"

I shook my head slowly, regretfully. I wanted more than anything to buoy up her spirit. But my inner turmoil at her imminent death did not allow for hope of anything. "I will miss you so much," I finally managed to choke out.

Then, as a tear trickled down Melodee's face, she whispered, "I love you."

I broke down unashamedly. I sobbed into her pillow, unable to meet the longing in her eyes, a longing which cried for a concurrence that everything would indeed be all right. "Oh, Melodee," I croaked through a constricted throat. "I love you too. I'm so sorry I couldn't do more—" My voice closed off as I held her tight, unable to even breathe.

Melodee closed her eyes. I felt her body go limp. Her breathing became slower, deeper. I wondered if she had heard my declaration of affection. I kissed her forehead and again whispered, "I love you."

As I climbed back onto my cot, I watched Ester measure another dose of the smelly amber liquid. I was still concerned it might be a toxic derivative of turpentine, some distillate of which I was unaware. Yet I held my tongue and did not protest. I no longer worried that continued dosing might build a lethal concentration in her adolescent system. Regretfully, I concluded it didn't matter. Her cancer had advanced to a point that nothing could be done to stop it.

These thoughts, as well as the words of Shemnon's prayer, continued to bounce around in my head as I tried to fall asleep. The rumbling thunder and gentle rain should have caressed me into a restful slumber, but instead, the sounds pummeled my frazzled nerves. What was it about Shemnon's prayer that had me so worried—and confused? He spoke of a devastating and sorrowful conclusion. And yet there was an unmistakable happiness lingering in the air.

I sat up, brought my knees to my chin, and buried my face in the folds of the blanket. Without thinking about it, I whispered repeatedly, "Father, help me understand. Father, help me believe . . ."

I don't remember when my prayer ended.

THIRTY

The wind whipped and complained, making sleep impossible. The curtain between Melodee and me remained drawn. I peeked in and saw Zeniff sitting next to her, holding her hand. He was asleep. Melodee looked terrible. Even in the semidarkness, I could see her condition had worsened. She was not going to make it.

Unable to bear any more, I left the room and wandered the halls of the building. I had to get my mind on something else before my heart broke in two. The petroglyphs moved, animated by occasional lightning and the flickering of wall sconces. What stories did they tell? What traditions carried on through their reliefs? I saw numerous images of feathered serpents, of people in the act of praying, and of star patterns representing the alignment of planets. One showed Saturn hovering above the North Pole, Jupiter below the South Pole. The pictograph made no sense, but I felt they were telling the story of things past and also foretelling things to come. To shift my thoughts from losing Melodee, I concentrated on deciphering the strange stone carvings. In fact, I was so lost in discerning their meaning that I did not hear Shemnon approach.

"They tell of the world and of my people," he said softly.

I jumped. "You scared me."

"I am sorry, David."

Regaining my composure, I asked, "What exactly do they say?"

"It is a sad story. It tells of good people turning bad and, sometimes, of bad people turning good. In the end, much good was lost, and many of my ancestors turned to evil ways and barbaric traditions."

"Who were your people?"

He shrugged. "Many of our ancient records are lost. Sadly, we do not know much about our forefathers. The traditions we hold onto are few, but they are plain and precious to us. That is why we do not wish to pollute them with influence from the outside world."

My mind, weary from the events of the day, did not lend itself to accepting things as they were. I felt I should trust this old man, but I was sick of mysteries and riddles. "Pollution—as in medicines that could help Melodee survive?" I grumbled.

He silently walked a few paces toward the veranda before answering. The wind played with wisps of his silver hair as he looked out on the grounds. "She is in God's hands now. Nothing would make me happier than to see her live."

"Then why don't you do something? Why can't I take her to a real doctor to get help?"

He stared without answering. I thought at first he hadn't heard me. When he finally spoke, his words carried a sharp undertone. "Did the child's doctors offer her any hope in *your* world?"

I was loath to admit it, but he had made a good point. "No, sir."

"Ester is a fine physician, but we do not rely on her skill alone. Faith must play a part in all things. Faith and trust."

Plopping angrily on a bench, I said, "How can you know that? Simply believing in something doesn't automatically make it happen. I would love to believe Melodee will not die, but that won't stop it from happening."

The village leader sat beside me. "I did not say *belief*. I said *faith*."

"Faith, belief—what's the difference?"

"You can believe anything you like, but until you act on that belief, it is nothing more than a wish. Faith requires a show of confidence, even in the midst of sorrow and doubt."

Something in the way this old man spoke made me feel I had heard the truth, even though I did not fully understand it. He was sure, confident, and without question. But there was a hesitancy also, a flicker of doubt that left an open end to his statement.

"I assume Ester has done all she can do. You even held a prayer service in Melodee's behalf, but Melodee still believes she is going to die." Then with much remorse, I added, "And so do I."

"Is that what your heart is telling you? That we should give up hope?" The old leader's gaze was penetrating.

I spit out, "I have. It would take a miracle to save her now."

He placed a gnarled hand on my knee. "David, my friend, you must give God a chance. We believe in miracles, but most miracles occur when we meet God halfway. Belief is required, but so is effort. Belief plus effort creates faith. We have done all we can. Now we must trust in God and let His will be done. If He chooses to call Melodee home, it will happen. If He chooses to let her stay, so it shall be."

"I wish I had your acceptance of things," I sighed.

Shemnon rose slowly and turned to face me. "Listen with your heart, with your spirit. Let your soul open to God's will, and you will find the comfort you seek. Do not give Him the answers you wish to hear, but hear the answers He wishes to give. Otherwise, you will be an unhappy man for a very long time."

I watched the village leader walk out into the rain and down the stone steps. His words echoed in my head. It ended up being a very long and sleepless night.

* * *

Morning brought a hard rain. The snapping of fat droplets against the lattice in the window and the moist gloominess beyond told me that the day was not one for a casual stroll along the river-bank. Then an ethereal sound pierced the thrumming drone of the rain. It was the tranquil, melodic voice of a child.

I am a child of God
And He has sent me here,
Has given me an earthly home
With parents kind and dear.

Melodee was singing. Her pure, sweet voice with its breathy overtone and slight vibrato carried the lyrics of her song as a whisper on the wind. It was a beautiful sound. I parted the curtain and peered in. She stopped singing, smiling at me sheepishly.

"Sorry. I hope I didn't wake you."

"You're alive," I blurted without thinking.

"I sure am. And it feels good."

"But—your leukemia, the turpentine—"

She frowned playfully. "Turpentine? What're you talking about?" she shrugged. "I still have leukemia, but . . . I think it's going to go away now."

I sat on the edge of her bed. "How can you be so sure?"

"I have faith in the Lord and trust in the skill of my doctor."

I couldn't think of anything with which to counter that simple logic. All my retorts would have been negative, and I wanted to offer nothing but positives from now on.

Physically, Melodee did look somewhat improved, but I knew she was still very ill. She looked at me with total innocence as she waited for me to respond.

"Please . . . don't stop singing," I muttered, struggling for anything to say.

"I'm a little embarrassed. Are you sure you wouldn't rather go for a walk or something?"

"It's raining cats and dogs and a few other critters I can't identify," I told her. "Please, I was touched by the words of your song."

"Okay."

She sang the words she had begun with and then continued through the rest of the song.

Lead me, guide me, walk beside me,
Help me find the way,
Teach me all that I must do
To live with Him someday.
I am a child of God,
And so my needs are great;
Help me to understand His words
Before it grows too late.
I am a child of God.
Rich blessings are in store,
If I but learn to do His will
I'll live with Him once more.

"I believe you already know all there is to know about His will, kiddo," I said. "Besides, I'm sure God wouldn't hesitate to help you learn if you didn't."

She favored me with a playful smirk and said, "That's not what the words are saying."

I mulled over what I had just heard and came up with the same conclusion as before. "It's not?"

"No. A lot of people think it's a song about a child asking Heavenly Father for guidance, but I don't think so."

"What's it about, then?"

"Listen to the chorus again: 'Lead me, guide me, walk beside me, help me find the way.' Who do you think is supposed to do all that for a child?"

It hit me like a ton of bricks. That's what a *parent* is supposed to do. This song was a child's plea to his or her earthly guardians. Melodee continued singing before I could answer.

"'Teach me all that I must do, to live with Him someday.' Who is supposed to do that teaching?"

"A mom and dad," I answered.

"Very good. A-plus, Professor Kirkham."

On a secular level, I fully accepted the responsibility of teaching Paige the knowledge of this world. I figured she would always get straight A's in school—one, because she was naturally brilliant (that's the proud father in me talking), and two, because both Dyana and I encouraged and assisted her whenever she struggled with a new concept. But what about teachings on a *spiritual* level? How many parents claiming a belief in God let others take the lead in religious learning and spiritual understanding? Did that task superficially fall to Sunday School teachers or pontificating ministers? Or—as in my case—was it conveniently ignored?

The words to Melodee's song rang through my head with a clarion call to repentance. It didn't matter that I wasn't a church-going sort myself. Because of my apathy in religious matters, the responsibility of teaching Paige about a loving God was something I had willingly neglected. I remembered my parents saying bedtime prayers and offering grace before meals. Regretfully, it was a tradition I had not continued. If I had failed my family as an earthly father, the realization that I had also failed in a spiritual sense grieved my soul as nothing had before.

"What's wrong, Uncle David?"

I felt like I was going to throw up. "Nothing."

As if reading my thoughts, Melodee said, "It's not too late to start, you know."

"Assuming we get home," I tried to jest. As soon as I said it, I remembered what old Shemnon had said several days ago.

"We will," Melodee said matter-of-factly.

"But Shemnon said he doubts we'll ever leave this place."

"That was before."

I waited, then asked, "Before what?"

"Before he saw the change in you. He is impressed with your willingness to learn about God—you know, reading the scriptures and all. He told me that before, he was concerned you were too worldly minded, and that you would unintentionally bring his people to ruin if you left."

"He knows what the Book of Mormon is?"

"No. I just told him it is a book of scripture. And he can see the difference it is making in you."

"But he doesn't even know me. How can he see a difference?"

She shrugged. "He is a very wise man."

"He told you he'll let us leave?"

"Well, not in those words. But I think he recognizes our faith in God. And because of his lineage, he trusts us enough to let us go."

"His lineage? You mean Mayan?"

"No. Nephite."

"Nephite—as in the Book of Mormon?" I asked, almost laughing. The idea seemed completely ludicrous.

"I don't know for sure, but it's possible."

The concept contradicted something I had read earlier. I grabbed Melodee's Book of Mormon and opened to the introduction. "Look here," I showed her. "It says all the Nephites were wiped out and only the Lamanites remained. They're the forefathers of the American Indians."

My evidence didn't faze her. "How far are you in the Book of Mormon?"

"Middle of Alma, why?"

"So you've already read about the Mulekites and the search parties sent out by Limhi and King Benjamin, and the records they found of a lost civilization, and the people of Zeniff and the priests of Noah—"

"Whoa, slow down," I interrupted. Her recap was impressive, but I didn't see how it explained anything. "Yes, I remember all that. So?"

"What I'm saying is that there are many cultures and civilizations and people that wandered off that are briefly mentioned but never fully talked about. I guess Mormon either didn't have access to their histories or they weren't important enough to be included in the final abridgement."

"But it says specifically that the people of Nephi were wiped out," I persisted.

"And that was probably true in the land where the record was being kept at the time. Just keep reading. Toward the end of Alma, you'll read about Corianton, who leads a large group of Nephites to the land northward. They are lost to everyone from then on. And about a man named Hagoth who sails off with some Nephites, then returns, then sails off a second time and is never heard from again. What it doesn't say is why those people left or where the Lord took them or what ever became of them."

Sailing off on some sacred voyage? "Maybe they went to Tahiti for a vacation," I quipped.

"That may be closer to the truth than you think," she answered with a twinkle in her eyes.

I didn't have anything with which to argue the point. "So you honestly think the people of this village are descendants of Nephi?"

"Some might be."

"Then this is the most important anthropologic discovery of the century," I announced with a good measure of awe.

"It would be if everyone accepted the Book of Mormon as true. Trouble is, even though scholars have proven the accuracy of Joseph Smith's translation, and that with his limited education he could not have written the Book of Mormon himself, not everyone believes it's true. Do you know why not?"

I shrugged my shoulders.

"Because that would mean everything else about Mormonism is true. Our church leaders have always said the Book of Mormon is the keystone of our religion. You do know what a keystone is, don't you?"

"Of course."

"Well?"

I pondered what Melodee was saying and saw the logic in it. However . . . it shouldn't be difficult to validate. "But if the book can be vindicated then why doesn't your church use those facts to prove its authenticity?"

She sighed heavily. I couldn't tell if it was from fatigue or from her frustration in explaining things to me. She closed her eyes and spoke more softly.

"How many times has a concept in science been accepted as fact and then later proven wrong?"

"More than I can count," I chuckled.

"So how would you feel if something you accepted as truth—because it was once proven true—was suddenly disproved?"

"Like I had been cheated, I guess."

"My dad says scholars have 'proven' Jesus never lived in the times and places the Bible says He did. Other scientists have come up with physical explanations for each of the ten plagues of Moses, proving they were not acts of God. Some are now saying that genetic samples from Middle Eastern and Native American cultures don't match, proving Lehi didn't bring his family here. What do you think of that?"

I shrugged, not knowing how to answer Melodee, but intrigued by the pattern of logic she pursued. I couldn't wait to see where it was leading, and yet I had a sinking feeling I already knew.

I offered, "So you're saying that someone will always come up with something to disprove someone else's beliefs."

"Always," she said, her eyes still closed.

I asked the next question without first forming it in my mind. "So how does anyone know for certain the Book of Mormon is true?" As soon as I asked it, I instantly recalled the promise mentioned in the introduction and knew I was trapped.

Melodee's eyes slowly opened and focused on me with such intensity I felt as if she were looking directly into my soul. "Keep reading. You'll see."

* * *

By noon the rain had passed. An hour or so later, Ester and Helam came to put us through our physical therapy. I didn't feel I needed it but went along for Melodee's sake. Ester gave her whatever potion she had brewed that morning, made her work up a sweat, then cleansed her in the sauna and rinsed her in a pool. Melodee swallowed more of the strong-smelling amber liquid, and then took a nap. I held little hope in the success of this therapy, but Melodee expressed such faith in these natives (whoever they were) and such profound faith in her God, that I didn't want to be the pessimist who brought her spirits back to reality. Each morning it seemed like we had taken one step forward, but by evening it felt as if we had moved two steps back.

As Melodee napped through the afternoon, I sat in the wisteria-cloaked arbor and read. Helam joined me and looked over my shoulder, as if he were reading along. He always had a ready smile on his weathered face and seemed pleased at my progress in the book. At one point I tried to turn a page and he stopped me, holding the page open as if needing to finish a particular passage.

"Can you read this?" I asked with playful annoyance.

His eyes twinkled and he shrugged.

"Is this story about you and your people?" I figured if anyone would know it would be him.

He said nothing.

"Do you even know what this book is?"

He took the book and pointed at the front jacket, which read *Book of Mormon, Another Testament of Jesus Christ*, and pointed to Jesus' name. Something in me warmed to the thought and told me that an understanding of the Son of God was more important than knowing Helam's genealogy or relationship to the people in this book. And despite my insatiable curiosity, I felt content with that answer.

I liked this old man and his simple way of expressing himself. I only wished I could communicate with him better. He turned back to the page we had stopped on and motioned for me to continue reading.

"Wait, how come you seem to understand me every once in a while? And don't give me the 'I don't know' blow-off, please."

Helam placed a hand on my shoulder and looked at me with a kindness I thought would melt my soul. Then he pulled me into a hug and held me tight. I didn't know how to respond, so I patted his back, indicating he could release me. I was admittedly uncomfortable with such an open show of affection. I moved to break the embrace, but he held on tenaciously. Then he moved his mouth to my ear and whispered a Bible passage in Spanish.

"If any man hath ears to hear, let him hear."

I chuffed. "You speak Spanish?" I asked in that language.

"No."

"But . . ."

Holding his index finger close to his thumb, Helam said, "Un poco." He then turned and walked away without further explanation.

My mind was befuddled. Nothing made sense, even though I was trying so hard to understand. Shemnon kept telling me to listen with my heart, not my mind. If I had ears to hear, let them hear. Don't overanalyze. Don't require proof of everything. Don't prejudge. And, most often, have more faith. In other words, to go against every teaching I had ever had. I was a man of science, for heaven's sake. Proving things was what I did. I had always tried to keep my mind open to new ideas, but not so far open that my brains fell out. What my new friends were asking went against everything that was in me, against my very nature.

THIRTY-ONE

I kept reading the Book of Mormon and pondering, and even praying, but the distractions were ubiquitous. Helam frequented my side, always smiling, clinging to me like a noonday shadow. Incessant ponderings over Dyana and Paige entered my mind trailing dark clouds of remorse. But most of my thoughts lingered on Melodee. She wasn't getting much better. She'd have her occasional bursts of energy in which her ailments lessened significantly, but then she'd lapse back into her near-catatonic state, and the sickly gray pallor would return to her skin. It worried me constantly and ate at me because I felt there was nothing I could do. I frequently asked Shemnon if he could show me the way to a modern village or city so I could bring back help and real medicine, but he always refused. I guess I couldn't blame him. The village leader wanted his people to remain a secret from the world, and bringing help would destroy that anonymity. I promised not to reveal anything about Cumorah but inwardly knew that would be impossible. Even most Third World countries place certain restrictions on modern medicines, and without proper identification and credentials, I wouldn't be able to get much more than some painkillers and perhaps some penicillin.

So I kept pondering, trying to ignore the threat of finding Melodee dead one morning, and trying desperately to piece together the events of the past few weeks to learn why I was going through all this.

That evening I decided to read again. We had a brief respite of pleasant weather, but it had begun to mist again. Ester had just given Melodee her supper: another bowl of the coarsely ground barley and rice porridge. Melodee asked me to say evening prayers with her, then turned over and went right to sleep.

I left the room and sat under the veranda of stone at the door to our hospital. A torch braced in a wall sconce illuminated the pages of Melodee's Book of Mormon. It was an evening conducive to study, and my mind seemed to focus as never before on the pages in my hands.

All day I had been struggling with the concept of faith. To me, faith was the inability to prove something. It was the religious person's scapegoat for living as they did. But Melodee and Shemnon kept referring to faith as a *means* of proof. That confused me. Proof was something tangible, something anyone could repeat over and over, and always achieve the same results. Two plus two would always equal four. That would never change. I believed in knowledge. They believed in faith. Somehow, the two had to connect—I simply couldn't see how. Then I read in Alma 32 verse 21: *And now as I said concerning faith—faith is not to have a perfect knowledge of things; therefore if ye have faith ye hope for things which are not seen, which are true.*

My heart thumped an arrhythmic beat. It made sense! I certainly did not have a perfect knowledge. I knew a lot—probably more than your average Joe—but my knowledge wasn't absolute. And just because I couldn't see or prove something didn't mean it was untrue. There were vast amounts of truth in the world, much discovered, much still hidden, but that didn't make the undiscovered portions false. It was all so simple.

I looked at the book in my hands with newfound respect. What was it about this tome, about the feelings I got each time I humbled myself, pushed my stubborn analytical nature aside, and absorbed the book's messages? What was it about Melodee's self-confidence, the solid assuredness she showed even in times of adversity that gave her strength beyond her years? What gave her the unshakable optimism that everything would be all right, regardless of the outcome? Was this faith? And if it was, how could I obtain it? My heart ached for this knowledge with an intensity I could not express. Who could I turn to for the answers? How could I learn to benefit from this awesome power?

A breeze fluttered the pages of the Book of Mormon. I continued to read. Alma mentioned that at first, no one could know for sure the truthfulness of his words. Then: "But behold, if ye will awake and arouse your faculties, even to an experiment upon my words . . ." I liked the sound of that. I didn't have to take anyone's word for it. I could experiment with these things myself. ". . . and exercise a particle of faith, yea, even if ye can do no more than desire to believe . . ."

That's exactly what I had been doing. I wanted to understand what made these things so incredible to some, so marvelous to others, and so life-changing to millions. More importantly, I wanted to *believe* in these things myself. ". . . let this desire work in you, even until ye believe in a manner that ye can give place for a portion of my words."

I felt confident I could believe—in my own manner, my own way of thinking—to allow a *place* in me for Alma's words to work. The prophet then went on to give an example of how to accomplish this. He used the analogy of a seed—something with which I, as a botanist, was very familiar. Alma said to plant the seed and allow it to grow. Don't kill it with unbelief but nourish it with hope; give it a chance. And when it begins to grow you will feel a swelling within you.

I flinched and drew a quick breath of amazement. I had felt those feelings! Several times, in fact. Was that what it was—the seed of faith beginning to grow? The verse went on to explain that this was a good sign, and if I treated it as a good thing and allowed it to grow, it would begin to enlarge my soul and would begin to enlighten my understanding. And it would become delicious to me.

A light burned in my soul and coursed through my body like a magnificent beacon. It filled my entire being with a comprehension that had me breathless. I tried to read more, but my eyes blurred with tears that appeared without warning. Suddenly, it was all clear to me. I quickly wiped my eyes and focused on the page. Alma said if the swelling enlightened your soul—which it did mine—then you could be assured it was a good seed. Then verse 34 explained how once you knew what was happening, your faith was now a perfect knowledge "in *that* thing."

And it was. My soul had swelled with emotion, my understanding had been enlightened, and my mind was beginning to venture into realms I had never before ventured. I continued reading, "O then, is this not real?" It most certainly was! It was more real than I thought I would ever admit. Faith wasn't the mindless wanderings of uneducated individuals. It wasn't the blind being led by the blind. It wasn't the scapegoat for things unproved. It was the doorway to greater understanding and knowledge and light. And I wanted to run through that doorway at full speed.

* * *

A gentle hand and a soft voice stirred me from my sleep. My eyes focused on a beautiful face, that of the young physician. I smiled weakly and said good morning.

Ester mentioned Melodee's name in a sentence dripping with pride.

"Something bad has happened to Melodee?" I said, holding my head and willing the morning brain-fog to clear.

"Not bad. Good," she said, flashing a proud thumbs-up.

"She's no longer sick? No, that can't be." I tried not to let Ester's confidence in an obvious medical error get me excited. I wanted her to be right, but I knew she was wrong. "I think you might be jumping to conclusions, doc. Melodee may be *feeling* better but she has terminal cancer. She's going to die."

The young physician put her fists on her hips and favored me with a look of exasperated condescension. "No," she snapped.

I lumbered out of bed and put on my shirt. "I'd like to believe you, but I don't think it's possible. You see, there is no known cure for her kind of cancer."

I pulled aside the curtain and found Melodee's bed empty.

Ester pantomimed eating. She then pointed at my stomach and asked something in her mysterious language.

"Yeah, I'm starved."

We found Melodee talking with Shemnon through mouthfuls of porridge. There were two banana peels beside her half-finished bowl and a partial cup of orange juice. The old man laughed with an overflowing dose of admiration as he conversed with the little girl.

"Good morning," I said tentatively.

"Morning, Uncle David," Melodee chirped. "Did you sleep well?"

"Fine. How're you feeling?"

"Great. Want some breakfast?"

Ignoring her question, I asked, "Great, as in okay for now . . . ?"

She smirked. "Great as in great. I think my cancer is almost gone."

"She is much better," Shemnon interjected. "And she has an amazing appetite."

I had to admit Melodee looked very well. Her skin had regained a rosy hue, and her eyes were clear and bright. Her cheeks were still hollow from a lack of nourishment, but the skin didn't sag from her bones with the same lifelessness it had yesterday. She looked as if she were ready for a day at the beach: perky, healthy, happy.

"How?" I asked no one in particular.

"Whole-grain food, lots of water, exercise, and Zypaka," the village leader answered.

"Zypaka?" I questioned.

As if understanding our conversation, Ester nodded.

"What is Zypaka?"

Shemnon stood and signaled to a server in the kitchen area. "You must eat first. You need to regain your strength. We can talk of medicine later."

Food sounded great right then, but I couldn't take my eyes off Melodee. I had been certain she would not live out the week. Yet, here she was, looking as if she had recovered from nothing more than the stomach flu. Her appetite was obvious; however, when someone placed a plate of fried leeks, scrambled eggs with sun-dried tomatoes and bell peppers, and a cup of goat's milk before me, my questions instantly took second place to my stomach. I was ravenous.

While we ate our breakfast, Ester excused herself. Shemnon continued to talk to us about his people and the village of Cumorah. Melodee asked all sorts of questions that I was sure came from her knowledge of the Book of Mormon. Shemnon knew nothing of that book but felt it might be a record of his ancestors. More importantly, he said they had records of their own, which they kept on thin metal plates of gold. *Just like the ones Joseph Smith had discovered and translated,* I mused.

"Platos de oro," Melodee said aloud.

"Yes," the old man chucked. "*Planchas* de oro. We keep them hidden, but I'll let you see them if you like."

Something sparked in my memory. The word *oro* echoed in my head, and I knew it answered a mystery that had bothered me for some time. Now suddenly it was wonderfully clear.

"That's what the drug men were asking Helam for," I blurted, as if everyone knew to what I was referring. When I saw the questioning looks, I laughed. "The men who took us captive; I thought they had asked him where the bull was—the *toro*. But they wanted the gold—the *oro*."

"Many people know of our village, but few have ever found it. With mystery comes much speculation. Cumorah is rumored to be paved with gold," Shemnon chuckled, "so many search for it all their lives."

"Like Ponce de Leon and the Fountain of Youth?" Melodee asked.

"I do not know that name," our old friend responded, "but many have let the desire for riches ruin their lives."

"How did they capture Helam?" I wanted to know.

"Occasionally, we go out to gather meat and other necessities. We always try to avoid contact with others, but it sometimes happens."

I was cautiously amazed. "But surely some outsiders have found their way to Cumorah, haven't they?"

He shrugged as if it wasn't important. "Yes, but we have ways of remaining hidden."

A brutal image came to mind, one of Aztec human sacrifices and blood rituals. "You don't . . . kill them?" I hesitated to ask.

Shemnon burst out laughing. "And risk eternal punishment? No. They live. They simply cannot remember how they got here."

I was about to open that cryptic can of worms when Ester returned with a small vial of her pungent, amber liquid. This she handed to Melodee and motioned for her to drink it.

"This stuff is yucky."

"It does not taste good, but it will make certain your healing," the village leader explained in a consoling tone.

Ester nodded as if confirming Shemnon's statement.

"Make certain her healing?" I asked, not understanding the gist of his words.

"Her cancer is sleeping, but it is still there. Melodee needs many more days, perhaps even months, before she is fully healed."

Since I had lost track of time, a few days didn't seem like that big a deal. Besides, I was currently enjoying my study of the Book of Mormon and didn't want to rush through it for anything.

I dipped my fingertip into the vial and held a drop of the liquid to the sunlight. Tiny, reddish particles remained suspended in the amber droplet, even though the liquid itself was not very viscous. "This is . . . ?"

"Zypaka," Ester said.

"It destroys Melodee's cancer," Shemnon explained.

His words slammed like a hammer to my chest. At first, I couldn't breathe, reciting the old man's last statement in my mind. "This stuff *cures* cancer?" I gasped. Why it hadn't occurred to me earlier, I didn't know. Not waiting for an answer, I barked, "Where does it come from?"

"A small tree. It grows far from here, high in the mountains."

I was on my feet. "Show me!" I nearly shouted.

"Perhaps later. The way is very dangerous, and today is not good."

My voice quavered from barely restrained excitement. "Please. I don't care how dangerous. I *need* to know what tree this comes from!"

"Zypaka," Ester said, shaking her head as if to emphasize the *we already told you* tone in her voice.

"Look, I know many trees and plants. A great many. But I don't recognize that name," I explained.

Ester stared at me with a furrowed brow for a long time. She then turned to Shemnon with eyebrows raised. He rattled off a Cumorish sentence that bounced off my brain. While speaking, he pointed to the vial in my hands and then to the mountains in the distance.

Ester eyed me with unmasked suspicion then slowly nodded. I shouted, "Yahoo!" like a child on a thrill ride. They exchanged a few more words before Shemnon turned back to me. I was dancing in place, unable to hold still. A few of the villagers close by could not contain their laughter at my antics. I didn't care.

"Tomorrow," the village leader said with a poorly restrained smile. "Now it is time for your exercise and bath."

I struggled to keep my emotions from exploding. I was literally shaking from nervous anticipation. If Ester was right and this Zypaka stuff actually could cure cancer, I didn't care how much gold the village of Cumorah hid. Suddenly my entire world revolved around one thing: how soon tomorrow would come.

THIRTY-TWO

When Ester explained through Shemnon that Zypaka grew year round and that the medicinal extract was derived from seeds found in a central conelike structure, I assumed it was an evergreen. When she mentioned that the cone formed in the center of a whorl of fronds, I suspected it was an *ancient* evergreen. When she said that it only blossomed every three to five years, I didn't know whether to be angry or disappointed, or to simply break down and cry. I brooded over the information most of the evening, and then decided it didn't matter. If I wasn't able to retrieve a cone sample right away, I could still identify the plant, and then could proceed from there.

From a detailed sketch Ester penned on a piece of parchment, I deduced that Zypaka was a type of primitive conifer, a gymnosperm along the order of *Cycadales,* the most ancient evergreen known. The plant actually resembles a cross between a fern and a small palm tree, but is not genetically related to either. At least not in the last million years. The reddish seeds produced in Zypaka's conelike strobilus contained the oil from which the medicine was derived.

Of course, all of this was purely speculative until I actually obtained a real specimen. But the anticipation of finding a species that heretofore had been undiscovered—and that, according to Ester, contained an anticancer chemical—had me indescribably excited.

After a sleepless night, I was wrested from bed before the sun was up. The physician had me dress quickly and quietly, then placed Zeniff in charge of Melodee's physical therapy while we were gone. Together—with Helam in tow—we headed out into the darkness.

The trail we took was brutal. It led almost straight up a very steep mountain—more like a cliff, actually. Many times, we climbed tree trunks and branches to reach the next narrow plateau of rock and dirt. I was panting heavily, but the excitement coursing through my veins kept me stimulated with enough adrenalin that I didn't mind the exertion. In a matter of minutes, we lost sight of Cumorah.

We finally crested the ridge and began a meandering trek through jungle so choked with vegetation that I couldn't tell north from south, east from west, or even what time of day it was. All too soon, we came to another cliff and began another grueling ascent. I wasn't shocked at Ester's abilities to tackle these slopes; she was lean and lithe and had a physique and stamina that would be the envy of most athletes. But the fact that old Helam wasn't even puffing hard lambasted my egocentric machismo and humbled me to a level slightly above that of total wimp.

Upon reaching the upper ridge, I half expected to get a view of the sky, but the towering canopy allowed only a brief glimpse or two of a blanket of dark clouds, and the treachery of the narrow trails kept my gaze focused on each footfall rather than the surrounding views. Finally, we began a descent that was just as painful as the journey up.

We paused when Ester noticed my wobbling legs and sweat-soaked shirt. Helam produced a flask from which we shared swallows of cool, refreshing water. He passed around slices of dried papaya to eat as we rested a few minutes. Just as my breathing slowed to a normal rhythm, we set out again. If I had entertained any thoughts as to memorizing the way to the Zypaka trees, they had been quelled long ago.

At one point Helam indicated that we should slow our pace and be as quiet as possible. In a few simple words, he explained that there were strange and mysterious people in this area, and we would be better off if we didn't bump into them. Helam calling a little-known group of people "strange and mysterious" was like the proverbial pot calling the kettle black, but I thought it best not to share that insight with him.

Later on, we crested a hill that offered a clear view of the surrounding landscape. I gave a low whistle of amazement as I saw nothing but a vast ocean of green: an undulating expanse of treetops as far as the eye could see, with no visible breaks to indicate a valley, river, or human civilization. It was easy to understand how Cumorah could remain a secret so easily in this ultradense milieu of tropical rain forest.

Again, we climbed upward. Forget the Tower of Babel; I felt certain that at any moment we'd pierce the veil of heaven.

I stumbled and found myself sitting on a log, breathing coarsely. Ester stopped and gave me a questioning thumbs-up, her deep green eyes filled with concern.

"Groovy," I answered, wondering if she would understand that enigmatic phrase from the sixties.

She smiled and patted my shoulder. "You good man, David." I assumed she had picked up those bits of English by listening to conversations between Melodee, Shemnon, and me. She obviously had a brilliant mind. Picking up a word or two of a foreign language would be nothing to her. "Melodee trust you."

I understood her words but didn't agree with them. *Melodee trusts me?* For the life of me, I couldn't figure out what inspired that trust. I had been the bumbling oaf of this adventure. She was the one who kept the positive attitude and showed more self-assured confidence than anyone I had ever met. And yet she was the one dying from leukemia.

Not anymore, I corrected myself. *Or, at least I hope that's the case.* After all, I was going on the word of a semiprimitive, disturbingly young though exceptionally pretty, tribal healer. Only time would tell.

Soon we found ourselves walking through mist-enshrouded, gloomy jungle the likes of which could have spawned a scene in *Jurassic Park.* The fog was so thick it was hard to tell it from rain. We were soaked to the bone in a matter of minutes. Ferns and mosses abounded along the vague trail, and flowering vines and huge orchids laced back and forth, creating a scene that was downright primordial.

At a junction in the trail, Ester chose the fainter path, which we followed to a scattering of small, murky pools. Immediately I noticed some brilliant colors that moved in and out of the pools: bright, fluorescent oranges, blues, reds, and purples in random shapes and patterns.

Ester cautioned me not to touch them when I realized the colors were actually tiny frogs. "Bad," she said.

"Malo," Helam concurred.

I nodded. "I know. They're poison dart frogs. Their skin secretes a neurotoxin that's the most lethal in the animal world, even more deadly than snakes and spiders."

I couldn't tell whether Ester caught any of that statement, but she recognized I knew of their potential danger and moved on.

Finally, we came to a patch of what she called Zypaka. It was a small copse of gymnosperms standing beneath a canopy of tree ferns. I was correct in my earlier guess: these were definitely an unknown species of primitive cycad. My pulse quickened as I began to analyze and classify the small conifers. What I wouldn't have given for a pencil and notebook, a camera and sterile collection box. I looked down the whorl of each of the three-foot-high trees and sighed heavily. I found no cones inside.

Ester shrugged her shoulders, stating the obvious.

"Just my luck," I said more to myself than to my companions. My heart sank, but I continued to scrutinize every detail of the rare trees before me. I tried to burn a visual record into my brain so I could sketch them out later. I asked question after question about their life cycle and reproduction, their habitat and growth patterns, and more importantly, the characteristics of their seeds and how the amber liquid was derived from the oils within. Ester was very patient and responded as best she could, but the depth of my queries was often rewarded with no more than a shrug and an apologetic look from her green eyes.

We stayed in the area for little more than an hour. While Helam and Ester rested, I wandered about like a child in a candy store, discovering one tantalizing find after another. Much sooner than I had hoped, Helam indicated it was time to head back.

The journey home was a blur as my mind rehearsed the images I had seen that afternoon.

* * *

That night I asked for a writing instrument and some parchment to catalogue as much as I could remember about the Zypaka. Melodee was already asleep. Oh, how I wanted to wake her and share the things I had learned! But her enthusiasm for botanical science was probably equal to that of mine for country-western music—which wavered between zero and negative numbers. Instead, I picked up the Book of Mormon and began to read. I was immediately engrossed in the words of Alma and the events of the Nephite and Lamanite people. I felt comfortable reading those sacred words, and I was able to attest to their validity without a second thought. That surprised me, because it was so opposite my usual nature. But I didn't fight it. I let the feeling wash through me, instilling me with a profound respect for the Nephite people and their astounding leaders. Such knowledge, such wisdom could be learned from those who had gone before. I scoffed at the thought of anthropologists who claimed that all ancient cultures were primitive. Look at what I had learned in just a few days among a seemingly "primitive" people.

As I continued to read, I came to a verse that seemed to jump from the page. Alma chapter 46, verse 40 read:

And there were some who died with fevers, which at some seasons of the year were very frequent in the land—but not so much so with fevers, because of the excellent qualities of the many plants and roots which God had prepared to remove the cause of diseases, to which men were subject by the nature of the climate . . .

I was witnessing a fulfillment of that scripture. I was seeing firsthand the tools of ancient times used in a modern dispensation. The scientific community had a lot to learn by looking forward, but I marveled at the vast amounts of knowledge to be gained by looking back.

In that instant, the blessings Melodee had promised me long ago came to mind. I had been following her Word of Wisdom—even if some of the time, it had not been by choice. I had not consumed my mini-bottle of vodka, and I was reading and pondering, and even praying. I had made Melodee a promise, and now I was gaining wisdom and knowledge—great treasures of knowledge.

* * *

"How's your reading coming, Uncle David?"

"Just finished Alma, getting into Helaman." I held a finger to my chin and looked skyward as if pondering a great mystery. "Hmm, now why does that name sound so familiar? Helam—an . . ."

Melodee laughed. It was a wonderful, healing sound. She was getting better—there was no doubt in my mind. Ester had prolonged her life—potentially even curing her leukemia, although the young physician could not have known the severity of the disease. Again, only time would tell.

"Good name, good book," Melodee said with certain knowledge. "This is where it really gets good."

I had devoured the stories to that point and couldn't imagine how the book could get any better. "Why, what happens?"

"Just keep reading."

"Melodee," I whined. "That's not fair."

"Sure it is. If you're going to learn the truthfulness of the Book of Mormon, you have to do it on your own. It's between you and Heavenly Father now."

"No pressure there," I moaned jokingly. "Thanks a lot."

I noted that my little friend never asked me for my feelings about the book, whether I believed it or not. She simply encouraged me to keep reading and praying, and left it at that. There was no pressure, and that allowed me to learn at my own pace. But because of what I'd seen in Cumorah and—more importantly—from my experiences of a few nights before, I already knew the Book of Mormon was an accurate record of the inhabitants of early America.

However, I knew that was not what Melodee's question would be when I finished the book. She would ask me if I felt it was the word of God. Truthfully, whenever I asked myself that question, something inside me answered with a comforting assertion of, *Yes, of course it is.* But I wanted more. I wanted to know for certain, without a doubt that it was the word of God. And if it was, I wanted the rock-solid assurance I needed to find out what else Mormonism had to offer. As Melodee had stated, if I accepted the Book of Mormon, I had to accept the whole religion.

That afternoon, I begged out of Ester's physical therapy routine and sat in a grassy nook up against the roots of an enormous ironwood tree. A stream trickled next to the grassy area and sang a soothing tune as I opened the Book of Mormon to a place I had marked earlier. A prophet named Samuel, a Lamanite, was preaching to a bunch of wicked Nephites.

Samuel the Lamanite was prophesying about the coming of Jesus Christ. I found it fascinating that the people of this continent would know of something happening thousands of miles away on another continent. But it made sense. If Jesus was Lord of the whole earth, why shouldn't the whole earth know of His coming?

Gadiantons, wickedness, some political intrigue, stripling warriors, righteous Lamanites, etc. Third Nephi started off with a bang. The sun passed overhead without my notice. I was so engrossed in the words of the book I didn't even stop to eat. I kept reading and reading. I felt as if I were actually wandering the streets of Zarahemla, listening to the warnings of the righteous and feeling remorse and frustration at the sins of those who should know better.

Chapter 8: worldwide destruction at Christ's crucifixion. I found my pulse quickening, my concentration rapt. Chapters 9 and 10: the voice of Christ speaks to the people of Zarahemla. My breathing turned shallow and staccato. The world around me ceased to exist. The voice of the stream faded into silence.

Then a chapter synopsis stated, "Jesus Christ did show himself unto the people of Nephi, as the multitude were gathered together in the land Bountiful, and did minister unto them; and on this wise did he show himself unto them."

My mouth was agape. *Jesus came here? To America?* A rush of
wonderment drenched me as if from a waterfall. I was inundated with
such an overwhelming feeling of joy that I could scarcely breathe. It
was beautiful, so real, and so right. That Jesus would come to this
continent to teach this people made so much sense that I didn't question it. I remembered the introduction mentioning Christ's ministry
among the Nephites, but I didn't think it was literal. I sat up straighter
and read as quickly as I could without missing anything. I finished the
third book of Nephi and the fourth, and was just into Mormon when
I noticed that a torch, not the sun, created the light on the pages.
Without my noticing, night had fallen, and someone had secured a
torch in a crook of the ironwood tree. I had read hours past sunset.

I eased to my feet, moving slowly because my legs were numb.
Upon returning to our room, I found Melodee sitting in her bed.
The drawn curtain created one large space.

Seeing the book in my hand, she asked, "Pretty cool, huh?"

That wasn't a fitting word for what I had just read, but from the
mouth of a preteen, I guess it worked. "Way cool," I answered.
"Why doesn't the rest of the world know about this?"

"Hey, we're working on it. My brother's on a mission in Japan,
remember?"

"Oh yeah," I admitted sheepishly.

"People hear the title 'Mormon' and immediately think of
nonsmoking, nondrinking weirdoes who still practice polygamy.
They seldom let us show them what we really have to offer."

"A better lifestyle?"

"No, silly. Another testimony of Jesus Christ. That's the purpose
of the Book of Mormon. It's not to prove Joseph Smith was a
prophet or that we're the only true church on earth. The main reason
is to convince everyone—including you, Dr. David Kirkham—that
Jesus is the Christ, that He died for our sins, and that we can live
with Him again. What better message could there be?"

My eyes misted and my heart swelled. This little girl's words
were pure and true. I couldn't respond to her question because my
throat had tightened, but it didn't matter. I couldn't think of a satis-
factory rebuttal, nor did I want to.

THIRTY-THREE

The next few days were reminiscent of my college years. I spent my time studying from sunup to sundown, my whole attention focused on learning. Ester was a gracious and patient teacher, but I sensed she was hesitant to divulge everything she knew. I learned bits of her language and she learned pieces of mine. I learned that much of what Ester knew had been handed down from healer to healer, and that she was reticent to admit that much of it was guess-work—trial by error—sometimes a surprising success, other times a disastrous failure. I tried to explain that many of the world's greatest discoveries were simply lucky guesses, but she only smirked at that, as if she knew I was trying to make her feel better. As a translator, Shemnon was a huge asset, although he seemed somewhat bored by the scientific nature of our discussions.

I also spent many hours reading the Book of Mormon. Here Melodee became my teacher. Although still a child, she fully understood the principles of faith and repentance and redemption through Jesus Christ. Dyana and I had discussed such things in the past and had many a minister in the churches she'd dragged me to try to explain them to us, but no religious teacher had ever come close to making the ideas plausible. Even though I knew faith had a lot to do with religion, I still felt it should make sense, too. None of this *God is a mystery and can't be comprehended* nonsense. Melodee helped confirm my feelings by quoting from her Doctrine and Covenants. She said the glory of God was intelligence, and whatever principle of intelligence we gained in this life would rise with us in the hereafter. And the more we learned now, the better off we'd be later. Now *that* made sense.

I wondered how Dyana would feel about me getting so involved in the Book of Mormon. I marveled at how caught up I was in learning about the mission of Jesus on the earth. The more I read, the more I wanted to learn. Just like Melodee's father had said, the more I knew, the more I knew I didn't know. And because of my insatiable inquisitiveness, I wanted to know everything.

At length I came to the book of Moroni. I felt a twinge of disappointment in that I realized I would soon be finished. But the feeling was also accompanied by a measure of anticipation and excitement to read the entire book again. I had been well into Alma's writings before I discovered *how* I should be reading the book. When I expressed this to Melodee, she told me that spiritual things could not be discerned with a temporal mind, but that the two often testified of and supported each other. Now that I understood that, I couldn't wait to start over and discover the things I missed before.

"That's very common in our church," she laughed.

"What is?"

"Discovering new things each time you open the Book of Mormon," she explained. "Ask anyone in the Church and they'll tell you every time they read it they learn something new. My dad says there've been times he's read a chapter for the fiftieth time and found a passage he swears was never there before."

I chuckled. "Then I can't wait to hurry through Moroni so I can start again."

A somber look came over her as her gaze pierced me. "Oh, don't do that, Uncle David. Don't rush through to the end. Some very important lessons are taught in Moroni. The most important has to do with you in particular."

I waited for further insight, but she remained silent. Finally, I asked, "What lessons?"

"You'll see."

I shook my head. "Somehow I knew you were going to say that."

"When you get to chapter 10, read the first five verses very carefully."

"Why?"

Another mischievous look.

"Never mind," I said.

I did as Melodee instructed and took my time. What a wonderful book. What an incredible man Moroni was. At last, I came to chapter 10 and paused. I was amused at how nervous I felt, like I was about to learn something that I knew would make a profound change in my life. If I chose to proceed, I knew I would be committed to follow through. If I chose to skip the last chapter, I knew I would never be able to face myself again. I took a deep breath and jumped in.

As I read, I discovered that Moroni sealed up the writings in the Book of Mormon for future generations. He exhorted those who read the words to ponder them in their hearts. Then he stated:

And when ye shall receive these things, I would exhort you that ye would ask God, the Eternal Father, in the name of Christ, if these things are not true; and if ye shall ask with a sincere heart, with real intent, having faith in Christ, he will manifest the truth of it unto you, by the power of the Holy Ghost.

That was it. The challenge. The ultimatum. The next step I had to take. I wondered how many people had breezed over those words without pondering their significance. I wondered if I would have done the same thing without Melodee's forewarning. It was the same challenge from the introduction that I thought would be my out-clause.

I had received these things, and read them. I was moved by the influence of the Spirit and felt they were true. But I still did not *know* like Melodee knew. And I wanted to. Oh, I wanted so desperately to know. Happily, I finally understood *how* I could. The formula was set, and all I had to do was follow it. I had to ask God, in the name of Jesus, if these things were true. However, it could not be done flippantly. I needed to ask with real intent. In other words, I had to ask with the understanding that I would continue to learn more about the Lord's gospel. I must ask, having faith that I would receive an answer—believing, anticipating, *expecting* an answer. And then I would obtain that answer.

I finished reading and slowly closed the book. It was almost as if I didn't need to ask. I knew. The feelings welling within me convinced me it was true. But I had committed to doing it the right way. I went back to the grassy nook by the creek and dropped to my knees. I bowed my head and took a deep, cleansing breath. I poured out my heart to a God I now knew was listening, a Father in Heaven I used to be so apathetic about. He wanted me to know the truth. He loved me enough to give me a friend like Melodee who had taught me these wonderful things. I felt so unworthy, so inept, so humbled.

"Father, God. I don't know why You have blessed me so much. Melodee has shown me the Book of Mormon and has testified to me. She is such an incredible little girl—a marvelous young woman, really. I love her with all my heart, as I'm sure You do. But I am at a crossroads. I feel these things are true, but I need to know. I need to know for certain. O God, Please tell me—"

My words choked off as my throat tightened. A comforting warmth poured over me, surrounded me, lifted my soul, radiated through me in a way that made me feel weightless, cleansed, free. A cool burning in my eyes and a wondrous searing in my chest filled me with such glory I could scarcely breathe.

"Please, my Father, let me know—"

"You already know."

My heart skipped a beat as I looked around quickly. Someone had spoken to me. Someone was listening in on my prayer.

Yet I saw no one. Nothing. I looked at the book in my hands and noticed it was covered with moisture. But it hadn't been raining. I realized at that moment that this book—this *true* book, this second witness to Jesus Christ—was moistened with my tears. I understood in that instant that the only person with me was the Holy Ghost. The intensity of my joy was beyond description. I knelt for I don't know how long, pouring out my heart, soaking in the Spirit, letting it teach and confirm, letting it testify that these things were true. I no longer needed to simply believe. I knew.

* * *

That evening I shared my good news with my friends. Shemnon simply nodded and walked away. Ester's countenance softened, and she indicated how happy she was for me. Helam took my hand in both of his and smiled at me with misty eyes. His expression showed me how proud he was of how far I'd come.

Melodee began to say something, but her words choked off in a sob of joy. Instead, she gave me a hug that would have melted the hardest steel. After a moment, she said, "I knew you'd find the truth, Uncle David. I just knew it. And to have the Spirit speak to you! Wow. What a great foundation for your testimony to grow from."

"You mean that isn't all there is?"

"Of course not, silly. A testimony is not a one-time thing. It's not like being 'born again' the way you usually hear about. A testimony grows line upon line, precept upon precept. It's something you have to work constantly to maintain or you'll lose it. And you still have so much to learn."

That was a fact I was all too aware of, and it gnawed at my conscience deeply. I dropped my gaze and shuffled my feet. "I know."

Sensing my hesitancy, Melodee asked, "What's the matter?"

"I feel so blessed to have found these things. But I can't help but wonder how this will affect my wife and daughter. They may have given up on me already. I can't wait to share this with them, but do they even know I'm still alive? And if I ever do get back, will they accept the Book of Mormon as I have?"

"I wish I had an answer for you," Melodee said. "Your family sounds like a great one. I'd love to meet your daughter someday."

"I'd like that too. But . . ."

"I have been speaking with Shemnon and the village elders," Melodee said. "I think they are convinced I am not a danger to them."

"But not me," I added remorsefully.

"Shemnon has told them of your growing faith. There may be a chance."

"A chance for what?"

She smiled. "For us to return home."

* * *

"You must never reveal anything about our village or our people," Shemnon said with a forcefulness that could easily have been a threat as well as a plea.

"We won't," Melodee answered for both of us.

He stared at us, through us, for a long while without speaking. "Yes, I believe that is true."

My heart was beating rapidly. "How will we find a way out? Last I checked we're in the center of an immense rain forest in the middle of nowhere."

"David, your faith is young and has much potential for growing," Shemnon said tenderly. "Allow it to grow."

"Yes, sir," I said, duly chastened.

"Also, you must never mention the experiences you have had in Cumorah," the village leader added. "Not even the things our healer has taught you."

"But . . . how will we explain Melodee's recovery?" I asked.

To Melodee he said, "Ester tells me you are not fully cured yet. You must use the elixir for several more weeks before you are free from the cancer. Even then, there is a chance it can come back."

"And if she does fully recover?" I asked, leading.

Shemnon winked at me. "Make something up."

I scoffed. "Look, I got A's in science and chemistry, and a C-minus in creative writing."

"The answer will come to you when needed," Shemnon assured me. "You have yet many discoveries to make."

Whatever he meant by that, I reluctantly agreed not to mention what Ester had shown me. "How long before we go then?"

"When the time is right," Shemnon said as he walked away.

* * *

I tossed and turned all night. There was so much I could bring from Cumorah, and yet I had promised to reveal nothing. How could I keep that promise? I had learned about a miracle drug. I had discovered a miraculous book. What *future* discoveries did Shemnon imply? What hidden treasures were yet to reveal themselves? And how long would that take? A week? A month? Ten years? What day was it now? Here in the tropics there really was no definitive way of telling the seasons apart. In a way, it was frustrating not knowing.

I eased out of bed and stood in front of the window. Melodee was sleeping soundly. Ester had given her a dose of something in addition to the Zypaka elixir. The moon was full and shimmering, and the village was resting peacefully. No sounds could be heard other than the occasional movement of leaves and branches stirred by the evening breezes, and the ubiquitous chorus of nocturnal creatures. Standing there, I fought conflicting emotions. I loved this place, this people, and the countless things I could learn here. I loved the fact that Melodee was growing stronger each day. But I longed for home, longed for the embrace of my wife and daughter. Despite my joy, I still felt like a prisoner in Cumorah. I tried to ignore the fact that our freedom hinged on the whims of the village elders, but it gnawed at my temper, urging it to boil over as it used to.

A soft rap sounded at the door. I opened it to find Ester standing there. She motioned for me to follow her. Under the stone veranda she paused and stared silently out at the moonlit courtyard below.

"You good man," she began softly. I didn't voice a thanks. I didn't feel she wanted one. "You give much."

"You've given me much more. You have saved my life as well as Melodee's. I will always be in your debt."

She shook her head. Did she not understand me? I put my hands on my heart then held them out in a giving gesture. "You give more."

Ducking her head, Ester blushed. "Thank you."

"When we do leave, I will miss you, Ester. You good woman," I said, lightly mimicking her stilted English.

She turned and smiled up at me. I smiled back. Nothing more needed to be said.

"You sleep, David," she stated in a suddenly more professional timbre.

I shook my head. "I am tired, but can't seem to slow my mind enough to sleep," I sighed.

She nodded and motioned for me to follow her.

We returned to the room, where she gave me some of the medicine she had dosed Melodee with earlier. "What is this?" I asked.

"Sleep," she winked at me.

"A sedative or some brainwashing hallucinogenic?"

That won me a confused look, but it was just what I was hoping for. "Never mind." I smiled.

I drank the stuff, which tasted rather chalky, and returned to my cot. Ester came over and tucked me in as if I were a small child afraid of the dark. She kissed her fingertips and placed them on my forehead. "You good man," she whispered again.

As I watched her leave, I thought, *You are a better person than I'll ever be*, but didn't speak it. In fact, the pasty numbness coating my mouth and thickening my tongue wouldn't allow me to say anything.

I closed my eyes for a moment. It ended up being a very long moment.

THIRTY-FOUR

Movement.

Slow motion.

I was being carried. My eyes wouldn't open. My tongue wouldn't move. I hated the lack of control but somehow knew I wasn't in immediate danger.

Then I was drifting as if in a boat. Then I was on land. It was day, then night.

Movement again. Daylight.

I tried to open my eyes and managed a brief glimpse of tree limbs and branches slowly passing over me. I heard water, the rhythmic sound of paddles surfacing, arching, submerging. A flash of blue sky. A fluffy, white cloud.

More drifting. A breath in my ear—someone whispering to me. Broken Spanish. "I will miss you, my friend. Farewell." It sounded like Helam.

Then we were motionless for a very long time.

* * *

A loud squawk pierced my ear. I forced one eye open and saw a large, blue macaw sitting on the rim of the canoe. It looked at me with the same curious expression I gave it. It squawked again, then left in a flurry of feathers.

I lay in a dugout canoe, beached in a small cove just off a wide river. Melodee lay at my feet, curled beneath a thin covering of cloth resembling burlap. Wrested from her sleep by the noisy bird, she moved slowly and stretched with concerted effort. I noticed oily beads of perspiration on her forehead and temples. She looked better but still not one hundred percent well. I sat up and looked around.

Thick, primordial jungle surrounded us. We were alone, abandoned. With only a few provisions at our feet and no one to guide us out of the rain forest, I suddenly felt afraid. I looked in vain for one of the people of Cumorah. They obviously had brought us to some remote location in the jungle and left us to fend for ourselves. So much for fond farewells.

"Where are we?" Melodee asked through a stifled yawn.

"I don't know. Somewhere other than Cumorah." On closer inspection, my little companion looked more haggard and worn than a simple day of canoeing would cause—assuming it had taken only one day to get to our current locale. "You okay?"

She nodded. I could tell it was a lie. What she needed was a dose of Zypaka. I began rummaging through the items in the canoe. I found a sack of dried meat, some fruit and nuts, a flask of water, and a small porcelain jar filled with Ester's amber elixir. I exhaled a long sigh of relief—then choked on a quick breath. Was this enough? Ester had indicated that Melodee would need continued dosing for weeks. The amount of medicine in the small jar looked to be about ten days' worth. Had she miscalculated?

"What's wrong, Uncle David?"

Now it was my turn to lie. "Nothing, kiddo. I just wish they hadn't left us like this."

"Yeah. I'm going to miss them."

I was glad that she misinterpreted my meaning. "Yeah. Me too."

Eyeing the provisions, she asked, "Is this enough to last us?"

"That depends on how quickly we can find our way out of here. I have no clue where we are."

Melodee picked up a banana and peeled it. I chose a strip of meat and gnawed on it. We munched in silence as we examined our surroundings. I tried to remain optimistic, but I felt the old anxieties of being lost frazzle my nerves and sour my stomach.

I got out of the canoe and stretched. My muscles were surprisingly sore, as if I had just finished a mega-workout and a 10K run. Melodee tried to exit the boat but didn't have the strength to stand. I helped her ashore and situated her under a large tree fern. I took the jar of elixir and, finding a small dish beneath the burlap, dosed a portion to her. I wasn't sure if I gave the correct amount, but I tried to mimic what I had seen Ester do. Melodee gagged it down without question.

As she rested, I wandered around a bit. I hesitated leaving her alone, but she was in no condition to accompany me, and she wanted to stay by the canoe just in case the Cumorans returned. The jungle was as thick as ever, and my hopes of finding a modern city nearby quickly vanished. After an hour of searching, however, I stumbled onto a fairly well-used trail, dimpled with footprints and shoe treads. A glimmer of hope returned. I followed the trail for a half mile, but got nowhere. Not wanting to leave Melodee alone for too long, I returned and told her what I had found.

"Do you suppose Helam left us here in hopes that we would find that trail?" she asked.

"Perhaps, but not likely. I had to do quite a bit of searching before I found it. If he wanted us to find it, he would have placed us closer to it."

"That makes sense. Should we follow it?" she asked while attempting to stand.

"Yeah, I think so. It's better than sitting around here just twiddling our thumbs."

I got a snicker out of that one, but nothing more. I debated the wisdom of taking Melodee on a hike through this inhospitable terrain, but decided we didn't have much option. I certainly did not want to leave her alone for long, and I had no idea how long it would take to find help following the trail.

We gathered our things from the canoe. I carried everything, including Melodee's backpack, and found her a stout pole to use as a walking stick. It took some time to find the trail again. When we did, it was well past midday, and we stopped for a rest. Melodee was stoic as ever, never complaining, but she was not her usual talkative self either. I offered her a drink from the water flask and some dried meat. I ate a papaya and some Brazil nuts. Luckily, billowing, white clouds blocked the sun, preventing it from raising the temperature to unbearable levels. For a tropical rain forest, it was a very pleasant day. Before long, Melodee was fast asleep. I took the opportunity to explore the trail.

I walked for nearly half an hour. Because of the agreeable nature of the day, I got careless in my wanderings. Instead of being cautious, I hiked along the trail as if I were enjoying a stroll in a shady park. Rounding a corner, I suddenly entered a clearing filled with trucks and men. The trucks carried slatted crates filled with white cellophane bags; the men carried rifles and shotguns. A large cinderblock building stood off to one side, and a small helicopter sat on a landing pad adjacent to the building. I instantly surmised that this wasn't the same complex in which I had met Helam. That building was a tiny outpost—this was a major drug-processing center. The dense isolation of this part of the jungle was ideal for it.

I dove for the cover of some underbrush, praying I had not been detected. Peering out from the vegetation, I found my prayers unanswered. Two of the men were pointing in my direction, one of them shouting rapidly in Spanish. The others in the compound began heading toward me, their guns at the ready.

I rejoined the main trail and ran as fast as I could. As I ran, question after question flashed through my mind. Why was this happening again? Why did Helam drop us off so close to a major drug outpost? Was Heavenly Father no longer watching out for us? I shook those negative thoughts from my mind and continued to run. It wasn't long before I found Melodee asleep where I had left her.

"Honey, wake up, quickly."

Her eyes opened slowly. "I don't feel so good," she said weakly. It was the first time I had ever heard her truly complain.

"You have to get up," I commanded, gathering our things as fast as I could. "Hurry."

She slowly rolled to her knees and used the walking stick to stand. She struggled for breath, as if the exertion from standing had sapped all her strength.

"Can you run?"

Her eyes swam. "I don't think I can even walk."

Shouts from the drug men filtered toward us. Rapid-fire Spanish, angry, bitter, obscene.

"I got careless and ran into more drug runners. A whole bunch of them. We have to go, now!"

She took a feeble step forward and stumbled. Tears pooled in her eyes. "I don't think I can."

"Melodee. We don't have a choice."

More shouts. Much closer.

Melodee began a slow, steady pace that headed toward the cove. She made it about thirty feet before collapsing to the ground. I knelt and shook her forcefully. "Melodee." She was out cold.

"This way!" a man called. "¡Rápido!"

I shrugged on the backpack, picked up Melodee, and headed down the trail. Even though she had lost a lot of weight, my arms soon burned with the awkward burden. Each step I took sent a jolt up my spine, causing the muscles in my back and legs to seize and knot. My breathing was instantly coarse, raspy. I sucked in the hot jungle air in huge, noisy gasps. My chest stung with every inhalation. Sweat poured from my brow.

Dropping down a small incline, my footsteps faltered and my legs wobbled and lost strength. I staggered, tripped, and fell. I twisted before hitting the ground so that Melodee would land on top of me instead of under me. Something broke, shattered, but it was too brittle a sound to be any of my bones. I lunged to my feet, picked up Melodee, and continued down the trail.

I soon lost track of where we were. Forcing my mind to stay focused, I lumbered along the trail at an awkward gait. I was no longer running—I didn't have the energy. I said a silent prayer, begging God to give me the strength to continue. I again wondered how this could be happening. We had already gone through so much. After our uplifting experiences in Cumorah, I assumed we were on God's good side. Now I wasn't so sure.

Skidding down a steep decline, I fell backwards. I paused to catch my breath. The air burned my lungs as if I were inhaling fire. I heard a shot ring out. Monkeys screeched. Birds squawked. The drug men were close and apparently shooting at anything that moved. Struggling to my feet, I pushed through a curtain of vines and stumbled into the clearing around the cove.

The canoe was only a few yards away. I tried to hurry but my legs faltered and wouldn't respond. It was like one of those dreams where you are running at full speed but are getting nowhere. Each step was painfully slow, agonizingly small. Finally, I reached the canoe and set Melodee in the bow. I shoved off and began paddling with all my might.

Another shot rang out. The water next to me erupted.

"Stop where you are!" an angry voice commanded in Spanish. I kept paddling. Faster.

Another shot. Another explosion of water. I entered the river channel.

"Kill him!"

A volley of gunfire shattered the tranquility of the forest. Startled birds filled the air in panicked flight. The canoe splintered as shotgun pellets riddled its side. A hot flash of pain slashed through my shoulder. I kept paddling, splashing more water than pushing it behind the oar. More gunfire. With each shot, the water churned as if suddenly boiling. The river's current grabbed the canoe. I stroked harder. We moved faster, smoother. Soon we were out of range. The gunfire ceased.

I kept paddling, but with less intensity. My shoulder grew weaker with each stroke. Every movement caused a searing pain. An angry, red splotch grew at the site of the wound, but I didn't slow our pace for a least three miles. Then, as the rhythms of the jungle slowly returned to normal, I let the current move us downstream and paused to examine my shoulder.

A deep gash channeled through the skin on my deltoid, and blood ran freely. But there was no serious penetration, no bullets or pellets left behind. I felt confident the wound would eventually stop bleeding. It would leave a scar, but it was not life threatening. I held the burlap tightly against the wound and began to examine Melodee. She looked terrible. I wiped her face and arms with a cloth dipped in the river. Her breathing was shallow and coarse, but steady. She needed her medicine. Apparently, I had not given her enough.

I opened the backpack—and my heart sank. The porcelain jar lay in pieces. The Zypaka elixir was gone, soaked into the inner lining of the backpack. Nothing remained of Melodee's cure.

* * *

By nightfall, we had covered several miles. Melodee slipped in and out of consciousness. Neither of us ate much, and our water flask had dried out long ago. The river widened even more and moved slow and steady. I was certain it would lead to the ocean, but what we would find there was anyone's guess.

I pulled onto a soft shore. By now, my head was spinning from dehydration and the loss of blood. My shoulder still seeped, but I knew the bleeding would soon stop. Melodee had awakened, and she sat in the bow looking like a ghost. That confused me—I had thought she was on the mend. But I knew her therapy was far from over. And now, with the elixir gone, I wasn't so sure she'd have much of a chance.

"I am so sorry about the Zypaka," I said for the umpteenth time.

Melodee shook her head in acceptance. "I told you not to worry about it. It was an accident."

"But it was helping so much. Your cancer was almost gone. I don't know what else to use."

Her smile was weak but comforting. "We'll use faith, okay?"

I nodded, no longer able to voice my remorse and lack of confidence.

I decided against a fire. With the threat of drug men close by, offering any signal of our presence would not be wise. Besides, I didn't have the energy to start a fire. The shore on which we beached was very small and faced a steep embankment that prevented anyone or anything from getting to us. Still, if the drug runners discovered our location, it would be like shooting fish in a barrel. We stretched out in the canoe and slowly drifted into a fitful slumber.

Toward midnight, Melodee cried out in pain, a convulsing whimper that ended in an anguished sob. I felt her skin; it was hot as a cinder. Cold sweat traced opaque rivulets down her face and neck. Her brow furrowed in a steady crease. Although my body complained with every movement, it was nothing compared to what she must be going through. I made my way to her side and wiped her forehead and neck.

"Shhh, Melodee. I'm right here. You'll be okay." The words sounded empty, patronizing.

She looked up at me with vacant eyes. I knew she could see me, but there was little recognition in her blank stare. She bit her lip and winced in pain. A trickle of blood seeped between her teeth. She had bitten clean through her lip.

"Oh, Melodee," I whispered. "Don't do this. Not here, not now." My pleading was selfish. I had gone through this once before. I could not bear it a second time.

Her jaw began to quiver as she drew in sharp breaths to quell the pain. She swallowed hard and stammered, "I—need—more—medicine."

Tears burned my eyes. "I know, sweetheart, but there isn't any."

My heart thumped bitterly, and my stomach felt as if it had clenched into a ball of lead. I wiped angrily at my eyes, knowing I may well have killed her when I broke the jar of elixir. "I am so sorry, Melodee."

I wanted to swear, to curse everything and everyone. I would do anything to alleviate her pain, to take it on myself so she wouldn't have to suffer, yet I could do nothing. I knew it and she knew it. I sobbed uncontrollably, hating myself. Hating the world. Hating God.

Then her clammy hand touched my wrist tenderly. Her lips moved in an effort to speak. Melodee's eyes were slightly open, beseeching me.

"Pray for me." It was barely more than a whisper.

"It's too late," I mumbled pathetically.

"Not too late. Have faith . . ."

That was all she could say. Her body went limp. Her breathing stilled to almost nothing. I rolled to my knees and clasped my hands so tightly they blanched. My throat constricted as I struggled to breathe. In a convulsing voice, I whispered, "Please, God. Not this one. Not Melodee. I will do anything. Anything. Please save her."

I don't know how long I stayed on my knees. I heard myself repeat the same words over and over. A strange but wonderful strength from within allowed me to continue praying, pouring my heart and soul out to God. I promised everything. I called on all the faith I could muster. I trembled uncontrollably. My head spun and my muscles had gone beyond fatigue, but I kept praying.

"Give me faith, Father. I now know Thou art real. Show me Thy love, Thy mercy and grace. Please, Father, spare this child. Please . . . please . . ."

I do not recall when my body collapsed. In my mind, I continued to pray all night. I didn't notice the tide change, or feel us shift from the muddy shore. The drifting of my mind masked the drifting of the canoe.

I had run out of strength. Out of tears. Out of faith.

THIRTY-FIVE

The susurration of tiny waves lapping against a shore filled my ears. The smell of salt and sand and seaweed teased my nose, and the cry of a gull woke me.

My head felt very heavy, so heavy that an extreme wave of vertigo hit me when I opened my eyes. I slammed them shut before the rising nausea in my throat erupted. I opened my mouth and forced myself to take long, deep breaths. Thankfully, the nausea subsided.

I listened to the sounds around me. Seagulls, terns, and other marine birds pierced the air with sharp, staccato cries. The laughter of children. I tried to focus my thoughts, to organize the sensory clues and paint some sort of coherent picture with them. But nothing seemed to fit.

The voice of a seasoned gentleman made its way through my cerebral fog. "Señor, are you okay?"

I licked my lips and swallowed hard to moisten my parched throat. "Helam? Is that you?"

"No, señor. It is Manuel."

"Who?"

"Manuel, señor. From the hotel Palacio de la Playa."

I felt hands under my arms, lifting me into a sitting position. "Here, señor, drink this."

A bottle—a plastic bottle—was placed to my lips, and I swallowed a few sips of delightfully refreshing water. I felt a damp cloth rubbed over my face and eyes, as I took a second pull from the bottle. I then heard the soft groans of a child waking and stretching.

"Uncle David, where are we?"

"You are on the beach, señorita, by the hotel Palacio de la Playa," Manuel said kindly. "Here, drink some water."

I finally managed to pry my eyes open and look around. The bright sun was dazzling against a pure white sand beach and a scintillating blue lagoon. Some two hundred yards down the shore, a crowd of beachcombers played in the minimal surf before a grand, multi-million-dollar hotel. Melodee and I were still in the dugout canoe.

"Did you drift out to sea, señor?" Manuel looked the quintessential Mexican cabana man, complete with a wide sombrero, gaudy Hawaiian shirt, and a bushy gray mustache.

"We drifted somewhere," I answered with a dry, scratchy voice.

He looked at Melodee. "Is the señorita okay?"

"Sí, estoy bien," she said with an equally scratchy throat.

An instant smile crinkled the edges of Manuel's dark eyes, and a burst of glee escaped from under his mustache. "Ah, bueno, princesa, bueno."

A smile creased my face too. Melodee looked worn and haggard, but alive. She was alive! I grabbed her in a huge hug and squeezed until she groaned. Tears again poured from my eyes as I looked her over and found her surprisingly well.

"Thanks, Uncle David. I'm glad to see you too."

"You're alive. I thought for sure you . . ."

"Were dying? I think I was."

"Is the señorita sick?" Manuel asked.

To Manuel, she said, "I was." To me, she said, "I'm feeling much better now, thanks to you."

"Melodee, I did nothing."

"You prayed for me. I heard you."

I was speechless. We looked at each other as the world ceased to exist. Then, somewhat embarrassed, she lowered her eyes. After a long moment of silence, and quiet prayers of thanks on my part, Manuel cleared his throat. "May I help you back to the hotel?"

It took some time to get our feet under us, but we managed to stumble along the beach. "Where did you get the canoe, señor?" Manuel asked along the way.

"We found it," Melodee answered. She flashed me a knowing look, and I nodded in return.

Manuel seemed to accept her answer without question. "I have not seen one like that since I was a *cabrito*."

"Me either," I said, which brought another burst of laughter from our host.

* * *

Neither Melodee nor I had an I.D. or passport, but we were obviously American, and the hotel was very accommodating. They had received word of the plane crash, and they knew that the search parties had come up empty. It was now the fifth of January. We had been missing for almost seven weeks.

After a quick cleanup and a cursory check by the Palacio de la Playa's nurse, the hotel concierge gave us a room and the use of the telephone. Melodee held the phone to her ear and waited patiently. Her smile ran from ear to ear.

"Hello, Dad?" Tears welled in her eyes. "It's me, Dad. It's Melodee." She listened in silence for a moment then stared at the handset. Holding it to her head again she said, "Hello? Dad, are you there? Oh, hi again. Yeah, it's me. I'm okay, Dad. Is anyone else home? No? Well, tell Mom and everyone I'm okay. Yeah. Yeah. I'm in Mexico. We crashed. Yeah. I'll fill you in on everything later, okay? I love you too, Dad. No, I think I'm getting better . . ."

At that point, I walked to the refrigerator to get another soda. I felt awkward listening in on her conversation. After twenty or so minutes, Melodee handed me the telephone. I punched in the numbers, clutched the handset to my ear, and listened to the steady ring as I quickly tried to figure out what I was going to say. A huge knot formed in my gut, and my mouth felt as dry as the Gobi Desert.

"Hello?"

Never did anyone's voice ever sound so sweet. "Hi, Paige, it's Daddy."

An empty silence filled the receiver. Hot tears formed at the corners of my eyes as I waited. Then I heard her calmly call out, "Mommy, it's Daddy," as if I were simply calling from the office.

A pause. Then a hesitant, "Hello?"

"Are you sitting down, hon?"

A gasp. "David?"

"Yeah, it's me, babe. I'm okay, too."

"David!" Her screech was one of joy, disbelief, and confusion. It was a lovely sound.

"Yes, Dyana, it's really me. Listen, there's a lot to explain and a whole lot more to make up for, but first I want you to know how much I love you."

"David? They said your plane crashed. That you were . . . dead."

"They *assumed* I was dead. What else could they think? But I survived the crash and have been . . . well, I've been sort of wandering through the jungle for the past two months."

"Oh, honey, are you sure you're all right?" Her voice was breathless, eager, and beautiful. I could hear her crying on the other end, and longed to wipe her tears and hold her in my arms.

"What is it, Mommy?" I heard Paige ask.

"It's Daddy, sweetheart. He's okay. He's coming home soon."

"Goody!" was her delighted cheer.

* * *

Two days later, BioCraft chartered a jet flight home. I was eternally grateful when I looked out the window and didn't see propellers. My mind raced over what I had been through . . . and what was still to come. There was so much to tell, and so much I couldn't tell. All my vows to be a better husband and father came to my mind, only this time I felt certain they weren't merely lip service. This time, I would actually see them to fruition.

During the flight home, the stewardess asked if I would like a mini-bottle to calm my obvious nerves. "No thanks. I don't need that anymore," I answered, smiling at Melodee.

I felt very apprehensive about sharing my testimony of the Book of Mormon with Dyana. I prayed many times during that flight that she would be receptive to my newfound beliefs. But I first had to start with our marital relationship. That would be a struggle; however, I would go about it differently this time. More give, less take. And I would exercise faith and trust in my Heavenly Father. If

He wanted things to work out—and I knew He did—then they *would* work out.

I also brooded over the fact that I couldn't utilize what I had learned from Ester. Without any samples, the company would treat my recalled data as mere anecdotal evidence, and it would go no further than my notebook. Additionally, although faith had saved Melodee's life for now, I still knew we had to meet the Lord halfway, and I wondered if she might slip back into her illness without continued dosing of Ester's elixir.

Midflight, Melodee began rummaging through her backpack and stopped short with a questioning mumble. "What's this?" she asked as she handed me a small leather pouch.

I opened the pouch and out tumbled my old mini-bottle—only it wasn't filled with vodka. In it sloshed a murky, amber elixir with little red flakes. *Ester! What have you done?* I stared at the bottle with a vacant expression. Melodee looked at it and commented, "Looks like it's gone bad. I knew that stuff was rotten."

"On the contrary," I breathed. "This is the most wonderful stuff in the world."

EPILOGUE

A year later, Melodee called just after returning from her last visit to her doctor. She said the man was speechless. It was a delight to hear her describe his dumbfounded reaction as her monthly tests continued to show a cessation of her cancer. Additional tests would be run, perhaps for another year or more, but the prognosis looked good. The cancer was still present, just in a dormant state.

Dyana and I sought out a reputable marriage counselor. Our meetings were revealing and humbling, yet productive. I hadn't realized how selfish I had been. Dyana felt the same way about herself. I gently exposed my new faith in God, which both the counselor and my wife applauded. Dyana was hesitant to jump into Mormonism, but after meeting Melodee's family, she was at least willing to take a cautious look at it. I couldn't ask for anything more.

BioCraft rewarded me with a state-of-the-art lab and a top-notch staff in New Compounds Research. No more open-field analysis or unexpected time away from my family.

I kept the mini-bottle of Zypaka elixir locked in my desk for a long time until the excitement of our adventure settled down. I had given my word not to tell about the things I had discovered in Cumorah, but I knew the chemicals within the amber elixir had helped save Melodee's life and could save many others. I prayed about what to do, and I finally got a clear answer to move ahead with it. In answer to another prayer, I knew that as regrettable as was the loss of life on the small commuter flight, without the crash, I never would have found the medicine that would eventually save countless other lives.

I removed the copy of Melodee's Book of Mormon (mine now—she had given it to me as a late Christmas present) from my desk drawer and again marveled at the blessings I had received. I held the mini-bottle of elixir next to the book and smiled. I silently thanked the Lord for knowledge, for understanding, and for allowing a sweet little girl the chance to share her testimony with me. Melodee's indomitable spirit had opened my eyes and my heart to the treasure of the gospel of Jesus Christ.

And perhaps—with the Lord's blessing—I could share a few of my own treasures with the world. Even hidden treasures.

ABOUT THE AUTHOR

Gregg R. Luke was raised in Santa Barbara, California. He served a two-year LDS mission in Wisconsin before studying biological sciences at the University of California at Santa Barbara. He graduated from the University of Utah College of Pharmacy and currently practices pharmacy in Logan, Utah. He enjoys reading, music, science, and nature. He and his wife, Julie, have three children and live in Mendon, Utah.